HACK/SLASH

OMNIBUS

VOLUME 2

A
Tim Seeley/Stefano Caselli
Production

Writer: Tim Seeley

Art Direction & Series Design: Sean K. Dove

Production: Sam Wells

Editor: Mike O'Sullivan

HACK/SLASH OMNIBUS Vol. 2. November 2010. Second Printing. Published by Image Comics, Inc. Office of publication: 2134 Allston Way, 2nd Floor, Berkeley, CA 94704. For information regarding the CPSIA on this printed material call: 203-595-3636 and provide reference # EAST – 69983.
PRINTED IN THE U.S.A. ISBN: 978-1-60706-274-5.

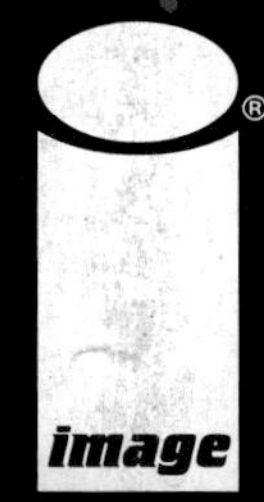

Gross Anatomy
Penciler: Emily Stone
Colorist: Courtney Via
Letters: Brian J. Crowley

Originally Issue 1

Shout at the Devil
Penciler: Emily Stone
Colorist: Courtney Via
Letters: Brian J. Crowley

Originally Issues 2-4

Love Stories
Penciler: Emily Stone
Letters: Brian J. Crowley

Originally Issue 5

Double Date
Artist: Fernando Pinto with
Stefano Caselli/Tim Seeley
& Splash!
Letters: Brian J. Crowley

Originally Issue 6

Tub Club
Penciler: Rebekah Isaacs
Colorists: Andrew Dalhouse
Letters: Crank!

Originally Issues 7-9

Little Children
Penciler: Emily Stone
Colorist: Courtney Via
Letters: Brian J. Crowley

Originally Issue 10

The Coldest Dish
Penciler: Emily Stone
Colorist: Courtney Via
Letters: Brian J. Crowley

Originally Issue 11

Murder/Suicide
Penciler: Tim Seeley
Colorist: Katie De Sousa
Letters: Crank!
Thanks to: Missy, Fractal,
Salome, Vivid, Kyra, Drake,
Sash, Brian Warmoth,
Alicia Li and Rion Vernon.

Originally Hack/Slash Annual

Interlude
Penciler: Emily Stone
Colorist: Courtney Via
Letters: Brian J Crowley
and Crank!
Writing Assists: Evan Dorkin

Originally Portions of Issues 12-13

Over the Rainbow
Penciler: Emily Stone
Colorist: Val Staples
Letters: Crank!

Originally Issue 14

Cassie & Vlad Meet the Re-Animator
Story by: Tim Seeley, Barry
Keating and Brian Yuzna
Penciler: Emily Stone with
Matt Merhoff
Colorist: Mark Englert
Letters: Crank!
Re-Animator Created by:
H.P. Lovecraft
Thanks to: Brian Yuzna, Barry
Keating, Steve Baron and
Stefan Hutchinson.

Originally Issues 15-17

GROSS ANATOMY

#1A by **STEFANO CASELLI & TIM SEELEY**

ATLANTA, GEORGIA.
NOW.
SVVVVNNNNNNNNNNN!
SVVVVNNNN-ZZZZRRRRRRR!
I WANT YOU TO FREE ASSOCIATE WITH ME.
COME NOW. TALK TO ME. PAIN. AGONY.
WHAT DOES IT UNLOCK, MS. HACK?

WEE WEE WEE...
WHAT?
I CAN'T HEAR YOU. SPEAK UP.
WHAT COMES TO YOUR MIND?

NNH... THIS LITTLE PIGGY WENT WEE WEE WEE...
...ALL THE WAY HOME.
MAKE YOUR JOKES. HIDE WITHIN YOUR CAGE OF FLESH. I STRIPPED AWAY MY OWN MASK TO FREE MYSELF.
AND I HAVE PEELED BACK THE LIES OF OTHERS UNTIL ALL THAT REMAINED WAS BONE.

MY TRUTH IS THIS: I DID THINGS TO MY STUDENTS... SICK THINGS. AND THEY TURNED ME IN. THEY RUINED ME.
SO, THERAPEUTICALLY, I TOOK THEM APART... REVEALED THE TRUTH ABOUT THEM.
YOU ARE NOT ONE OF MY STUDENTS. YET YOU SOUGHT ME OUT. WHY?
DID YOU HOPE TO STOP ME? IS THAT IT?
OR DID YOU SIMPLY NEED A PSYCHOLOGIST?
IF THAT IS THE CASE, THEN, LET US DO THIS PROPERLY. MS. HACK...
...TELL ME ABOUT YOUR MOTHER.

CHIPPEWA FALLS, WISCONSIN.
THEN.
WHATCHA DOIN', HACK?
SPREADIN' COOTIES ONTO THE SWING SET AGAIN?

FUCKIN' DIRTY, UGLY CUNT. SHE SMELLS.
I'M SORRY... I'LL LEAVE... I JUST WANTED TO SWING...
WHERE YA GONNA GO, STINKY?
HOME?

YEAH... SHE'S GONNA GO TELL HER BIG, FAT BITCH MOM.
OOH YEAH... WATCH OUT FOR THE LUNCH LADY!

HEY HACK. MAYBE YOU'D STINK LESS IF YOU TOOK A BATH.
SPLOOSH!

HUNH
HUNH
HUNH

AHUHHH...
AHUHHHHH...

HAH. LOOKIT THAT CRYBABY.
YEAH... JOE, MAYBE WE SHOULD LEAVE HER ALONE NOW, MAN.
WHAT ARE YOU BOYS DOING!?

GET OUT OF MY WAY, YOU BOYS! LEAVE HER ALONE!

GET UP HONEY. GET UP.
WHAT'D THEY DO TO YOU?
UN HUNNH... NOTHIN', MOMMA, NOTHIN'...

WHY'D YOU LEAVE THE HOUSE!?
I TOLD YOU NOT TO LEAVE THE HOUSE.
BU-BUT... MOMMA.

YOU GOTTA LISTEN TO YOUR MOMMY. I TOLD YOU NOT TO LEAVE...
...LOOK WHAT HAPPENS WHEN YOU DO! YOU GET HURT, THAT'S WHAT!

THE WORLD IS FULL OF PEOPLE WHO WANT TO HURT YOU, CASSANDRA.
ALL WE'VE GOT IS EACH OTHER. EVEN YOUR FATHER LEFT US ALL ALONE!
I JUST DON'T WANT YOU GETTING HURT, HONEY.

MOM... NOT... NOT HERE.

NOW.
FUCK YOU.
I'VE BEEN SAYING IT FOR AWHILE... I BELIEVE THE DAYS OF THE SIMPLE SLASH AND STAB ARE ENDING.
THERE'S NO STATEMENT IN IT. THESE DAYS IT'S ALL ABOUT THE GORE AND THE TORTURE.
IT'S DIFFICULT TO BE AN INNOVATOR LIKE MYSELF. BUT IT'S OBVIOUS I'M ON TO SOMETHING.
PHYSICAL PAIN UNLOCKS PSYCHOLOGICAL PAIN.
THE LOOK ON YOUR FACE WHEN I MENTIONED YOUR MOTHER WAS PERHAPS EVEN MORE DELIGHTFUL THAN YOUR VISAGE WHEN I REMOVED YOUR TOE.

WHAT KIND OF PERSON SEEKS OUT KILLERS AND SADISTS, MS. HACK?

SVVVVNNNN!
WHAT KIND OF PERSON FOLLOWS A TRAIL...

...OF BLOOD?

THEN.
AAAAAH!
AHNN HUNH
OH GOD...
...PLEASE STOP, MS. HACK... PLEASE...
NOT SO BRAVE NOW, ARE YA JOE FITCH?
YOU WERE AWFUL TOUGH WHEN YOU WERE TERRORIZING MY LITTLE GIRL WEREN'T YOU?
WEREN'T YOU?!
MOM...
...MOM, YOU HAVE TO STOP THIS.
THIS ISN'T RIGHT MOM!
YOU CAN'T JUST KILL EVERYONE!

NOW CASSIE...
...YOUR MOTHER KNOWS BEST.
THOSE OTHER KIDS AND THIS BOY...
THEY WERE BEING SO CRUEL TO YOU. YOU'RE SUCH A SWEET GIRL CASSIE.
NEVER HARMED ANYONE. BUT THE WAY THEY TREATED YOU.
THEY LIKED TO HURT YOU. SOULESS CREATURES THEY ARE.
JUST SO MUCH MEAT.

NO!
UNF
CASSANDRA. WHY?
DROP THE AXE!
THIS IS WRONG MOM. I... I CALLED THE POLICE.
BUT, I'M YOUR MOTHER. ALL WE'VE EVER HAD IS EACH OTHER...
... I LOVE YOU, CASSIE.
TSSSSSSSS

NOW.
ANOTHER ONE DOWN.
-UNGHHH-
LET'S SEE... AN IMPULSIVE ATTRACTION TO VIOLENCE, A LACK OF CONCERN FOR OWN WELL-BEING.
A FAILURE TO CONFORM TO SOCIAL NORMS. NOT TO MENTION THAT FLAT VOICE AND THE DISPLAY OF LOW AFFECT.
I'D SAY YOU'RE A PRIME CANDIDATE FOR A DIAGNOSIS OF ANTISOCIAL PERSONALITY DISORDER.
A DIFFICULT DISORDER TO LIVE WITH.
WHEN NOT PROPERLY TREATED, THOSE WITH THIS CONDITION OFTEN END UP IMPRISONED OR ENGAGING IN RISKY BEHAVIOR THAT COULD LEAD THEM TO BEING INJURED. MAIMED EVEN.

THERE'S ALSO THE INTERPERSONAL RELATIONSHIPS.
THOSE SUFFERING FROM THIS DISORDER HAVE DIFFICULTY MAKING AND MAINTAINING FRIENDSHIPS.
TELL ME MS. HACK...
...DO YOU HAVE ANY *FRIENDS?*

CHICAGO, ILLINOIS.
THEN.
JESUS. WHO THE HELL DID YOU HIT?
SHIT, MAN... I DUNNO. BUT FROM WHAT WAS GOIN' ON UP HERE...
THIS IS EITHER A VICTIM OF THE MEATMAN KILLER OR IT IS THE MEATMAN KILLER...
WE DID IT... WE GOT THE REAL KILLER.
HURR... YES. WE GOT HIM.
I'M SORRY I ATTACKED YOU.
EVERYONE WAS SAYING THE MEATMAN KILLED ALL THOSE KIDS.
I... GOT CAUGHT UP IN IT.
OFTEN I AM BLAMED.
I HAVE LEARNED THAT MY FACE CAN FIND ME MANY TRUFFLES.
TROUBLES.
YES. ALSO THOSE.
WELL, THE SLASHER IS PASTED ALL OVER THE FRONT OF A TRAIN. I'M DONE HERE.
IT WAS... UH... GOOD TO MEET YOU, MEATMAN.

VLAD. MY NAME...
...IT IS VLAD.
LOOK... VLAD. I'M TRAVELING THE COUNTRY TAKING CARE OF SLASHERS.
AND, WELL, YOU WERE REALLY HELPFUL UP THERE WITH JULIAN...
...I COULD USE THE EXTRA MUSCLE. IT'S NO PARTY, BUT...
HURR... I DO NOT... HURR...
YES. I WILL GO.
WE CAN HELP EACH OTHER WITH OUR TRUFFLES.

NOW.
CAN I GET A SOY CHAI LATTE?
AND ALSO YOUR PHONE NUMBER?

OH.
THAT'S NOT THE REACTION I WAS...

HOLY SHIT.

HURR...
...DO YOU HAVE WIFEY ACCESS?

WIFEY?
OH, WI-FI...
...YEAH ...YES.

GOOD. I WILL NEED TO BORROW SOME, YES?

IT IS A VERY IMPORTANT MATTER.

PET TRACKS.com
KEEPING TRACK OF YOUR PETS
I MUST FIND MY FRIEND.

HE'S FREAKING OUT THE CUSTOMERS. GO TELL HIM TO LEAVE.
BUT...
PLEASE!

HEY, UM... MAN?
YOU'LL HAVE TO UH... LEAVE?
Y'KNOW, CUZ, YOU UH... CAN'T BE HERE.

HURR... I APOLOGIZE.
IT IS RUDE OF ME TO USE YOUR WI-FI AND NOT BE A PAYING CUSTOMER.
I WILL HAVE A COFFEE YES?
UM... BUT... OKAY.

PET TRACKS
COLLAR LOCATION
THIS ADDRESS. IT IS NEAR, YES?
UM... YEAH... THREE BLOCKS NORTH.
CONDOS, I THINK.
GIVE THIS MAN MY COFFEE.
I MUST LEAVE. THANK YOU.
UM... ONE COFFEE FOR THAT GUY.
MY HERO.
I AM COMING, CASSANDRA.

HMM... STILL NOT TALKING, MS. HACK?
PERHAPS IT'S TIME TO SWITCH FROM THE TOES TO YOUR TONGUE SINCE YOU AREN'T USING IT MUCH ANY--
WHOOOF
UHHHH... SUCH VIGOROUS DISDAIN FOR THE MALE SEXUAL ORGAN.
HUNNNH
PERHAPS I HAD YOU FIGURED WRONG...

...PERHAPS YOUR DISORDER STEMS FROM A DISLIKE OF MALES.
A RAMPANT CASE OF PENIS ENVY.
A STIFLED ELECTRA COMPLEX.

WHAT'S WRONG, MS. HACK? DID DADDY NOT HUG YOU ENOUGH?

THEN.
HI DEB. YEAH... THIS IS DELILAH.
I WAS JUST WONDERING IF YOU'D SEEN JACK DOWN THERE AT THE PUB.
NO? YEAH. OKAY. NO... NOTHING SERIOUS.
HE JUST... WELL, HE WAS SUPPOSED TO BE HOME A FEW HOURS AGO. SURE.
WELL, LET ME KNOW IF HE SHOWS UP.
MR. PINK. MOMMY'S WORRIED CUZ DADDY DIDN'T COME HOME FROM WORK.
I'M NOT WORRIED.
DADDY WILL BE HERE ANY SECOND.
ANY SECOND...

I'M AFRAID THAT LAST BIT OF ACTING OUT HAS CONVINCED ME THAT YOU ARE UNTREATABLE MS. HACK.
TIME'S UP. THIS SESSION IS OVER.

WHA--?
HURR...

WHO'S HERE? COME OUT!
HURR...

COME OUT, OR I'LL CUT THE GIRL FROM CHIN TO BELLY BUTTON...

...AND LET HER WATCH HER INSIDES SPILL OUT.

GHUH
SCHLIKT!
SCHLIKT!

CASSANDRA!
YOUR FOOT!
I'M FINE. UNTIE ME. HE'S ALL MINE.

YA WANNA KNOW THE TRUTH ABOUT ME, DOC?

I'M **REALLY** FUCKED UP.

NOOOOOOOOOOOOOOOOOOOOOO!

LATER.
OTEL
ELLO
I DO NOT THINK WE SHOULD USE YOU AS BAIT ANY MORE. IT IS TOO RISKY.
DAMN IT. T'S ANOTHER THAT I CAN'T WEAR OUT IN PUBLIC.
WE GOTTA STOP BLEEDING THESE GUYS OUT SO BAD. WE CAN'T AFFORD THE WARDROBE COSTS.
DAMN, DAMN, DAMN! I TOTALLY LOVED THESE STOCKINGS!
I SAID I AM CONCERNED. THIS PLAN WAS TOO DANGEROUS.
YOU COULD HAVE BEEN KILLED. NOT TO MENTION WHAT ELSE HE COULD HAVE DONE TO YOU.
CASSANDRA?
CASSANDRA?
AHUHHH... AHUHHHHH...
IT IS... OKAY LITTLE CASSANDRA. IT IS OKAY.
AHUNNH...

THE CRANE CENTER.
NORTHERN CALIFORNIA.
THIS IS DR. WHITE.
I'M FOLLOWING UP ON REPORT #6064...
...YOU'VE FOUND NO EVIDENCE THAT CEUTOTECH IS CARRYING ANY FURTHER RESEARCH INTO THE PHENOMENON?*
*SEE HACK/SLASH: SLICE HARD.
GOOD. ARRANGE FOR ANYONE WITH ANY KNOWLEDGE OF THE MINNESOTA BRANCH'S ACTIVITIES TO GO INTO "RETIREMENT". YES. THE USUAL.
BAG AND TAG EVERYTHING YOU FIND IN THE MINNESOTA FACILITY AND HAVE IT SENT HERE.
I DON'T CARE HOW CRISPY IT IS. I WANT IT.
YES. THANK YOU. GOOD NIGHT.
DR. JACK HACK, PSYD.

NEW YORK CITY.
WHOOOOO!!!
I TELL YA WHAT. I NEVER BOOKED YOU GUYS CUZ YOU SUCKED. BUT, YOU GOT SOMETHING GOIN' NOW.
YOU REALLY PACKED 'EM IN. HOW'D YOU DO IT, SIXX?

SIMPLE, MAN. I MADE A DEAL WITH THE DEVIL.
YEAAAHHHHH!

HAH. YEAH. THE DEVIL.

MMMFF
MMMFF
SIX SIXX Dressing room

MMMFF
MMMFF
TO BE CONTINUED...

SHOUT AT THE DEVIL

HACK/SLASH

#4A by **TIM SEELEY & SEAN K. DOVE**

19 MILES OUTSIDE OF TAMPA BAY, FLORIDA...
9 MONTHS AGO.
Jim & Edna's
TONIGHT: ACID WASHED
BEER
BÜZ LIGHT
Mullet HIGH LIFE
YOUR LOVE EATS THROUGH MY ARMOR!
ACID WASHED! YOU DISSOLVE MY RESTRAAAAAINT! ACID WASHED! YOUR LOVE LEAVES A STAIN!
MELT MEEEEEEE, BABY!
WOO! PLAY SOME SKYNARD!
YEAH!!
THESE ARE ALL YOURS, BOYS!
SIGH

I DON'T GET IT. WHERE'S THE FAME?
WHERE'S THE DRUGS? WHERE'S THE GROUPIES?
WE GOT GERTRUDE.
WE PLAY MUSIC THAT MAKES PEOPLE FORGET THEIR PROBLEMS.
OUR SONGS WILL MAKE PEOPLE BELIEVE IN ROCK AND ROLL AGAIN.
WE SHOULD BE TOURING STADIUMS, NOT SHIT HOLES IN TAMPA.
WE SHOULD BE GETTIN' MORE ASS THAN A CHURCH PEW.
YEAH... WELL, I CALL FIRST DIBS ON GERTRUDE.

YOU EVER STOP TO THINK MAYBE IT'S BECAUSE WE SUCK?
I MEAN, "YOUR LOVE LEAVES A STAIN"?
WHAT THE HELL IS THAT?
MAYBE WE COULD, Y'KNOW, PRACTICE?

PRACTICE? WE DON'T NEED IT. THIS MUSIC IS IN US. I WAS CONCEIVED TO A KISS RECORD.
I GOT BREAST FED TO MOTLEY CRUE. WE'VE ALL GOT ROCK IN OUR SOULS.
DID SOMEONE MENTION SOULS?

I BELIEVE YOU'RE CORRECT, MR. SIXX. YOU HAVE POTENTIAL.
IT JUST NEEDS THE PROPER INCENTIVE TO BE UNLEASHED.
YEAH, AND WHO ARE YOU? A RECORD EXECUTIVE?

SOMETHING LIKE THAT.

CHATTANOOGA, TENNESSEE.
TODAY.
99¢ CASTLE
NOTHING OVER A DOLLAR!
URM... THEY MATCH YOUR HAIR, YES?
99¢
SIGH CAN'T I EVEN SHOP FOR UNDERWEAR WITHOUT YOU?
GO LOOK AT THE TOYS OR SOMETHING.
BAIT
SPECIAL
HOTGUN SHELLS
25/BOX

THEY HAVE NOTHING GOOD HERE.
ALL THE SPIDER-MANS ARE COLORED WRONG.
YEAH? AND HERE I THOUGHT IT WAS BECAUSE YOU HAVEN'T LET ME OUT OF YOUR SIGHT SINCE THAT NUT BAG LOPPED OFF MY TOES.*
*SEE ISSUE #1! --MASOCHISTIC MIKE

I'M BUYING LINGERIE IN A FUCKING DOLLAR STORE.
PLEASE, LET ME WALK ON MY OWN AND SAVE MY LAST SHRED OF DIGNITY.

SEE? I'M NOT A CRIPP--
AGHK!!
GODDAMN COCKSUCKING MOTHERFUCKING CHRIST IN A TREE!

GOD'S XXL PROPERTY

WHAAAAAH!

YOU MUST EXCUSE HER.
SHE HAS ONLY A SMALL SHRED OF DIGNITY.
GOD'S XXL PROPERTY
BEEP BEEP

CHRIS.
YOU CALLED AT A GOOD TIME.
I BET YOU SAY THAT TO ALL THE GUYS.
WHAT'S THAT?
NOTHIN', LISA! JUST TALKING TO CASSIE.
LISA?
UM. YEAH... I'M AT HER PLACE IN INDIANA. AFTER THAT WHOLE CHUCKY ORDEAL* SHE ASKED IF I'D STAY FOR A FEW DAYS.
SINCE I'M STILL UNEMPLOYED, I FIGURED I COULD KEEP AN EYE ON HER.
*SEE HACK/SLASH VS. CHUCKY --CHARLES RAY O'SULLIVAN.
ANYHEY, I WANTED TO GIVE YOU A LITTLE HEADS UP. I STUMBLED ON A POTENTIAL CASE.
I FOUND EIGHT RECENT CASES OF MISSING TEENAGERS AROUND THE U.S., AND I CROSS-REFERENCED THEM.
THE CASES JUST SO HAPPEN TO CORRESPOND TO THE TOUR SCHEDULE OF A BAND CALLED ACID WASHED.
WHAT THE HELL IS "ACID WASHED"?

THEY'RE SOME KINDA RETRO METAL GROUP FROM FLORIDA. BIG HAIR, TIGHT PANTS, GUITAR SOLOS.
THEY'VE EVEN GOT A ONE-ARMED DRUMMER AND A ROOM UNDER THE STAGE FOR GROUPIES.

COPS CHECKED IT OUT, BUT COULDN'T FIND ANY EVIDENCE OF THEIR INVOLVEMENT. I FIGURE YOU'D BE MORE QUALIFIED IN KNOWING WHAT TO LOOK FOR.
WELL, MISSING DOESN'T MEAN SLASHED TO PIECES. NORMALLY, I'D SKIP THIS ONE.

BUT MY RESEARCH INTO 80s SLASHER CASES DID SEEM TO INDICATE SOME SORT OF HAIR METAL/SLASHER CONNECTION.
I'LL THINK ABOUT IT. SEND ME THE INFO.

WILL DO, BOSS. ONCE WE GET ALL OF US INTO ONE HOUSE, HACK/SLASH, INC. WILL BE ABLE TO DO STUFF LIKE THIS FOR YOU EVERY TIME.
Hack/Slash, Inc.
HACK/SLASH WHAT?

HACK/SLASH, INC.!
I MEAN... IT'S STILL IN THE PLANNING STAGES, BUT A LOT OF SLASHER SURVIVORS WANT TO HELP YOU ON YOUR MISSION.
I FIGURE WE GET US ALL IN ONE PLACE... MAKE IT LIKE A SUPERTEAM, Y'KNOW? WE'LL BE YOUR Q.
GOOD IDEA, CHRIS.
SO WHEN SOME PSYCHO WE BUST COMES BACK FROM THE DEAD AND GOES GUNNING FOR REVENGE, HE CAN DO ALL HIS SHOPPING IN ONE PLACE.
I APPRECIATE THE HELP, BUT THIS ISN'T A FUCKING TEAM EFFORT.
THE SECOND WE SET UP A HALL OF JUSTICE IS THE SECOND EVERY SLASHER LOOKING FOR A SEQUEL KNOWS WHERE TO GO!

OKAY, SO MAYBE NOT ALL IN ONE PLACE, BUT I STILL THINK YOU COULD USE A HELPLINE EVERY ONCE IN AWHILE.
I MEAN, YOU'RE GOOD, BUT YOU HAVEN'T SAVED EVERYONE.
THINK OF JASON...*
*SEE HACK/SLASH: DEATH BY SEQUEL TPB --G.I. MIKE.

LISTEN, YOU SLEAZY LITTLE FUCK! WHY DON'T YOU SUCK MY BIG, WET, HAIRY, PINK--

--POPSICLE.
GOD'S XXL PROPERTY

C'MON, VLAD. WE'RE GOING TO FLORIDA.
AGAIN? HURR... MORE BEAUTIFUL SCENERY?

WHAT'D CASSIE HAVE TO SAY?
OH... UH... NOTHIN'. SHE SAYS, UH... HI.
TOO LATE TO SOAP YOUR BACK?
YEP.
DAMN.

BUT THERE'S ALWAYS LOTION.

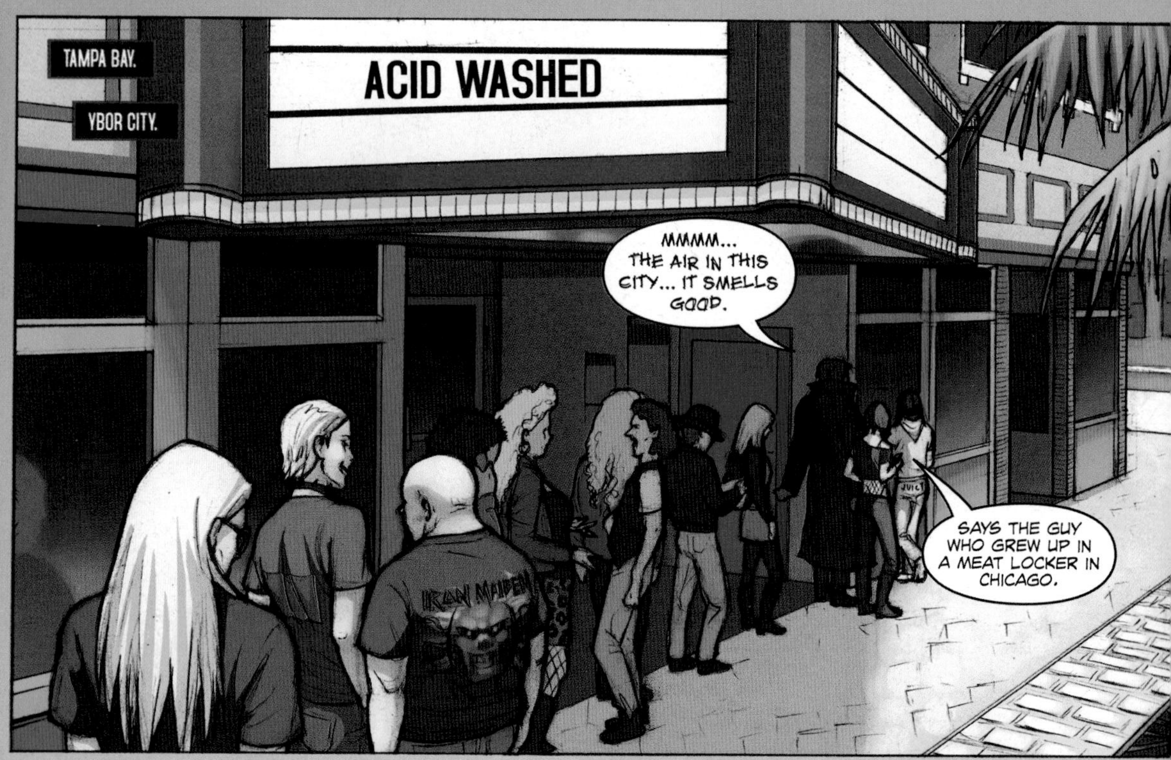
TAMPA BAY.
YBOR CITY.
ACID WASHED
MMMM... THE AIR IN THIS CITY... IT SMELLS GOOD.
SAYS THE GUY WHO GREW UP IN A MEAT LOCKER IN CHICAGO.

I HAVE NEVER SEEN MUSIC PLAYED FOR REAL.
DON'T GET TOO STARRY-EYED. WE AIN'T GETTIN' LUNCH, AND WE'RE SLEEPING IN THE VAN TONIGHT.
BETWEEN THE GAS FOR THE EIGHT HOUR DRIVE AND THE TICKETS, WE JUST BLEW THE REST OF OUR MONEY.
ISN'T ACID WASHED JUST TOTALLY WORTH IT?!

THEY JUST GOT BACK FROM A MINI U.S. TOUR, AND NOW THEY'RE KICKING OFF THEIR BIG TOUR HERE IN TAMPA WITH A TWO NIGHT SHOW FOR THEIR HOMETOWN FANS!
SO, EIGHT HOURS OF DRIVIN'?
WHERE'D Y'ALL COME FROM?
WHAT'S IT TO Y--

CHATTANOOGA. IN TENNESSEE.

CHATTANOOGA? WHY, I'M FROM CHICKAMAUGA, RIGHT ACROSS THE BORDER FROM CHATANOOGA... IN GEORGIA!
I EVEN TOOK MY NAME FROM IT.
YOUR NAME IS CHICKAMAUGA?
HA HA! NO, NO. I'M GEORGIA. GEORGIA PEACHES.

LOOK, WE'RE NOT FROM CHA--
SAVE YOURSELF! DO NOT ATTEND THIS SHOW!

THIS BAND HAS MADE A PACT WITH THE DEVIL HIMSELF!
OH, COME ON, NOW...
ACID WASHED: SATAN

THEIR MUSIC TAINTS EVEN THE PUREST OF SOULS! THEY EXIST TO DENY SALVATION TO THE PURE OF HEART!
OW, LADY! YOU'RE HURTING ME!

LET. HER. GO.
ACID WASHED: SATAN

YOU WILL SEE! ACID WASHED WILL TAKE YOU TO HELL WITH THEM!

I WISH I COULD SAY I WAS SURPRISED, BUT THIS IS FLORIDA. CRAZIES EVERYWHERE. THANKS FOR THE ASSIST, BIG GUY.
I TELL YOU WHAT... I KNOW YOU'RE BOTH HUNGRY. I'M ON THE WAY TO WORK, ANYWAY. HOW 'BOUT I GET Y'ALL A FREE LUNCH?
WE GOT A REAL NICE BUFFET.
HURM. YES... WONDERFUL.

COME, CASSANDRA! FOOD!
ACID WASHED: SATAN
YEAH... I'M COMIN'...

TOP BRASS GENTLEMEN'S CLUB.
HIGH NOON BUFFET.
A BUFFET TABLE AT A STRIP CLUB SEEMS... SO... WRONG.
MMMM... BACON BITS.
GEORGIA IS NICE. SHE IS VERY HAPPY UNLIKE...
YEAH, SO I'VE BEEN IN A PISSY MOOD.
SHE IS AWFUL FRIENDLY...
SHE DIDN'T EVEN SEEM TO NOTICE THAT YOU'RE, Y'KNOW... YOU.
HURR... GEORGIA IS VERY NICE.
GIVE IT UP, EVERYONE...
...FOR MS. GEORGIA PEACHES!!!
GIRL, IF YOU LOVE ME, WHY DO YOU PUSH ME AWAY?
GIRL, IF YOU LOVE ME, WHY DO YOU LET ME BURN?

EVERY TIME I ASK YOU, YOU SAY SOMETHIN' CAUSTIC.
EVERY TIME I TOUCH YOU, YOU ERODE MY LIFE AWAY.
YOUR LOVE EATS THROUGH MY ARMOR! ACID WASHED!
SOON...
DIDJA' GET ENOUGH TO EAT?
YES. AND MUCH TO SEE.
I GUESS YOU REALLY DO LIKE ACID WASHED.

HA HA. YEAH... THEY KINDA MOVE ME, Y'KNOW?
NEVER SEEN THEM LIVE BEFORE?
NOPE. I'M ALWAYS WORKIN'.
I HEAR THEY'RE GOING ALL OUT FOR THIS ONE THOUGH... SOME KIND OF CRAZY PYROTECHNICS DISPLAY AND EVERYTHING. GONNA BE TIGHT.
SO, YOU ALWAYS GIVE STRIP-CLUB BUFFET MEALS TO COMPLETE STRANGERS?
HAH! NO, NOT REALLY. BUT Y'ALL ARE NICE.
I HAVEN'T MET TOO MANY PEOPLE SINCE I MOVED HERE... OUTSIDE OF WORK, I MEAN.
THE GIRLS ARE REAL NICE, BUT, THERE'S... Y'KNOW... POLITICS.
I CAN IMAGINE.
WHEN I WAS A KID, I USED TO ACT IN THE CIVIL WAR ERA REENACTMENTS THEY HAD IN MY TOWN.
WASN'T A WHOLE LOTTA ROOM FOR ACTING WHEN YOU'RE "SLAVE GIRL #4"... BUT THAT BUG SORTA BIT ME ANYWAY.
I TOOK THIS GIG TO SAVE UP MONEY TO MOVE OUT TO L.A., GIVE HOLLYWOOD A TRY. HELL, IF *STRIPPIN'* AIN'T GOOD PRACTICE FOR *HOLLYWOOD*, I DUNNO WHAT IS!
SO, SMALL TOWN GIRL MOVES TO L.A. CLASSIC TALE.

YEAH, YEAH, I KNOW WHAT YOU'RE THINKING: THIS IS GONNA END UP AS A "WELCOME TO THE JUNGLE" VIDEO.
BUT I HAVE CERTAIN *ADVANTAGES*-- INCLUDIN' A FIRM MORAL CENTER. NO DRUGS. NO ALCOHOL.
PEACHES! CAN I GET A DANCE?
AND NO *SEX*.
AT LEAST UNTIL I GET MY CO-STARRING ROLE WITH *DENZEL*.

HOLEEE SHIT! SIX SIXX! AND OUT OF MAKE UP EVEN!
AGO I'D NEVER HEARD OF YOU GUYS. NOW I'M A HUGE FAN!
YOU GUYS BROUGHT METAL BACK.
I ALMOST SHIT WHEN I FOUND OUT YOU WERE PLAYIN' THE ORPH. I EVEN TRADED SHIFTS SO I COULD WORK TONIGHT!
THAT'S AWESOME. THANKS FOR LISTENIN'. NOW, I GOTTA...
WHERE'S THE OTHER GUYS? I'D LOVE TO GET Y'ALL TO SIGN MY BACK!
COME BACK IN A FEW MINUTES... I HAVE A FEELING THEY'LL BE HERE REAL SOON.
SWEET. THANKS, SIX. ROCK ON!
YEAH, ROCK ON YOU FUCKIN' DOUCHE...
ALL RIGHT, BAND...
...IT'S TIME. TIME TO PLEASE OUR BENEFACTORS.
SOUND CHECK.
TESTING, TESTING...
PLEASE, NO!
SORRY, BABY. WE GOTTA TRADE YOUR SOUL FOR SOME ROCK 'N ROLL!
"...I EVOKE THE WORDS OF THE GREAT WIZARDS!"
THRUMMMMMMM!

THERE'S JUST FIVE WORDS TO SAY AS YOU GO DOWN, DOWN, DOWN.
YOU'RE GONNA BURN IN HELL!*
*LYRICS BY TWISTED SISTER.
I CARRY MY CRUCIFIX UNDER MY DEATHLIST.
FORWARD MY MAIL TO ME IN HELL . . . OUR FATHER, WHO AIN'T IN HEAVEN!*
*LYRICS BY MOTLEY CRUE.

HEY, SATAN-- PAID MY DUES...
FCHOO!
FCHOO!
UHHHHH...
FCHOO!
I'M ON THE WAY TO THE PROMISED LAND! I'M ON THE HIGHWAY TO HELL!*
*LYRICS BY AC/DC.
TASTE THE LOVE, THE LUCIFER'S MAGIC!*
ZZZZZZZKKKLLLKK
OOOH, YEAH! BABY! DEMONIZE ME!
*LYRICS BY W.A.S.P.
YESSS!!!
ARE YOU READY TO ROCK!?

SORRY, LADIES... FRONT ROW IS FOR V.I.P.s ONLY.
DOES THAT INCLUDE LIL' OL' ME?
GEORGIA!

FIRST SEATS? THIS IS GOOD, YES?
YEAH, MOST OF THE GUARDS COME TO THE CLUB, SO I HAVE A FEW CONNECTIONS.

OH, HELL NO!
I'M GERTUDE HALL, THE ORGINAL ACID WASHED FAN!
HOW THE HELL IS SIX GONNA SEE THESE BEAUTIES WITH THIS MAN-MOUNTAIN STANDING IN FRONT OF ME!?
IT'S BAD ENOUGH THEY DON'T GIVE ME A BACKSTAGE PASS ANYMORE!

AND THIS ISN'T SOME GOAT-ROAPER SHOW!
IT'S PURE ROCK! SO AT LEAST TAKE OFF THE HAT, YA BIG, INBRED *HICK!*
HURR?
ER... SORRY. I DIDN'T KNOW YOU WERE...
...YEAH.
THANK YOU.
OH! MY! GOSH! THEY'RE STARTING!

HELLOOOOO, TAMPA!
WE ARE HOME, AND WE ARE HERE *TO MELT YOUR FACE!*

ARE YOU READY TO GET DOWN WITH ME?
ARE YOU READY TO GO DOWN WITH ME?
DOWN, DOWN, DOWN TO THE DEVIL!!
SMELL THE BLOOD, FEEL THE FIRE, WE'RE GONNA MAKE LOVE, NEVER TIRE!
MEH.

DOWN TO THE DEVIL
TRICK OR TREAT
GRASS ON THE FIELD (I SAY PLAY)
BLACK ROSES
EVERYBODY WANTS THE KITTY MASSAGE
TERROR ON TOUR
WET MOON
ROCK 'N' ROLL NIGHTMARE
DIRTY PILLOW TALK
ACID WASHED
ACID WASHED! YOU DISSOLVE MY RESTRAAAAAINT! ACID WASHED! YOUR LOVE LEAVES A STAIN!
NOW IS THE TIME, MY FRIENDS! THE TIME FOR THE GIVING OF FLESH IN THE FORM OF A SACRIFICE!
SACRIFICE!
SACRIFICE!
SACRIFICE!
BUT THIS ISN'T JUST ANY SACRIFICE. WE ONLY WANT THE PUREST!
THE UNTAINTED! FOR THE GODS OF ROCK DEMAND...
...A VIRGIN SACRIFICE!

COME FORWARD, VIRGINS! COME FORWARD TO THE ALTAR BENEATH THE STAGE!
ONLY THE MOST PURE WILL BE CHOSEN. ONLY THE MOST PURE WILL GIVE THEMSELVES FOR ACID WASHED!
ACID WASHED!
ACID WASHED!
ACID WASHED!
HOLD UP, HULK. YOU'RE TOO BIG AND UGLY FOR THEIR TASTES. WE'VE GOT ENOUGH.
THANK YOU, TAMPA!
GOOD NIGHT!

OW...
...MY EARS ARE RINGING.
WHERE ARE WE?
OH, SHIT... THAT OLD LADY WAS RIGHT...
...ACID WASHED BROUGHT US TO HELL.

HEH... LOOK AT THIS! SOME KINDA STONED RETARD!
CASSANDRA! NO!
ELEVEN
AGH!!
URGGHGH... CASSANDRA...
VLAD? WHAT'S UP? GET THE HAIR METAL KILLERS?
CHRIS. I NEED YOUR HELP.
THE BAND... THEY USED A SPELL. THEY WERE TALKING OF UNTAINTED SOULS AND SACRIFICE.
CASSANDRA, I, AND A GIRL NAMED GEORGIA WERE UNABLE TO RESIST.
CONTROLLED IN THE MIND. THE GIRLS... THEY DISAPPEARED.
"UNTAINTED"? I KNOW CASS IS, AND I ASSUME YOU ARE... WAS THIS GEORGIA CHICK A VIRGIN TOO?
YES. I BELIEVE SHE SAID SHE HAD NOT HAD THE SEX.
I READ ABOUT THIS IN ONE OF JASON'S BOOKS...
...SOUNDS LIKE THESE GUYS ARE USING SOME KIND OF ENCHANTMENT.
HELPS THEM GET THE PURE SOULS THEY NEED. ONLY WORKS ON VIRGINS.
IF YOU WANT TO GET THEM BACK NOW... JESUS! YOU KNOW WHAT THIS MEANS?
YOU HAVE TO GET LAID.

YBOR CITY, FLORIDA.
SIXX
YOU GUYS, WERE, LIKE, SO AWESOME TONIGHT.
YEAH, I COULD REALLY FEEL IT TONIGHT.
WE'RE GOING TO BE HUGE. LEGENDS, EVEN.
WHICH ONE OF YOU HOT LITTLE BITCHES WANTS TO JOIN OUR MÉNAGE À TWAT?
KEEP YOUR HANDS OFF MY GIRLS, STU, OR I'LL PUT YOU BACK IN THE CRATE.
HEE HEE.

I PROMISE YOU, THEY'LL WANT ME BACK THERE.
JUST TELL THEM... TELL THEM GERTUDE IS HERE.
LADY, THE BAND HAS REAL SPECIFIC TYPES AND NOT ONE OF 'EM GOES FOR THE GNAWGAHYDE LOOK. SO, JUST WALK AWAY.
LISTEN SHITFERBRAINS. I HAVE FUCKED EVERY GUY WITH A GUITAR FROM GENE SIMMONS TO TINY TIM.
I'M ROCK ROYALTY! I'M NOT A GROUPIE, I'M AN INSTITUTION.
I HAVE FOLLOWED THIS BAND SINCE THEIR FIRST SHOW.
THEY WERE MINE LONG BEFORE ANY OF THESE LITTLE WHORES SHOWED UP!
PLEASE, IF YOU KNOW WHAT'S GOOD FOR ROCK 'N ROLL, LET ME BACKSTAGE!
NOPE.
HOW ABOUT I SHOW YOU MY TITS?

OUTSIDE.
ALL I KNOW IS THAT MY DAUGHTER WALKED IN TO SEE THIS BAND, AND SHE HASN'T WALKED OUT.
I NEVER WOULD HAVE LET HER GO TO SEE THIS ATROCITY; BUT HER MOTHER NAGGED ME TO DEATH ABOUT IT.
WELL, THE SHOW IS OVER, BUT SOMETIMES GIRLS STAY TO MEET THE BAND...
...AUTOGRAPHS... THAT SORT OF THING.
ARE YOU SAYING MY DAUGHTER IS SOME KIND OF GROUPIE?! I SWEAR IF THAT BAND TOUCHES HER...
CALM DOWN, SIR.
WE'D BEEN WARNED THAT A NUMBER OF DISAPPEARANCES HAVE BEEN ASSOCIATED WITH THIS GROUP. WE JUST WANT TO MAKE SURE EVERYONE IS SAFE...
YOU MIND IF WE TAKE A LOOK AROUND?
OF COURSE NOT. COME ON IN.
HURRRM...

ELSEWHERE.
DON'T YOU FUCKING TOUCH HER!

C-CASSIE... JUST DO WHAT THEY WANT...

NEVER DID WHAT PEOPLE WANTED... NOT ABOUT TO START...

THUK!

GULLOCK
EYYYAAAH!

GRAAAA!

Goha na Jafa!
KRRZTTTT!

Kuma rom qua zaad.
OH GOD, OH GOD, OH GOD...

AHHHHHH!
GUNARTA! GUNARTA!
OH GOD...
AHUH
WHERE THE HELL AM I?!
OH...
AAAAAAAH!

Voo Roff Kirreeta.
KUMOK!

Mi daramma gumarta. Pash pah maratta!

Paf!
COFF
COFF

You. Are. LUCKY. NOW we go.

EMINENCE, INDIANA.
SO A HOOKER IS OUT OF THE QUESTION THEN?
YES. NO MONEY.
BUT, I CANNOT FACE THIS DEMON BAND IF I AM VIRGIN.
1:15
OKAY. WE'LL FIGURE OUT A WAY TO WIRE YOU SOME GIRL-MONEY...
WORST CASE SCENARIO, I CAN GET A RED EYE FLIGHT DOWN THERE AND... Y'KNOW... DO HIM.
EXCUSE ME, VLAD.
UH... WHAT?
WHAT?! IT'S AN EMERGENCY!
CASSIE COULD BE ANYWHERE. WE BOTH OWE HER OUR LIVES.
TOUCHÉ.
ALRIGHT VLAD, WE'RE GONNA WORK ON OUR END TO GET YOU MONEY.
IN THE MEANTIME, SEE IF YOU CAN FIND OUT WHERE THE HOOKERS ARE, OKAY?

SO... I SHOULD NOT TRY THE... URR? REGULAR WAY?
I... WELL...
LOOK MAN... YOU'RE AN AWESOME GUY. THE BEST.
BUT TALKING TO WOMEN, GETTING THEM TO LIKE YOU, GETTING THEM HOME... WELL, IT'S REALLY HARD. IT'S REALLY HARD FOR NORMAL GUYS EVEN.
NORMAL. HURR...
BUT... CASSIE LIKES ME. AND SHE IS A GIRL.
IT'S JUST, THIS WHOLE THING... IT'S KIND OF A GAME.
IT'S NOT AN EASY GAME, ESPECIALLY IF YOU'VE NEVER PLAYED. AND PEOPLE, ESPECIALLY IN THIS GAME, ARE REALLY JUDGEMENTAL ABOUT...
SIGH
VLAD. YOU GO FIND A GIRL. DO THIS THE REGULAR WAY. WE'LL FIND A WAY TO WIRE YOU CASH, JUST IN CASE.
EVERYTHING OKAY?
GOD HELP ME, I THINK VLAD MIGHT BE IN MORE DANGER THAN CASSIE.

ELSEWHERE.
THIS HERE'S TWO GIRLS, KUMOK. THE BIG GUYS ASKED FOR THREE.
Munta cah vok.
YEAH YEAH, MATH AIN'T A REAL STRONG SUBJECT 'ROUND THESE PARTS.
GUESS IT'LL HAVE TO DO. BRING 'EM IN , AND WE'LL CALL IT EVEN.
Sha barnah coo.
Marnah po! Move.
GOD! OW!
HEY, KUMOK...
Yes?
...YOU'RE THE ONE THAT'S LUCKY.

THAT SIX HAS SURE GOT SOME PRETTY FANS. GUESS THE APPEAL OF THE BARGAIN WOULDN'T BE SO STRONG IF WEREN'T FOR LADIES LIKE YOURSELF.
DARLIN', YOU IN PARTICULAR ARE ONE SMOKIN' LITTLE FILLY. THERE WAS A TIME, I COULDA HAD YOU TREMBLIN' IN YOUR SHORTS.
THOSE WERE THE GOOD OL' DAYS. ALMOST SEEMS LIKE ANOTHER LIFE BY NOW.
WHERE ARE WE? WHAT'S GOING ON HERE?
HONEY, THAT IS A LONG STORY, AND I'M JUST PLUM TIRED.
YOU AND YOUR FRIEND JUST SIT TIGHT AND IT'LL ALL BE OVER REAL SOON.
POOCH, KEEP AN EYE ON THEM. I'M GONNA GRAB SOME SHUT EYE 'FORE THEY ARRIVE.
WAIT! DON'T LEAVE US!
WHO ARE THESE PEOPLE?! WHAT DO THEY WANT!?
SHHHH IT'S... IT'S OKAY, HON. WE'LL GET THROUGH.
ONE WAY OR ANOTHER, WE'LL GET THOUGH.
WHY WON'T THEY TELL US WHAT THEY WANT...?
Pet me.

HOLY FUCK! THE... THING! IT TALKS!
Pet me. Pet me and I will tells you what Master not tell you.
I AM NOT TOUCHING THAT THING.
FUCK.
UNH LIKE... LIKE THIS?
Ooooh yes. yessssss. Ask. Ask. Pooch will tell?
LET'S START WITH THE BASICS.
WHERE THE FUCK ARE WE, WHO WAS THAT GUY, WHAT DOES HE WANT WITH US, AND WHAT DOES IT HAVE TO DO WITH THAT SHITTY FUCKING BAND?
Oooohhh... yesssssss...

This place is... Nef. Home. Nef is ruled by great and powerful gods. Our Gods cannot create.
They are only good for sufferings and deaths. To make, they need creatures from your world.
Pure ones. Good ones. Virgin ones.
They find a hero from your world to help them. They offer him great gifts. Talents. Musics.
This human uses talents. Becomes big famous. Finds glory. Is love by all.
In trade, this human is taught our magicks. This human sends us pure ones for the Gods.
And when his deal is done, his skills go away. Then he finds others. Others who wants the musics and the love.
mmm. Yess... My Master. In your world, he was a King. Here is a hero.
And soon. Soon, you will be mothers.

FLORIDA.
I TELL YA WHAT: NIGHTS LIKE THESE, I WISH I WOULDA STAYED WITH BARRY.
AIN'T NO GOOD REASON IN THE WORLD TO STAY WITH THAT BUM.
AT MY AGE, ALL THE GOOD ONES ARE TAKEN OR GAY.
THERE'S ONE GOOD REASON. AT LEAST I DIDN'T HAVE TO DO THIS. GO OUT TO BARS, TRYING TO MEET MEN.
DON'T I KNOW IT.
OKAY. SCREW IT. IT'S LATE, AND I'VE GOTTEN NOWHERE.
JOSE, MARK MY WORDS, I'M GOING TO GO HOME WITH THE NEXT GUY THAT HITS ON ME.
HELLO. MY NAME IS VLAD...
GOTTA GO! G'NIGHT!
HURR...

LADY, YOU'VE HAD TOO MUCH TO DRINK. I CAN'T LET YOU IN.
I JUS WAN' ONE MORE DRINK. JUST ONE MORE.
I'M SORRY LADY. YOU'VE HAD ENOUGH--
I WILL WALK HER HOME.
HEEEEYYY. I REMEMMER YOOOUU.
WHERE WE GONNA GET ANOTHER DRINK?
WE ARE NOT. I AM HELPING YOU HOME.
SSSS RIGHT DOWN THERE.
Y'KNOW WHAT? THE BAND LEFT ME. LEFT ME ALL ALONE. JUST LIKE EVERYONE ELSE.
YES. I SAW.
OPEN

SEEMS LIKE IT'S ALWAYS THAT WAY. I JUST GIVE AND GIVE. AND THEY JUST USE ME UP AND THROW ME AWAY.
EVERYONE ALWAYS SAID I WAS A SLUT. A GROUPIE. BUT, I WOULDN'T HAVE SLEPT WITH ALL OF THEM IF JUST ONE HAD LOVED ME BACK.
I JUST LOVE MUSIC SO MUCH. I JUST WANTED ONE MUSICIAN TO LOOK AND ME AND LOVE ME LIKE HE LOVED THE MUSIC.
I WANTED SOMEONE TO BE SO INSPIRED THEY'D WRITE A BALLAD ABOUT ME. LIKE "BETH" OR "MADALAINE", Y'KNOW? I JUST WANTED TO BE "HAIR-ENADED".
THIS ISH MY PLACE HERE.

SOMETIMES I THINK NO ONE'S EVER GONNA LOVE ME.
I SH'POSE YOU KNOW WHAT THAT'S LIKE...
...WITH THAT FACE OF YOURS.

HURRR... I MUST LEAVE.

YOU'RE NOT GOING ANYWHERE.

AHUNH
SNIFF
I DON'T THINK I CAN CRY ANYMORE. I'M OUT.
I KNOW THE FEELING.
SO... SO I GUESS YOU'RE A VIRGIN, TOO.
YEAH. 100% PURE. THAT'S ME.
BUT MY REASONS AREN'T AS NOBLE AS YOURS. WELL, IF WAITING FOR DENZEL WASHINGTON IS NOBLE...
...I WAS ALWAYS THE "FREAK" IN SCHOOL. NO ONE LIKED ME, ESPECIALLY NOT THE GUYS.
I'M STILL A VIRGIN BECAUSE I EMIT SOME KIND OF PENIS REPELLANT. SERIOUSLY. I'M LIKE RAID TO COCK.
WHAT?! COME ON. THAT'S BULLSHIT. YOU'RE A HOT GIRL.
AND THOSE CLOTHES... YOU HAVEN'T DONE IT BECAUSE YOU DON'T WANT TO.
I MEAN, SERIOUSLY, HAVE YOU MET MEN?
GIRLS HALF AS SEXY AS YOU HAVE TO USE A STICK TO KEEP GUYS AWAY.
HEH...
...I DUNNO... JUST WITH GUYS... IT NEVER FEELS RIGHT. THEY MAKE ME FEEL WEIRD.
LIKE... I DON'T KNOW... LIKE I DON'T UNDERSTAND THEM. AND SOMETIMES I DON'T WANT TO UNDERSTAND THEM.

MAYBE YOU'RE...
...GAY.
MAYBE. SOMETIMES I THINK IT'S POSSIBLE. OR I THINK I JUST DON'T KNOW WHAT I AM.
I THINK I LIKE GUYS. SOMETIMES. I DON'T KNOW. MAYBE I'M JUST NOTHING.
WELL, IF IT WASN'T FOR THESE CHAINS, I KNOW HOW WE COULD MAYBE GET US SENT HOME.
IF I COULD, I'D MAKE US GOOD AND IMPURE AND HAVE SEX WITH YOU RIGHT NOW.
REALLY?
SEE, NOW *THAT* SOUNDED A LITTLE *TOO* EXCITED. YOU ARE *DEFINITELY* GAY.
HEY NOW LITTLE MAMAS...
...IT'S TIME TO GET READY FOR THE BIG SHOW.

EMINENCE, INDIANA.
24 HOU
WESTERN UNION
VLAD. WE FOUND A PLACE. WE'RE SENDING YOU SOME DE-VIRGINIFYING MONEY RIGHT NOW.
URR... YES... I MAY NOT NEED THE MONEY. I HAVE FOUND A FRIEND.
CHRIS-- I NEED TO KNOW HOW TO HAVE THE SEX. WHAT DO I DO?
WAIT... WHAT!? WHAT DO YOU MEAN... ?
WHO ARE YOU CALLING, YOU BIG SEXY MAN? PUT THAT DOWN AND FOLLOW ME.
VLAD?!
MMMH... MM... OH YESSS...
HURR!
VLAD? YOU THERE?

YBOR CITY, FLORIDA.
I HOPE YOU ALL HAVE A GOOD NIGHT'S REST, 'CUZ TOMORROW NIGHT IS AN EVEN BIGGER SHOW.
WE'RE ON THE VERGE OF ROCK ROYALTY. SABBATH. MAIDEN. PRIEST. THEY WON'T HAVE NOTHIN' ON US.
WHATEVER, MAN. THIS SUCKS. WE GOT THE BUNK END OF THIS DEAL, SIX.
HOW COME *YOU* GET TO TURN BACK TO HUMAN FORM, AND WE GOTTA BE UNLIVING, SOULESS THRALLS?
IT'S VERY SIMPLE.
I'M THE FRONTMAN.

ELSEWHERE.
GETTING' DRESSED AND NOT PLANNING ANYTHING IN THERE.
WANNA SEE ME ALL SHOOK UP.
YOU GOTTA BE KIDDING ME! WHAT ARE THESE GUYS? THE GODS OF LAS VEGAS?
FUNNY. NOW YOU TIE HER UP.
THEY GOT ALL KINDS O' STORIES 'ROUND HERE ABOUT WHERE THESE GODS CAME FROM.
ME, I GOT MY OWN THEORY: SEE, GOD CREATED THE UNIVERSE, RIGHT?
I FIGURE THERE MUST HAVE BEEN SOMETHING THERE BEFORE. AN OLD UNIVERSE. PROBABLY A REAL NASTY PLACE... ALL CHAOS, BLACK MAGICKS AND DARKNESS.
THESE FELLAS, WHO'RE GONNA BE THE FATHERS OF YOUR BABIES... I THINK THEY CAME FROM THAT OLD UNIVERSE.
KNOWIN' THAT, YA GOTTA UNDERSTAND WHY THEY MIGHT BE A LIL' OLD FASHIONED...

I DON'T WANT TO BE A MOTHER... I DON'T WANT TO BE HERE...
...PLEASE, SIR... JUST LET US GO HOME.
AW, DARLIN', NOW YOU JUST CALM YOURSELF. DONCHA KNOW?
AIN'T NOTHING MORE GLORIOUS THAN CREATIN' LIFE.
TO BE IMPREGNATED?

EMINENCE, INDIANA.
ELSTEN ANIMAL SHELTER
YOU SPENT THE NIGHT?! THAT'S GREAT!
YES. BUT... I AM NOT SURE THAT I HAVE LOST IT.
YOU AREN'T SURE YOU HAD SEX?
HOW CAN HE NOT KNOW IF HE'S HAD SEX?!
QUIET, CHRIS. IT WAS HIS FIRST TIME FOR CHRIST'S SAKE.
NOW, VLAD, DID YOU PUT YOUR PENIS INSIDE HER VAGINA?
URRR... VAH-GINUH?
VLAD!!
HURR? I MUST LEAVE. I WILL CALL LATER.
VLAD?
CLICK!
THE COPS ARE LEAVING. GUESS THEY DIDN'T FIND THE GIRLS. IT'S JUST LIKE YOU SAID. THIS WHOLE TIME I'VE BEEN SUCKING DEMON COCK.
YES. NOW, I MUST FIND MY FRIEND.

INSIDE...
KNOK KNOK KNOK
MR. SIXX? MR. SIXX?
CHRIST ON A FUCKIN' CRUTCH... WHAT?! IT'S EARLY AS SHIT, MAN. WE AIN'T EVEN GOT SOUND CHECK UNTIL TWO!
THE COPS WERE HERE. THEY WERE ASKING AROUND.
GUESS A GIRL FROM THE SHOW DIDN'T MAKE IT HOME LAST NIGHT. I TOLD THE BOSS YOU GUYS HAD FOLLOWED "FRIENDS" TO A FEW HOTELS AROUND TOWN.
SO, I WAS WONDERING IF MAYBE I COULD GET THOSE AUTOGRAPHS?
Y'KNOW, I SCRATCH YOUR BACK, YOU SIGN MY AXE. OTHERWISE, I GUESS I COULD MENTION I'D SEEN YOU WALKIN' AROUND THIS MORNING.
SIGH
ALL RIGHT. LET ME MAKE SURE EVERYONE'S UP.
FZZRRRAAKSH!
THEY'RE READY. JUST SO Y'KNOW, THE BAND CAN BE A LITTLE IRRITABLE IN THE MORNING...
...HUH?

WHERE DID YOU TAKE MY FRIENDS?!
GHYAH!
GOOD BOY. NOT A WORD.
WHERE!? TELL ME!
I SENT 'EM AWAY, MAN. BUT IF YOU LET ME GRAB MY GUITAR I CAN BRING 'EM BACK.
OF COURSE, WE PROBABLY SHOULDN'T DO THIS IN FULL VIEW OF THE PUBLIC.

GERTRUDE. STAY HERE.
SURE THING.

HANGING OUT WITH OUR CAST-OFFS NOW?
SHUT UP. FRIENDS BACK. NOW.
THEY'RE OFF LIVING THE ULTIMATE GROUPIE FANTASY. THEY'RE GIVING UP THEIR VIRGINITY FOR ROCK 'N ROLL.

YOU, ON THE OTHER HAND...
...ARE GONNA LIVE YOUR LAST FEW SECONDS IN A HEAVY METAL NIGHTMARE!
FZZRRRAAKSH!
RAGHG!
TEAR THIS UGLY FUCKER INTO LITTLE PIECES...
HEH HEH HEH.

YOU THINK YOU HAVE ME IN A TRAP.
HURR HURR HURR.
GHYAH!
SWOK!
DIE QUICKLY, PLEASE.
YOU'VE GOT A GOOD LOOK. YOU COULD'VE BEEN ON ONE OF OUR ALBUM COVERS.
TOO BAD YOU'RE ABOUT TO BE DEADER THAN GRUNGE.
SHRIIISSH
SHRIIISSH
RRRARGH!
UNF
THWAK!
YOU SHOULDN'TA COME HERE, FUGLY--!
HUK
SHUK!!
SHUK!!

AW, MAN! STU MAY HAVE BEEN THE WORLD'S BIGGEST COCK-BLOCK...
...BUT EVEN HE DIDN'T DESERVE THAT!
FUCKIN' A! IT'S JUST ONE GUY! NO WONDER WE ALWAYS SUCKED! YOU GUYS CAN'T WORK TOGETHER FOR SHIT.
GUESS IT'S UP TO ME LIKE ALWAYS.
HAVE A POWER CHORD, MOTHERFUCKER!
FZZKRRRAASH!!
FCHOOM!
AGHGH
OORF

ENOUGH OF THIS.
I WANT CASSIE. I WANT GEORGIA.
KRAK!
NOW.
AH! FUCK, MAN! FUCK!
SIX, YOU PUSSY!
GRAH!
THIS FREAK WAS AT THE SHOW THE OTHER NIGHT.
THE VIRGIN CULL WORKED ON HIM! HE'S PURE! PLAY THE FUCKING TONE!
MRRUH

AWESOME. THE *SHIT* I AM GONNA *MAKE* HIM DO...
THRUMMMM

HURR?

?!

SHIT.
HE'S NOT A VIRGIN ANYMORE.

HUR HUR HUR.
I'VE HAD THE SEX!

HURR HURR.
VAH-GII-NUH.
AHHH!
SHUK!!
SHUK!!
NOO!
YOU TRADED MY SOUL FOR FAME, SIX. MAYBE, I SHOULD LET HIM KILL YOU.
I SHOULD.
BUT, IT *WAS* A FUCKING GREAT RIDE.
THWAK!
CHROOOM
SHITSHIT SHITSHITSHIT SHITSHIT.
STILL GOT THE MAGICK. I CAN START OVER. START A NEW BAND...

OR A SOLO PROJECT. YEAH, THAT'S IT...
=ENK=
WHAK!
SIX SIXX. I REMEMBER WHEN I FIRST SAW YOU. I THOUGHT YOU WERE JUST THE HOTTEST THING.
OH. MY BABY.
NOW I SEE, YOU'RE JUST A MISERABLE, SELF CENTERED ASSHOLE WHO THINKS HE'S HOT SHIT ON A SILVER PLATTER.
BUT YOU'RE REALLY JUST COLD DIARRHEA ON A PAPER PLATE. I'M DONE WITH YOU, SIX SIXX.
HERE'S A COUPLE OF THINGS TO REMEMBER ME BY.
=MMMF=
LAST TIME I ASKED NICE.
NOW, WHERE ARE MY FRIENDS?

NEF.
AHUH. HUNH... YEAH.
HYAAH!
MASTERS! I HAVE FINISHED THE DANCE OF BAPTISM.
COME MASTERS! COME AND SPREAD YOUR GLORY ACROSS THIS LAND.
ZZZZAKKK
ZZZZAKKK
HOLY--

ZZZZAKK
ZZZZAKK
COME, MY MASTERS!
ZZZZAKK
ZZZZAKK
FUCK, FUCK, FUCK...
THE VESSELS ARE READY FOR YOUR SEED!
SSSSHLOOOP!
HEY, KUMOK... YOU STILL MAD ABOUT THAT MARK I GAVE YOU ON THE FACE?

THAT'S GOTTA PISS YOU OFF, RIGHT? SOME LOWLY HUMAN GIRL, DAMAGING YOU LIKE THAT?
I MEAN, YOU SERVE THE GODS. YOU'RE BIG SHIT.
AND YOU DON'T GET TO EVEN UP.
SILENCE! RA FOK!
RAH!
OUK!
YEAH...
...RA FOK YOU, TOO.
BRZAKAK!

URRR AK!
AHH!
HEY, KUMOK!
BRZAKAK!
YOUR LUCK JUST RAN OUT.
RRRRRR...
Stop human. Master needs you.
RRRRRR...
YEAH, LIKE I'M GONNA LISTEN TO A TALKING DOG.
YIPE
NO! THEY'RE ESCAPIN'! TAKE THEM NOW!
GREAT WORK BACK THERE. BUT THIS IS WHERE WE'RE *REALLY* GOING TO HAVE TO GET CREATIVE.
BRZAKAK!

NO ONE IS GETTING ALL TENTACLE PORN ON ME, FUCKER!
BRZAKAK!
GHYAH!
SLUURP!
OH GOD... THEY'RE GONNA GET US!
SQUOOCH!
JUST RUN! WE NEED SOME COVER!
THIS FAT FUCK WILL DO FOR NOW.
GET OFFA ME! YOU GOTTA ACCEPT THEIR--
SHUK!!
--SEED.
URR

GURRGULLL
OHNO NONONO NO!
SHLOOP
GEORGIA!
ERRRRGH I'M SO SORRY GEORGIA. I TRIED.
I KNOW.
I KNOW YOU DID.
SPLORGH

OOOF
WHAT?!
RUN! RUN NOW!
VLAD! THANK YOU!
HOW'D YOU FIND US?!
SIX! NEED A DOOR! OPEN!
IT TOOK MANY TRIES. THIS PLACE SUCKS MUCH ASS.
OH. SHIT. THAT'S WHAT I WAS WORKING FOR?
WHEN I MADE A DEAL WITH THE DEVIL, I WAS THINKING HE'D LOOK LIKE THE GUY FROM MAIDEN'S "NUMBER OF THE BEAST". BUT THAT--
SHUT UP! GO!

SON OF A... I AM CLOSING THIS, MAN!
NOT YET!
FWOOOP!
GRAA!
NOW! CLOSE IT!
VLAD!
FZZRRRAAKSH!
VRRRMMM
SQUIT
SPLORCH

IT'S BEEN REAL, SUCKERS. BUT I GOTTA GO.
GOOD.

WHA?!
AND DON'T COME BACK. YOUR SONGS SUCK ANYWAY.

"YOUR LOVE LEAVES A STAIN"? WHAT THE HELL IS THAT?
GHYAAAH!

ASSHOLE HAS LEFT THE BUILDING.
VRRRMMM

YOU DON'T HANG AROUND MUSICIANS FOR FIFTEEN YEARS WITHOUT PICKING UP A FEW CHORDS.

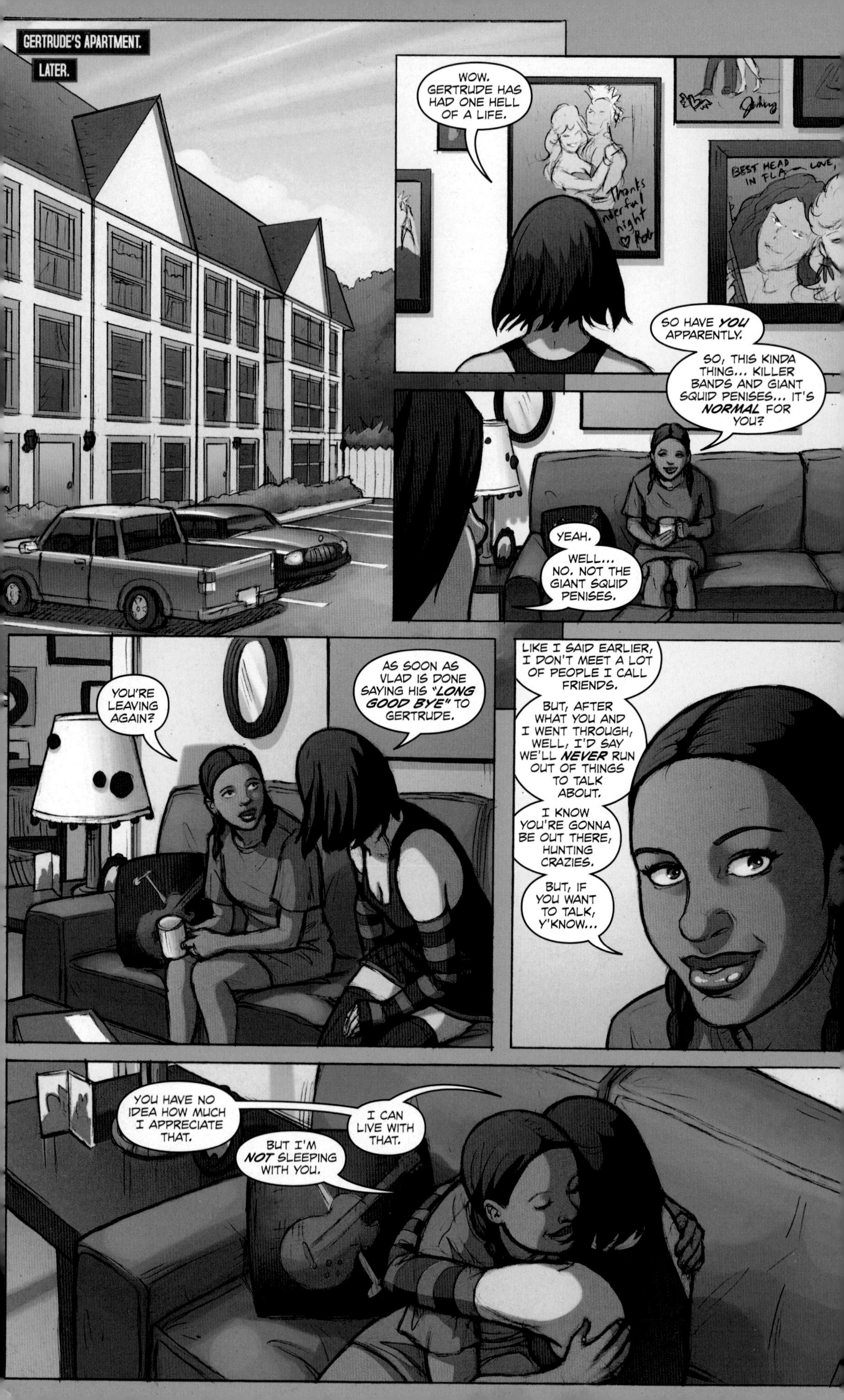
GERTRUDE'S APARTMENT.
LATER.
WOW. GERTRUDE HAS HAD ONE HELL OF A LIFE.
Thanks wonderful night ♡ Rob
BEST HEAD IN FLA — LOVE,
SO HAVE YOU APPARENTLY.
SO, THIS KINDA THING... KILLER BANDS AND GIANT SQUID PENISES... IT'S NORMAL FOR YOU?
YEAH.
WELL... NO. NOT THE GIANT SQUID PENISES.
YOU'RE LEAVING AGAIN?
AS SOON AS VLAD IS DONE SAYING HIS "LONG GOOD BYE" TO GERTRUDE.
LIKE I SAID EARLIER, I DON'T MEET A LOT OF PEOPLE I CALL FRIENDS.
BUT, AFTER WHAT YOU AND I WENT THROUGH, WELL, I'D SAY WE'LL NEVER RUN OUT OF THINGS TO TALK ABOUT.
I KNOW YOU'RE GONNA BE OUT THERE, HUNTING CRAZIES.
BUT, IF YOU WANT TO TALK, Y'KNOW...
YOU HAVE NO IDEA HOW MUCH I APPRECIATE THAT.
I CAN LIVE WITH THAT.
BUT I'M NOT SLEEPING WITH YOU.

SO, YOU HAVE A GIRLFRIEND NOW?
NO. SHE IS "MARRIED TO THE ROCK 'N ROLL". BUT IF I AM IN THE AREA, I AM IN TO STOP IN FOR A "HOT 'N SLOPPY". COOL, YES?
I CAN'T BELIEVE YOU HAD SEX BEFORE ME.
BEEEP BEEEP

HEY, CHRIS.
EVERYTHING TURNED OUT OKAY? THE FORCES OF EVIL HAVE BEEN THWARTED ANOTHER DAY?
YEAH, THANKS TO YOU AND A COUPLE OF NEWBIES.
YOU KNOW THAT HACK/SLASH, INC. IDEA YOU WERE YAMMERIN' ON ABOUT?
YEAH?

I'LL THINK ABOUT IT.

ELSEWHERE.
Jim & Edna's
TONIGHT:
ACID W
BEER
YOU'RE UP, MR. SIXX.
THEY'RE WAITING. IT'S YOUR CHANCE AT THE BIG TIME.
WHUU--?! WHERE AM I?

PLAY SOME SKYNARD!
IT'S YOUR OWN PERSONAL HELL, MR. SIXX.
AND WE'VE BOOKED YOU FOR AN EXTENDED ENGAGEMENT.
NO! NOOO!!!
AND THESE ARE THE LAST TITS YER EVER GONNA SEE!

THE CRANE CENTER.
NORTHERN CALIFORNIA.

GOOD NIGHT, DR. TUREK.
MAKE SURE TO LET SECURITY KNOW YOU'RE STILL HERE.
NO PROBLEM. G' NIGHT DR. WHITE.

WE'RE ALONE NOW, HONEY.
I WANT YOU TO KNOW... DR. WHITE AND I ARE CLOSE. WE'RE SO CLOSE TO UNDERSTANDING WHAT'S HAPPENED TO YOUR BODY.
I THINK WE CAN RESTORE YOU, EMILY.
SOMETIMES... SOMETIMES, I HAVE THOUGHTS... THESE FANTASIES WHERE YOU FALL IN LOVE WITH ME FOR MAKING YOU GORGEOUS AGAIN.
WOULDN'T I BE LUCKY? A MAN WITH THE LOVE OF THE MOST BEAUTIFUL WOMAN IN THE WORLD...

SIGH
I CAN DREAM, CAN'T I?

NEXT ISSUE:
THE RETURN O
MS. AMERICA

'Sexiest man' Vlad: "Hurr."
LOVE STORIES
TM
"I'm more than just another bad girl."
Cassie Hack speaks
IS BEAUTY REALLY JUST SKIN DEEP?
Unleash The Inner You!
TIPS FROM MS. AMERICA
EMILY CRISTY
see p.250
TM
#5A by CRANK! MODLED BY SANDRA KAMMERER

1989.
I DON'T KNOW, DAVID. IT ISN'T *THAT* HIGH.
OH. WELL, I REALLY DO FEEL PRETTY AWFUL. MAYBE IT'S JUST IN THE EARLY STAGES.
IF I STAY HOME TODAY I'LL AVOID BEING SICK LATER.
OKAY. YOU CAN STAY HOME *TODAY.* BUT, WHEN I GET HOME FROM WORK I WANT YOU TO DO WHATEVER HOMEWORK YOU'VE MISSED.
YES, MOTHER.
YES!
HEH... ≡SNORT≡ SICK DAYS ARE THE *BEST!*
DAD'S
GIRLIE
GIRLIE
GIRLIE
OH... OH MY...

EMILY CRISTY. MS. NOVEMBER.
I-I...
I LOVE YOU.

EMINENCE, INDIANA.
TWO WEEKS AGO.
I DON'T THINK I'VE EVER BEEN SO GLAD TO GET HOME.
YEAH, GETTING KIDNAPPED BY A MUMMY-WRAPPED SCHOOL GIRL AND TAKEN TO NEW ORLEANS HELPS BRING THINGS INTO PERSPECTIVE DOESN'T IT?*
* SEE HACK/SLASH VS. CHUCKY.
WELL, THANKS FOR THE RIDE BACK TO OUR NECK OF THE WOODS. I CAN WALK DOWNTOWN AND FIGURE OUT A WAY TO CATCH A BUS BACK TO MOUNT HEALTHY.
OH, DON'T BE RIDICULOUS. WE'RE BOTH EXHAUSTED. IT'S BEEN A TRYING COUPLE OF DAYS. WHY DON'T YOU JUST STAY HERE AND CATCH A BUS TOMORROW?
JUST MAKING SURE. I KNOW YOU SAID YOU THOUGHT WE SHOULD JUST BE FRIENDS. DIDN'T WANT ANYTHING TO BE "WEIRD".
FRIENDS CAN CRASH AT EACH OTHER'S HOUSES AFTER A KIDNAPPING, CHRIS.
OKAY. BUT JUST FOR TONI--
HEY, YOUR DOOR IS OPEN.
OH, NO! IT WAS NEVER CLOSED AFTER LAURA TOOK ME! IT'S BEEN OPEN THIS WHOLE TIME!
YOU'D BETTER STAY BEHIND ME, SO I CAN MAKE SURE IT'S SAFE.
OVER

HRRREEEK!
AHHH! CHUCKY'S BACK!
IT'S... IT'S A RACCOON.
CHIT CHIT CHIT
OH FUCK! A RACCOON?! HA! HA! HA!
HA HA HA HA HA HA!
OH GOD! YES! CHRIS... OH...

NEAR KANSAS CITY, MISSOURI.
NOW.
HURR
HURR
HURR
HURR
C'MON, VLAD... KEEP BREATHING.
HURR
EXHALE.
HURR
INHALE.
EXHALE.
INHALE.
VLAD?
COFF
COFF
COFF
COFF

IT'S GETTING WORSE.
NO... IS FINE... ≡ERRM≡ I HAVE HAD THIS MANY TIMES.
I KNOW. EVER SINCE YOU WERE A KID YOU'VE GOTTEN RESPIRATORY INFECTIONS.
YOU'VE GOT SENSITIVE LUNGS. IT'S HALF THE REASON YOU WEAR THAT CREEPY MASK.
THIS TIME IT SOUNDS BAD. SLEEPING IN THIS LEAKY VAN IN THE RAIN ISN'T HELPING.
WE NEED TO GET YOU SOMEWHERE DRY. A HOTEL.
BUT, CASSANDRA. ≡KRRRF≡ WE ARE OUT OF ≡WHEEEZZ≡ MONEY.
I SAW A PAWNSHOP ON THE WAY IN, JUST DOWN THE STREET. I'LL HOCK SOME OF OUR "PRIZES".
WE'LL BE KICKING IT AT THE HOLIDAY INN IN NO TIME.

THE CRANE INSTITUTE.
ONE MONTH AGO.
BWEE OOP BWEE OOP
WHAT'S GOING ON?!
THEY'VE GOT ONE, DAVID. FROM THE MINNESOTA CEUTOTECH INCIDENT. A LIVE ONE.
BWEE OOP BWEE OOP
DISCOVERED IT WANDERING AROUND OUTSIDE! COME ON!
I NEED THE HEAD DOC TO SIGN FOR THIS.
MOST BEAUTIFUL WOMAN... MOST BEAUTIFUL...
THAT WOULD BE ME.
GOOD GOD! IT'S CONSCIOUS AND SPEAKING?!
YEAH, WON'T SHUT UP. THINKS IT'S MS. AMERICA. SAYS IT WAS IN GIRLIE MAGAZINE AND EVERYTHING.

EMILY RISTY.
YEAH, THAT'S HER. HOW'D YOU KNOW?
I-I WAS A... UH... FAN. HAD A... Y'KNOW, CHILDHOOD CRUSH I GUESS.
HEH. WELL, IF YOU LIKED HER *THEN,* YOU'LL ***LOVE*** HER NOW. HER NEW LOOK IS PRETTY NICE. SOMEWHERE BETWEEN COURTNEY LOVE...
...AND A MEDIUM COOKED STEAK.
GYEEEAAH!!
EMILY...

NEAR EMINENCE, INDIANA.
5 DAYS AGO.
YOU'RE ASKING ME TO LEAVE?
NO, I'M NOT ASKING YOU TO LEAVE. I WAS ASKING WHEN YOU THOUGHT YOU WERE ***HEADING HOME.*** IT'S A TOTALLY DIFFERENT QUESTION.

I DUNNO... I JUST FIGURED SINCE WE'D BEEN, Y'KNOW, ***DOING IT,*** I'D STICK AROUND. IT SEEMS LIKE WE SORT OF HAVE A "THING".
GEEZ! DO YOU HAVE TO TELL EVERYONE WE'RE...
...DOING IT?
WHAT, ARE YOU ASHAMED?
NO, I'M NOT ASHAMED! I JUST... IT'S NO ONE'S BUSINESS.

BESIDES, I THINK WE SHOULD TALK ABOUT THIS BEFORE ONE OF US MOVES IN WITH THE OTHER. I MEAN, WHAT ARE YOU GOING TO DO FOR A ***JOB...***
OH, ***THAT'S*** WHAT IT'S ABOUT...
LOOK, I ***KNOW*** I DON'T HAVE THE BEST TRACK RECORD AS A BREAD EARNER, BUT I'M GONNA WORK ON...
...YOU'RE NOT EVEN LISTENING.
OH, NO.

KYLE.
YOUR EX? THE ASSHOLE THAT BASICALLY CAUSED THE BOBBY BRUNSWICK DEAD PET ATTACK?*
SHIT. HE SAW US.
* SEE HACK/SLASH: FIRST CUT TRADE PAPERBACK.

LISA! WOW, IT'S BEEN A WHILE.
WHAT ARE YOU DOING HERE?
JUST OUT WITH MY BOYS. WE'RE DOING A LITTLE CELEBRATING.
YOU'RE LOOKING HOT. SO, WHO'S THIS GUY?

I'M CHRIS. I--
I DIDN'T ASK YOU, FAG.
SO, IS THIS YOUR NEW BOYFRIEND, LEES? HE LOOKS LIKE A LITTLE BITCH.

AW... WHAT'S WRONG, KYLE? DON'T KNOW HOW TO IMPRESS A GIRL UNLESS YOU CAN GAS A RETARDED GUY?

NEAR KANSAS CITY, MISSOURI.
NOW.
PAWN SHOP
GUNS
SALE
JEWELRY
I'LL GIVE YA TWENTY-FIVE FOR ALL OF IT.

TWENTY-FIVE?! THESE KNIVES ARE ALL IN PERFECT SHAPE! I THINK THEY'RE THE KIND THAT CAN CUT A CAN.
AND THE CHAINSAW? THAT'S SOME QUALITY MACHINERY, MAN...
DAMN SEAGULLS

DAMN SEAGULLS
HONEY, EVERYTHING YOU HAVE LOOKS LIKE IT'S BEEN THROUGH A WAR.
AND, I GOTTA SAY, THIS IS THE FIRST TIME ANYONE'S EVER TRIED TO SELL ME A CHAINSAW WITH A BLOODSTAIN ON IT.
I'LL GIVE YA THIRTY, CUZ I'M FEELING GENEROUS.
I ***NEED*** MORE THAN THAT!

WELL, UNLESS YOU GOT MORE STUFF, I DON'T HAVE ANY MORE FOR YOU.
DAMMIT.

I'LL BE BACK.
I'VE GOT ONE MORE THING...

THE CRANE INSTITUTE.
LAST WEEK.
INTERESTING.
MS. CRISTY'S CELLS ARE COMPLETELY UNLIKE THE OTHER SUBJECTS. IT'S OBVIOUS THAT SHE HAD UNDERGONE THE SAME PHYSICAL CHANGE BROUGHT ON BY THE ADDITION OF THE "HATE JUICE" TO HER SYSTEM.
BUT, THE CELL STRUCTURE IMPLIES A HIGHER LEVEL OF STRESS, SUGGESTING THAT THE CHANGE MAY NOT HAVE TAKEN PLACE OVER TIME AS MOST OF DR. HACK'S RESEARCH HAS SHOWN.
IN THIS CASE, THE ADDITION OF THE CHEMICAL MAY HAVE BEEN IMMEDIATE. PERHAPS INGESTED IN SOME WAY.
SO SHE MADE HERSELF INTO A REV ON PURPOSE?
OR... SOMEONE ELSE DID IT FOR HER.

WHAT'S MORE INTERESTING TO ME THAN HOW SHE ENDED UP THIS WAY, IS WHAT IT MEANS TO OUR RESEARCH.
WHAT IF MS. CRISTY BECAME A REVENANT WHILE STILL ALIVE? DOES THAT MEAN WE CAN CONTROL THE METAMORPHOSIS? WHO KNOWS?
PERHAPS WE'LL FIGURE OUT HOW TO CREATE REVENANTS.
I'M GOING TO LUNCH. I THINK BETTER ON A FULL STOMACH.
PERHAPS WHEN I GET BACK WE'LL MAKE SOME MAJOR DISCOVERIES.
OR, PERHAPS WE'LL FIGURE OUT HOW TO RETURN MS. CRISTY TO HER FORMER GORGEOUS SELF.

NEAR EMINENCE, INDIANA.
5 DAYS AGO.
HA! HA! AND THE LOOK ON HIS FACE?
I CAN'T BELIEVE HOW QUICKLY HE GOT OUT OF THERE. HE PROB'LY WEN' HOME TO LICK HIS WOUNDS.
CHRIS: 1. MALE NURSE: 0.
WHERE YA WANN' GO NEXT, SEXY? HOME, MAYBE?
CHRIIIIS... STOP IT.
YOU LITTLE FAGGOT!
WHOMP!
UNNNF
FUCKIN' BITCH! I WAS TRYING TO BE CIVIL AN' SHIT! I DIDN'T EVEN BRING UP HOW YOU RUINED MY GODDAMN LIFE!
NO!
I CAN TAKE WHATEVER YOU CAN THROW AT ME, BITCH.
BUT IF YOU THINK I'M GONNA LET SOME LITTLE FAG TRASH-TALK ME WITHOUT SOME CONSEQUENCES, YOU'RE WRONG.

KYLE!
IF YOU KNOW WHAT'S GOOD FOR YOU, YOU'LL TAKE YOUR FRIENDS AND GO SLEEP IT OFF SOMEWHERE.
NOW THAT YOUR BUDDY DONOVAN DOESN'T RUN THE SHOW, NO ONE'S GONNA TURN THEIR BACK TO YOUR SHENANIGANS.
GO ON. SHOO!
GOOD EVENIN', MS.ELSTEN. HE GONNA BE ALRIGHT?
YEAH... I THINK SO...
I TELL YA WHAT: WHY DON'T I TAKE YOU FOLKS HOME? MAKE SURE YOU GET IN SAFE. WE'LL GET YER CAR INNA MORNIN'.
THANKS, RAY.
SO HOW'S THINGS GOIN' AT THE SHELTER?
MS. ELSTEN?
=SIGH= KIDS.

THEN.
AHUNNNH AHUNH
MS. HACK... UH... CASSIE?
I KNOW WHAT HAPPENED WITH YOUR MOM WAS PRETTY... UNPLEASANT.
BUT, I THOUGHT MAYBE YOU'D WANT THIS.
MAYBE IT'LL HELP YOU REMEMBER HER IN BETTER TIMES.
IT'S A REAL NICE WEDDING RING. YOUR DAD MUST HAVE LOVED YOUR MOM A WHOLE LOT.
NOW.
COFF
COFF
WHEEEEZZZ
PAWN
GUNS

THE CRANE INSTITUTE.
ONE WEEK AGO.
2300 HOURS. FRIDAY. ANOTHER LATE NIGHT WITH THE MYSTERIES OF MS. CRISTY. I SHOULD BE HOME BY NOW, BUT MY CURIOSITY HAS GOTTEN THE BEST OF ME YET AGAIN. *AHEM*
ENTRY #0307. BLOOD CELLS OF SUBJECT ARE EXTREMELY UNUSUAL, VARYING BOTH FROM NORMAL HUMAN AND THOSE FOUND IN THE REVENANTS.
THE MAJORITY OF THE PROTEINS APPEAR TO BE GONE, BUT LEUKOCYTE AND FIBRINOGEN FORMATION IS UP, PERHAPS FUELED BY THE ADDITION BY THE REVENANT "HATE JUICE".
CELLS APPEAR INERT, SHOWING LEVELS OF OXYGEN AND CELL ACTIVITY ATTRIBUTED TO CELLULAR DEATH.
CONDUCTING TEST #8: PLASMA FROM HEALTHY HUMAN SUBJECT IS ADDED TO SUBJECT SAMPLE.
SWEET JESUS.
DAVID! YOU MUST SEE THIS!!
IT'S AMAZING! CRISTY'S BLOOD IS SOMEHOW ABLE TO OVERTAKE THE HEALTHY CE--
DAVID!?
DR. WHITE?! I THOUGHT YOU'D LEFT... UH... I...
I KNOW WHAT IT LOOKS LIKE... BUT I...
SHIT.

NEAR EMINENCE, INDIANA.
5 DAYS AGO.
YOU KIDS HAVE A GOOD NIGHT. I'LL SEE YA IN THE MORNIN'.
LOOK, I KNOW I'M NOT THE GREATEST CATCH AS A BOYFRIEND. BUT I...
SHHHH
LET'S GO TO BED.

NEAR KANSAS CITY, MISSOURI.
NOW.
GOLDEN INN
HURR
EXHALE.
HURR
INHALE.
HURR
EXHALE.

THE CRANE INSTITUTE.
ONE DAY AGO.
OH GOD. OH GOD. I DID IT.
HI. IT'S ME. I'VE BEEN AWAY.
DR. WHITE HAD ME TRANSFERRED TO ANOTHER FACILITY. HE SAID I WAS GETTING TOO PERSONAL ON THIS CASE.
I SHOULD CONSIDER MYSELF LUCKY, I GUESS. HE COULD HAVE FIRED ME OUTRIGHT AND TOLD EVERYONE ABOUT... Y'KNOW.
ANYWAY, THIS IS THE LAST TIME I'LL BE ABLE TO SEE YOU. I COULD GET KILLED USING MY EXTRA BADGE TO SNEAK IN HERE LIKE THIS. BUT I HAD TO... JUST ONE MORE TIME.
THE DOC DISCOVERED THAT YOUR CELLS REGENERATE WHEN EXPOSED TO LIVING TISSUE. HE'S PLANNING ON ADDING SOME BLOOD TO YOU IN LIMITED AMOUNTS TO TEST YOUR SKIN AND MUSCLE REGROWTH.
POTENTIALLY, WITH ENOUGH TISSUE, IT MIGHT BE POSSIBLE FOR YOU TO REGENERATE ALL YOUR SKIN... YOUR HAIR... EVERYTHING FROM YOUR LIPS AND EYELASHES, TO YOUR BREASTS AND TOENAILS.

YOU... YOU WERE THE FIRST WOMAN I EVER FELL IN LOVE WITH. WHEN I SAW YOU IN THAT MAGAZINE... YOU WERE SO BEAUTIFUL, SO *PERFECT.*
YOU HAD THIS SMILE ON YOUR FACE... YOU SEEMED GOOD AND SWEET. LIKE YOU'D NEVER JUDGE ME LIKE EVERYONE ELSE DID.
EVER SINCE THEY BROUGHT YOU HERE, I'VE BEEN THINKING ABOUT THE DAY THEY'D REVIVE YOU... *FIX* YOU. YOU'D BE SO HAPPY TO HAVE YOUR LIFE BACK.... YOU'D SMILE THAT SMILE. MAYBE YOU'D FALL IN LOVE WITH *ME.*
I DECIDED THAT IF ANYONE'S TISSUE IS GOING TO BE USED TO REVIVE YOU, IT SHOULD BE *MINE.* YOU HAVE MY *HEART...*
...YOU SHOULD HAVE MY *BLOOD.*
PLP
PLP
PLP
PLP
PLP
SSSSSSSSSSSSS
OH GOD. YES. IT'S BEAUTIFUL. SO...
=UCK=
SNAP!

OH YES... THAT FEELS SO NICE.
I WAS FEELING SO NAKED. THANK YOU, DAVID.
SPLORCH
YOU'VE DONE SO MUCH FOR ME. I'M GOING TO REMEMBER YOU ALWAYS.
I LOVE YOU, DAVID.
TO BE CONTINUED...

DOUBLE DATE

Hack/Slash

CASSIE, DID YOU HAVE ANY TROUBLE RESCUING ME?

I SURE DID! I HAD TO **BEAT OFF** A PRIEST!

#6 A by **TIM SEELEY**

NEAR STONE COUNTY...
OH GOD. OH GOD. OH GOD. OH GOD.
OH GOD. OH GOD. OH GOD. OH GOD.
OH... RAUL...
WHO'S THERE?! D-DON'T COME ANY CLOSER!
KRIK
DON'T COME ANY...
ARE YOU ALRIGHT?
AIEEEE!

LATER...
I DROPPED HER OFF AT THE HOSPITAL, BUT SHE WAS TOO SCARED TO SAY MUCH.
DEFINITELY LOOKED LIKE SHE'D BEEN ENGAGED IN A LITTLE SINNING.
SO, I'D SAY THE BIG METAL CROSS CUTS OUR LIST OF SUSPECTS DOWN TO JUST ONE.
YES. FATHER WRATH IS BACK.
OKAY, I MARKED ON THE MAP WHERE THE LAST THREE MURDERS HAPPENED. IT'S A PRETTY STRAIGHT LINE.
FATHER WRATH NEVER WAS MUCH FOR CREATIVITY, SO I'M GUESSING THE NEXT STOP ON THE "BLUDGEON ALL SINNERS" TOUR WILL BE RIGHT HERE...
Clever
265
411
Marionville
Aurora
HAVERHILL
STONE
HAVERHILL.
C'MON, VLAD. WE'VE GOT SOME SINNERS TO SAVE.

OUR BOY Taber in DOUBLE DATE!

HAVERHILL HIGH.
CHRIS TABER, YOU'RE A SCOUNDREL!
GOSH, LINCOLN! DON'T SAY THAT!
WHY? I MEANT IT AS A COMPLIMENT.
BUT I DIDN'T *MEAN* TO ASK BOTH TRISH *AND* ANGELA TO THE DANCE TONIGHT!

I ASKED *ANGELA* BECAUSE I DIDN'T THINK SHE'D ACTUALLY SAY YES. SHE'S ALWAYS SAYING I'M TOO NICE FOR HER.
BUT *TRISH* IS A SWEETHEART. SHE'D HAVE BEEN *CRUSHED* IF I DIDN'T ASK HER.
AND NOW I DON'T KNOW *WHAT* I'M GONNA DO!

DO ABOUT WHAT, TABER?
OH! HEY *TRISH!*
UM, I WAS JUST TELLIN' THE GUYS ABOUT HOW MUCH FUN THE *SPIRIT COSTUME DANCE* WAS GONNA BE WITH MY FAVORITE GAL.

AW, TABER, YOU SAY THE SWEETEST THINGS. SEE YA IN MS. GOLDBERG'S CLASS!
KISS

I'LL FIGURE THIS OUT. DON'T YOU GUYS TELL ANYONE!

OF COURSE! MY LIPS ARE SEALED!

C'MON, LUNK! WE GOTTA GET TO SCIENCE CLASS!
REMEMBER, LINCOLN: MUMS THE WORD!

I WON'T TELL. BUT THAT DOESN'T MEAN I CAN'T MAKE THIS MORE INTERESTING!

IS IT JUST ME...
HATS
...OR DOES EVERYTHING LOOK KIND OF WEIRD?
Nora's Soda Shop
IT'S SO CLEAN. AND, LIKE, BRIGHT.
YES.
HEY, WERE YOU LOOKIN' AT MY GIRL?!
GULP
Nora's Soda Shop
THAT NORA'S PLACE HAS FILLED UP SINCE SCHOOL GOT OUT. I'M GONNA POP IN, DO A LITTLE 007 WORK.
I'LL FIND OUT WHERE TEENS GO TO DO TEEN STUFF.
AND ME?
IT SHOULDN'T BE TOO HARD TO FIND THE CHURCHES IN THIS TOWN. TAKE A PEEK... MAYBE FATHER WRATH NEEDS TO STOP IN ONE AND GET COMMUNION OR PICK UP A NEW CROSS...
BE CAREFUL.
THANKS...
"...BUT I THINK I CAN HANDLE WHATEVER THIS TOWN THROWS AT ME."
DON'T LOOK NOW, LUNK, BUT MY SPIRIT DANCE DATE IS ABOUT TO WALK IN...

AT A NEARBY PARK...
SO WHAT'S THIS YOU WANT TO TELL ME, TABER?
WELL, YA SEE, ANGELA... IT'S ABOUT THE SPIRIT DANCE TONIGHT...
YES?

UH, IT'S JUST THAT...
GULP

UH! LET'S GO OVER HERE!
HEY!

WHAT WAS THAT FOR?!
WELL... I... SORRY...

NO, NO... I LIKE A MAN WHO TAKES CONTROL.
NOW WHAT DID YOU WANT TO TELL ME?
UHM... I... UHM...

YESS... SINNNERSSSS... SIN, AND BE PUNISHED...
I... I JUST CAN'T WAIT TO SEE YOU DRESSED UP TONIGHT!
I'LL PICK YOU UP AT SEVEN!
AWWWWW! THANKS, TABER. I'LL BE WAITING!

MWAH
KISS
GOSH.

GO. SIN!
SEE YA LATER, ALLIGATOR.
GOSH.

LA LA LA LA! I'M A LUCKY GUY. LA LA LA LA!
LIVE IN A NICE OLD TOWN. LA LA LA LA!

GOT A KISS FROM A PRETTY GIRL. LA LA LA LA!
SIGH

BACK AT NORA'S!
...THAT'S WHEN I TURNED TO MY FATHER AND SAID, "ALL DUE RESPECT, SIR, BUT POLO IS FOR HORSES, NOT PONIES".

HE TOOK ONE LOOK AT ME, AND HE BOUGHT ME THE BENZ SLR! CONTINENTAL GT, PLEASE.

HMMMM... I SHOULD GET INTO THAT DANCE SOMEHOW. THAT *IS* WHERE FATHER WRATH IS MOSTLY LIKELY TO STRIKE.
BUT, IF I GO WITH THIS ASSHOLE, I'LL BEAT WRATH TO THE PUNCH AND BLUDGEON HIM MYSELF. THINK FAST, CASSIE...
SO... LASSIE, RIGHT? SHOULD I PICK YOU UP FOR THE DANCE AT SEVEN?

ACTUALLY, I CAN'T...
BECAUSE I'M GOING WITH *THIS* GUY.
LUNK?!

YUP. ME AND... UH... LUNK. HERE'S MY PHONE NUMBER. CALL ME AND I'LL TELL YOU WHERE TO PICK ME UP.
SEE YOU TONIGHT, GUYS.

=SIGH=
WHAT'S GOT YA DOWN, CHUM?
AW... NOTHING.
LADY PROBLEMS?
HOW DID YOU KNOW?
GUYS CAN JUST TELL.
I WISH MY FRIENDS WOULD SAY THAT. ONE DOESN'T TALK AND THE OTHER IS ALWAYS TRYING TO STAB ME IN THE BACK.
THE SHORT VERSION OF THE STORY IS: I ACCIDENTALLY ASKED TWO GIRLS TO THE COSTUME BALL TONIGHT AND I DON'T KNOW WHICH ONE TO TAKE!
TWO GIRLS AND A COSTUME BALL? YOU ARE ONE LUCKY GUY. WE NEVER GOT DANCES OR GIRLS AT MY SCHOOL.
SAY, HOW TALL ARE YOU?
HUH? WHY DO YOU ASK?
WHAT IF I TOLD YOU THERE MAY BE A WAY THAT YOU DIDN'T HAVE TO PICK JUST ONE?

HURRR...
SO FAR, NOTHING HAS HAPPENED AT CHURCH.

BUT MUCH IS GOING ON ACROSS THE STREET.
EVER SINCE I MADE THE SEX*, I WOULD LIKE TO MAKE IT SOME MORE.
ST. HARTLEY
CAR WASH
YOUTH GROUP
FUNDRAISER!
*SEE ISSUE #3
--VOYEURISTIC MIKE

NO... I MUST CONCENTRATE... WASH SOAPY GIRLS FROM BRAIN...
WHAT ARE YOU DOIN', YA CREEP?!

ARE YOU SPYING ON MY GIRL?! NO ONE LOOKS AT PINKY BUT ME!
NO... I WAS... WATCHING NUNS...
STAND UP YA UGLY CREEP. NO ONE SPIES ON MY GIRL!
OR MY NAME AIN'T GORILLA McMANN...
GULP
I DID NOT MEAN TO LOOK...
I WAS TRYING TO WATCH CHURCH, NOT GIRLS.
OH, NO... MAN... UH... MY FAULT... SORRY ABOUT THAT... UH... "FREAK" THING...

LATER.
STUPID LUNK. AND STUPID LASSIE. I DIDN'T WANNA GO WITH HER ANYWAY!
KICK!
NOW I DON'T HAVE A DATE FOR THE SPIRIT DANCE AND I HAVEN'T THOUGHT OF A WAY TO RUIN TABER'S DOUBLE DATE!
I THINK I CAN HELP WITH THAT...
YEAH, AND WHO'RE YOU SUPPOSED TO BE?
JUST A GUY TRYING TO HELP ANOTHER GUY.
SO YOU'VE GOT A GIRL THAT DOESN'T LIKE YOU, AND A BUDDY WITH TOO MANY GIRLS. I HAVE JUST THE THING.
NICELY DRESSED FELLA LIKE YOURSELF, I'M GUESSING YOU COULD EASILY PAY FIFTY DOLLARS FOR IT.
FIFTY DOLLARS? WELL, I AM RICH...
PUT THESE LIL' BABIES IN THE PUNCH...
...AND YOU CAN PUT A NICE, BIG X THROUGH YOUR PROBLEMS...

Havernhi
Inn

OKAY, YOU CAN LOOK NOW.

WHAT BETTER WAY TO CATCH A PRIEST, RIGHT?
HURR...

WHAT? DON'T YOU LIKE IT?
I LIKE... JUST FINE... I... NEED FRESH AIR.
BREEEP! BREEEP!
THAT'S MY RIDE. REMEMBER, TAKE THE VAN AND PARK AROUND THE BLOCK. IF WRATH IS IN THIS TOWN, WE'LL GET THAT ASS TONIGHT.

SLAM
YES. GET... THAT ASS.

MASQUERADE PROM!!
Come on baby,
Let's do the twist.
Come on babyyy...

ISN'T THIS GREAT, TRISH? THEY SURE MADE THE GYM LOOK GROOVY!
YES, TABER. IT SURE IS.
SOMETHING WRONG, TRISH?

I'M TRYING TO FIGURE OUT WHY YOU'RE DRESSED IN THIS KIND OF CREEPY COSTUME.
UH... IT'S THE NEWEST THING... ONE OF THOSE POPULAR CHARACTERS FROM JAPAN!
UM... I'LL GET YA' SOME PUNCH.

HEY LINCOLN!
WHY, HELLO, TABER. NICE COSTUME. HAVE SOME PUNCH.
A-listen people what I'm telling you,
stay away from runaround sue...

I'M NOT THIRSTY. THIS IS FOR TRISH.
AH, SO YOU CHOSE A DATE?
UH... NO... NOT EXACTLY.
SIGH. YOU WITH TWO DATES, AND ME WITH NONE. OH WELL, I WON'T COMPLAIN...

THERE'S ENOUGH LOVE IN THIS ROOM FOR EVERYONE.

VERY KITSCH, WOULDN'T YOU SAY?
UH HUH.
YOU'VE BEEN AWFUL QUIET. ARE YOU OKAY, TABER?
♫ go, go Johnny go. ♫ go, Johnny B. goode.

UH HUH.

LET'S GO OVER HERE.

WELL, HELLO, PINKY.
HIIIIIII LINCOLN. WHEW... I NEED MORE PUNCH. IT'S REEEEEALLY GOOD.
THERE'S ALWAYS MORE PUNCH FOR CUTE LIL' KITTIES LIKE YOU.
MMM... I WISH I WAS A CAT SO I COULD LICK MYSELF! HEE HEE.

ALRIGHT, LUNK. I'M GOING TO TAKE A LOOK AROUND. I'LL MEET YOU BACK HERE IN A SECOND.
BULLS
23

♫ go, go shawty, it's your birthday.. ♫ we gon' party like it's your birthday...

we gon' sip Bacardi like it's your birthday. And you know we don't give a fuck...
UH...
HUMP! HUMP!

THIS PLAN IS GREAT! GOOD LUCK WITH TRISH!
HEH.
cause it's not your birthday!

DOWN, MAN, DOWN...
HOLY SHIT. *WRATH.*
you can find me in the club. bottle full of bub. look mami. i got the x. if you into takin' drugs...

BACK THE FUCK OFF!
HEY! YOU GOOFED UP MY JITTERBUG!
i'm into havin' sex. i ain't into makin' love. so come give me a hug if you into getting rubbed.

UPTIGHT WHITE CHICK.

WRATH!
WHOMP!
GHYAH!

GOSH, HOW'D I END UP OUTSIDE? HEE HEE.
MMM... EVERYTHING IS SO SPINNY. I THINK I'LL LEAN AGAINST THIS TREE.
UR?
OOOOOH.
THIS TREE HAS MUSCLES. MMMMMM!
HEY, TRISH. WHERE'S YOUR DATE?
I-I DUNNO. HE WAS HERE... AND THEN HE WALKED AWAY... BUT THEN HE WALKED BACK THIS WAY... BUT... I DON'T KNOW IF IT WAS HIM.
OH... UH... WELL, WOULD YOU LIKE TO DANCE?
MMMMM... OKAY!

YOU KNOW WHAT?
WE ALL SPEND SO MUCH TIME COMPETING FOR TABER, TRADING EACH OTHER BACK AND FORTH, OR WATER SKIING WITH THE GODDAMN PRINCIPAL...
...WE JUST DON'T SPEND ENOUGH TIME **FUCKING.**

TAKE ME SOMEWHERE AND TEAR MY **PANTIES** OFF WITH YOUR **TEETH.**

COME ON, YOU FUCK! WHERE'RE ALL YOUR EVANGELICAL BULLSHIT SPEECHES?!
AHHH! WHY ARE YOU HITTING ME?!
I'M SORRY! I JUST DIDN'T KNOW WHICH GIRL TO PICK IS ALL!
FWAK!

HUH?
WOAH! HOLD ON THERE!
LET ME GO!

GET HER OUT OF HERE. I WON'T HAVE ANY FIGHTING AT MY SCHOOL!
YESSIREE, MR. CRUNK.

I'M TRYING TO HELP YOU--
WRATH?!

GO. SIN.

LET ME GO, GODDAMMIT!
USING THE LORD'S NAME IN VAIN WILL GET YOU NOWHERE, MY DEAR!

MMMM... OH YEAH... OH...
DO IT, HARD!

YOU GOT IT, BABY.
THUNK!
SINNERS!

HURR!? CASSANDRA?
FORGET ME! GO! LOCKER ROOM!

WHO WAS SHE YELLIN' TO--?!
WHA--? PINKY?!
HEE HEE HEY! WHERE'D THE SEXY TREE GO?

EEEEEEEE!
GO AHEAD AND SCREAM ALL YOU LIKE. THE MUSIC IS SO LOUD, NO ONE WILL HEAR YOU.
IT'S ABOUT FUCKING TIME! I DIDN'T THINK ANY OF YOU GOODY TWO SHOES WERE GOING TO COMMIT A *PUNISHABLE* OFFENSE.
AFTER A WHILE, THE ONLY THING KEEPING ME HERE WAS THE CHALLENGE...

SHRIIISSH
OH SHIT!
KRAK!
WRAAAUGH!
UK

PFAW
WHO THE HELL ARE YOU?!
I AM VLAD. I KILLED FATHER WRATH. YOU ARE NOT HIM.

YOU WILL TELL ME WHO YOU ARE AND WHY YOU WEAR THAT MASK.

MY NAME... MY NAME IS SAM. SAMUEL LAWRENCE.

"I'M FROM TENNESSEE. MY UNCLE... HE WAS A PREACHER.
OD TES AGS
"HE WENT FROM TOWN TO TOWN, TELLIN' PEOPLE ABOUT GOD AND WHAT THE POWER OF GOD'S LOVE HAD IN STORE FOR THEM.
"HE TOLD ABOUT THE PEOPLE GOD DIDN'T LOVE TOO, AND WHY WE NEEDED TO GET RID OF 'EM.

"HE WAS A GREAT MAN MY UNCLE... A GREAT SOLDIER IN GOD'S ARMY.
"BUT, THE DEVIL GOT TO HIM... MADE HIM A SODOMITE AND A FAGGOT.
"AND HE WANTED TO SHARE HIS SIN WITH ME.

"I DID THE ONLY I COULD... I FREED HIM FROM HIS SIN.

"AFTER THAT, I WAS DISILLUSIONED, RIGHT? SO, I DID WHAT A YOUNG SINNER DOES. I DID DRUGS, I DANCED, I FORNICATED... I LET THE DEVIL HAVE ME.

"BUT IT DON'T TAKE LONG AND I CAME TO MY SENSES. I REALIZED THE WORLD IS A WORSE PLACE WITHOUT MY UNCLE. I REALIZED I HAVE TO MAKE UP FOR MY OWN SIN AND HIS.
"SO I DECIDED IT WAS UP TO ME TO BEAR THE WEIGHT OF THAT CROSS, AND STOP THE SINNERS..."

SINNERS LIKE THAT UNCHRISTIAN PIECE OF SHIT BLEEDING OUT ON THE FLOOR...
...AND THAT LITTLE BITCH COWERING IN THE CORNER.

HURR.
I AM SORRY FOR YOU.
SORRY FOR ME?! HA! I AM HIGH AS KITE.
I AM FULL OF GOD'S LOVE AND YOU FEEL SORRY FOR--

CRACK
UGK

THANK... T-THANK YOU. YOU SAVED MY LIFE.

IT IS NO PROBLEM. I NEEDED A COLD SHOWER.

HAVERHILL
CHRISTIA COUNTY
FW
MAYBE WE'LL GET LUCKY AND WE WON'T GET ANOTHER FATHER WRATH SEQUEL.
I AM GLAD TO BE AWAY FROM HAVERHILL. MY MIND IS... CLEARER.
YOU THOUGHT IT WAS A PRETTY LAME TOWN, HUH?
URR... UH... YES. LAME.
WELL... I'M GONNA TELL YOU A SECRET. I LIKED IT.
I MEAN, SURE, IT'S AS VANILLA AND SHALLOW AS HELL. BUT, SOMETIMES...
...SOMETIMES I JUST WANT SOMETHING SWEET AND GOOD AND SIMPLE.
Y'KNOW?
HURR... MAY I TELL A SECRET THEN?
YEAH. SURE.
I AM... HORNY.
...
GODDAMMIT, VLAD.
THE END.

TUB CLUB
TUB CLUB
#7A by TIM SEELEY & SPLASH!

OOKLINE, MASSACHUSETTS.
WO MONTHS AGO.
FRANCO-BELLE COLLEGE FOR WOMEN est. 1873
ELIZA. WAKE UP, HONEY.
IT'S TIME.
I CAN'T BELIEVE WE'RE DOING THIS!
SHHHH. KEEP IT COOL...
WE DON'T WANNA LOOK LIKE ROOKIES.
HAH. NERD.
WITH ALL THE PRACTICE WE'VE HAD?

UMM... HI.
WE'RE HERE FOR THE... UH... MEETING.
OF COURSE YOU ARE.
LOOKS LIKE WE'RE ALL HERE. GOOD GIRLS.
I HERE-BY CALL TO ORDER A MEETING OF THE MOST EXCLUSIVE CLUB ON FRANCO-BELLE CAMPUS.
FIRST ORDER OF BUSINESS:
TAKE OFF THOSE CLOTHES, GIRLS.

SECOND ORDER OF BUSINESS: TASTE THE FORBIDDEN FRUIT.
HOT TUB + SPA. AUTHORIZED USE ONLY.
WELCOME TO *TUB CLUB*.
COME... THIS IS THE GARDEN OF EDEN...
...AND I AM THE *SNAKE*.

WILLIAMS APPLE ORCHARD.
POUGHKEEPSIE NEW YORK.

YOU'VE GOT THAT "THINKING TOO HARD" LOOK ON YOUR FACE. WHAT'S ON YOUR MIND, BIG GUY?
HRM. I WAS WONDERING. ARE UNICORNS REAL OR MAKE-BELIEVE?

MAKE-BELIEVE, VLAD. UNICORNS ARE MAKE-BELIEVE.
AH. BUT ZEBRAS ARE REAL, YES?
YEAH.

I THINK THAT'S THE END OF OUR SHIFT. LET'S GO GET OUR MONEY AND GET THE HELL OUTTA POUGH-KEEPSIE.

Y'KNOW WHAT THEY CALL IT WHEN A ZEBRA AND A HORSE BREED?
NO.
ZORSE.
HURR HURR.
ZORSE.
BEEP BEEP

GEORGIA. HEY.

NAH, JUST GOT DONE PICKING FRUIT.
HA HA HA! NO, THAT'S NOT A EUPHEMISM.

MARYLAND.
DID YOU NEED ANYTHING ELSE, ANNA-LEE?

NOPE. JUST MY INSULIN, NURSE MARSH.
OKAY, GOOD. WELL, I'VE GOT ONE MONTH'S SUPPLY HERE AND--

WHOOPS!

OH JEEZ! I'M SORRY, I'LL ORDER SOME MORE. I'M SUCH A...

...CLUTZ...

EMINENCE, INDIANA.
NOW THAT'S ART.
HEH. YEAH... ART.
ORIGINAL THUNDERGUARD MAGAZINE SPECIAL EDITION MAIL-AWAY POSTER.
TOTALLY COLLECTIBLE. THESE THINGS GO FOR 300 BUCKS ON EBAY.
THAT'S GREAT, CHRIS.
YOU HATE IT.
NO... NO, IF YOU'RE GOING TO MOVE IN, AND PAY HALF THE MORTGAGE, IT'S ONLY FAIR THAT YOU SHOULD GET TO MAKE IT YOUR HOME TOO.
AND IF THE WAY YO DO THAT IS B PUTTING UP, THIS... THE THAT'S THE WAY IT'LL BE.

AW, LISA, YOU ARE THE GREAT-EST.
YEAH... WELL, LET'S AT LEAST KEEP THE ACTION FIGURES IN THE *HACK/SLASH INC.* OFFICE, OKAY?

THAT REMINDS ME! I HAD A MEDICAL EXAMINER IN ALBERT CITY WHO WAS GONNA EMAIL ME SOME PHOTOS OF A BIZARRE BODY. WANNA CHECK IT OUT?
I CAN'T THINK OF *ANYTHING* MORE RO-MANTIC.

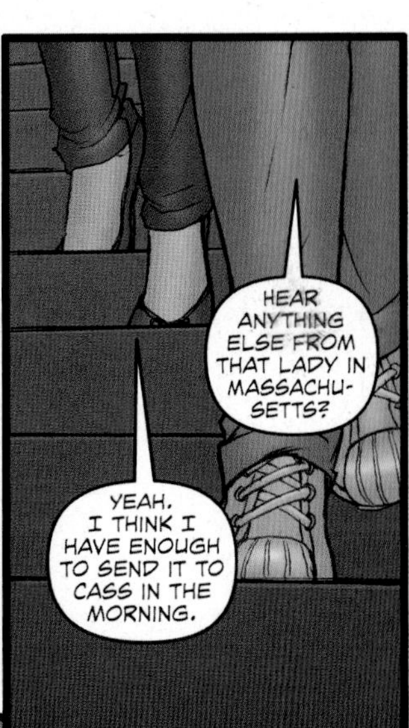
HEAR ANYTHING ELSE FROM THAT LADY IN MASSACHU-SETTS?
YEAH. I THINK I HAVE ENOUGH TO SEND IT TO CASS IN THE MORNING.

THERE'S NO BODIES OR ANYTHING... JUST A LEGEND... BUT IT COULD BE SOMETHING.
COOL. WELL, LET'S TAKE A LOOK AT WHAT I GOT AND SEE IF *MINE'S* SOMETHING.

HERE WE GO. LET'S OPEN THIS UP...

SHIT!
THAT'S DEFINITELY... SOMETHING.

MANSFIELD, PENNSYLVANIA.
ALMOST DONE, VLAD?
AL'S
MMM. POTTED MEAT PRODUCT.
NOW, I AM DONE.

YOU HAVE NOT EVEN STARTED?
OH, NO... I'M DONE.
BUT WE MADE MONEY TODAY. WE SHOULD STOCK UP WITH FOODS.
THIS'LL HOLD ME OVER. I FIGURED I'D SAVE THE CASH FOR SOMETHING ELSE.
CASSANDRA. YOU MUST EAT BETTER. YOU KNOW WHAT HAPPENS WHEN YOU LIVE ON SUCH FOOD.
THE KILLER DAIRY MEN DREAM.
YEAH, YEAH...

YOU ARE SAVING THE MONEY TO BUY MORE MINUTES ON THE PHONE.
YEAH, I S'POSE.
THE PHONE IS FOR BUSINESS, CASSANDRA.
YES, MOM.
HUUUURN.
YOU HAVE SPENT MUCH TIME ON THE PHONE WITH GEORGIA LATELY.

AL'S
HEY, SHE CALLS ME.
I KNOW. BUT YOU TALK FOR HOURS. WE DO NOT HAVE THE MINUTES FOR IT.
I'M TAKING CARE OF IT. BESIDES, THIS IS SORTA BUSINESS, RIGHT? I MEAN, SHE'S A CONTACT.
NO. SHE IS YOUR FRIEND. YOU LIKE HER. SHE LIKES YOU. AND THAT IS GOOD. BUT YOU SPEND SO MUCH TIME TALKING TO HER...
BRRING
CASSIE.
GOOD. TALK TO ME...
SIGH.
IT'S JUST LISA. SAY HI, GRUMPY.
HELLO.
AN UNUSUAL CORPSE YOU SAY?

BROOKLINE, MASSACHUSETTS.
HEY LADIES, WE COULDN'T HELP BUT NOTICE THAT YOU COULD BOTH USE ANOTHER BEER.
WE'RE FINE, THANKS.
NOW IF YOU DON'T MIND...
FUCKIN' FRANCO-BULL DYKES.
WOAH... I'M ALREADY BUZZED. I CAN'T DRINK LIKE I USED TO.
WELL, KEEP IN MIND YOU'RE DOING THE EQUIVALENT OF GIVING BLOOD AT EVERY CEREMONY.
OH... RIGHT.
SO IS THAT HER?
YEAH.
IT'S GETTING LATE. YOU BETTER GO NOW BEFORE SHE LEAVES.
I DUNNO...
YOU'RE READY FOR ASCENSION, 'LIZA. KATHY IS READY FOR THE ***KUNDALINI***. SHE CHOSE YOU TO REPLACE HER.
YOU'RE GONNA BE ***YOGINI***. YOU JUST HAVE TO INITIATE ***YOUR*** REPLACEMENT.
SHH. WE DON'T WANT THESE POSERS TO OVERHEAR.
YOU REALLY THINK SHE'S THE ONE? DO YOU THINK SHE EVEN LIKES GIRLS?
ANNALEE SAID SHE DID.

WELL...
...SHE DEFINITELY LIKES ***YOU***.

FREDERICK COUNTY SHERIFF'S OFFICE.
MARYLAND.

MMMMPH!
SHHH. WE ONLY WANT TO SEE YOUR BODY.
MMMMMPH!!

DON'T GET TOO EXCITED. HE MEANS THE ONE YOU'VE GOT IN YOUR MORGUE.

A FRIEND TELLS ME IT'S GOOD AND FREAKY.

THAT'S IT. ON THE TABLE.
WHERE WAS IT FOUND?
NEAR A CORNFIELD. PARTY PLACE FOR KIDS. ONE OF YOURS?
STICK TO THE ANSWERS. YOU'LL BE BACK TO YOUR PODUNK POLICE WORK IN NO TIME. WE JUST WANT A PEEK.
CAREFUL. IT'S... IT'S NASTY.
HURM... WE ARE USED TO--
ZZZZZP
...NASTY.

EMINENCE, INDIANA.
YEAH, THAT'S EXACTLY WHAT THE BODY IN ALBERT CITY LOOKED LIKE.
THEY IDENTIFIED IT AS SOME FIRST YEAR DOCTOR. TUREK, I THINK HIS NAME WAS. CHRIS'LL SEND YOU THE INFO.
COOL. ANYTHING ELSE?
THERE WAS ANOTHER ONE THAT CAME IN WHILE YOU AND VLAD WERE OFF FIGHTING ROCK N' ROLL CHOLULA.*
*SEE ISSUE 4.
IT'S CTHULU, LISA. CTHULU. "CHOLULA" IS A HOT SAUCE.
IN ANY CASE, A WOMAN EMAILED ME FROM A GIRL'S COLLEGE IN MASSACHUSETTS. I DUNNO... IT MIGHT BE WORTH JUST STOPPING BY AS LONG AS YOU'RE IN THE AREA.
HOOK ME UP. ANYWAY, I THINK WE'RE GONNA BED DOWN FOR THE NIGHT.
'NIGHT CASS.
LOGGING ROAD
TRUCKS ENTERING HIGHWAY
THINK WE'RE FAR ENOUGH FROM THE COP WE JUST ASSAULTED?
YES. HE DID NOT SEE THE VAN. NO ONE WILL LOOK FOR US HERE.
JUST ME AND YOU, AND ANOTHER NIGHT ON THE VAN FLOOR.
UP FOR A ROUND OF "SLAP JACK" BEFORE WE SETTLE DOWN FOR ANOTHER UNCOMFORTABLE NIGHT?
YES. I WILL SLAP MANY JACKS.
BZRING

FLORIDA.
CASSIE.
HEY, WOMAN. I'M ON A BREAK. BUSY?
99% 3 Angel
NAH... JUST ABOUT TO HIT THE SACK. WHAT'S UP, GEORGIA?
NOPE. NO PSYCHOS TONIGHT. JUST GROCERIES AND A GROSS CORPSE.
HEH... NOT AT THE SAME TIME. HOW ABOUT YOU?
THE SAME RICH GUY AGAIN? WOW... DES-PERATE...

ALBERT CITY POLICE DEPARTMENT.
CAN I HELP YOU?

WE'D LIKE TO SPEAK WITH A DR. GENUNG.
OH.

SHIT! FEDS!

C'MON, C'MON! MAIL HISTORY... ERASE!!!

FREEZE!
BACK AWAY FROM THE COMPUTER!
I DIDN'T DO ANY-THING!

SETTLE DOWN, DOCTOR. WE UNDERSTAND YOU'RE IN POSSESSION OF A VERY INTERESTING BODY...

MORNING.
I'M HERE TO SEE A NURSE MARSH?

MRS. MARSH? IT'S CASSIE HACK. LISA'S FRIEND...
SHH! IN HERE!
I'M IN HERE!
10 Easy Steps

BETTER SAFE THAN SORRY. EARS HAVE WALLS, Y'KNOW.
YEAH... SURE.
MY, YOU'RE YOUNGER THAN I EXPECTED. BUT IF MS. ELSTEN SAYS YOU'RE WHAT YOU ARE, THAN I'M WILLING TO BELIEVE HER.
EVEN IF YOU DO DRESS LIKE THAT MARILYN MANSON WOMAN. THERE AREN'T MANY OF US, WHO... YOU KNOW... BELIEVE.

DID LISA TELL YOU ABOUT ME?
NO... I JUST WOKE UP AND...
...MY NECK IS SORE...
WELL, I GUESS YOU COULD SAY I'M A LOT LIKE YOU. A PARANORMAL INVESTI-GATOR.
I'M NOT--

NOW, I'M SURE YOU'RE FAMILIAR WITH THE STORIES ABOUT FRANCO-BELLE. IT'S CONSIDERED ONE OF THE MOST HAUNTED PLACES IN AMERICA. RIGHT AFTER THE WAVERLEY HILLS SANITORIUM.
(I WOULD KNOW... I'VE BEEN THERE.)

FRANCO-BELLE IS KNOWN FOR THE DISAPPEARANCE OF SIX GIRLS IN 1907 AND ANOTHER SIX IN 1961. COMPLETELY UNEX-PLAINED. *POOF!*

WHEN A JOB AS NURSE OPENED HERE, I TOOK IT. IT GAVE ME THE CHANCE TO DO MY PARANORMAL STUDIES.
I THINK I KNOW WHAT'S CAUSED THESE GIRLS TO DISAPPEAR.

"YOU SEE, BACK THEN, GIRLS WEREN'T USUALLY ALLOWED AN EDUCATION. SO, THE GIRLS WHO ATTENDED FRANCO-BELLE, WELL, THEY WANTED TO STUDY OTHER FAMOUS WOMEN.
WOMENS STUDIES
"POWERFUL WOMEN TO LOOK UP TO. THAT'S WHEN ONE GROUP OF GIRLS DISCOVERED *ELIZABETH BATHORY*.
"DO YOU KNOW WHO THAT IS?"

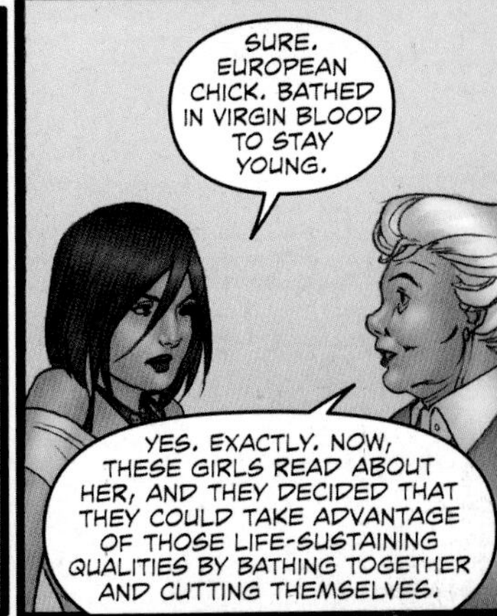
SURE. EUROPEAN CHICK. BATHED IN VIRGIN BLOOD TO STAY YOUNG.
YES. EXACTLY. NOW, THESE GIRLS READ ABOUT HER, AND THEY DECIDED THAT THEY COULD TAKE ADVANTAGE OF THOSE LIFE-SUSTAINING QUALITIES BY BATHING TOGETHER AND CUTTING THEMSELVES.

"NOW, NATURALLY, ALL THAT BATHING, AND BODILY FLUIDS...
"WELL, PRETTY SOON THE GIRLS WERE INVOLVED IN ALL KINDS OF KINKY SEX AND SUCH."

I BELIEVE THAT THESE GIRLS, THROUGH THEIR ACTIONS, AROUSED THE GHOST OF ELIZABETH BATHORY. AND SHE CAUSED THEIR DEATHS. SAME THING HAPPENED IN '61.
NOW, I'M SEEING THINGS. CLUES. I THINK IT'S STARTING AGAIN.
BUT I'M TOO OLD TO CHASE SPOOKS LIKE I USED TO.

LOOK, I'M NOT SOME KIND OF "GHOSTBUSTER". I DON'T THINK--
I'LL SET YOU UP WITH A GUEST DORM ROOM AND A MEAL PLAN FOR A WEEK.
JUST CALL ME RAY PARKER JR.

WE ARE SURROUNDED BY GIRLS.
SETTLE DOWN, BOY. DON'T GET YOURSELF ALL WORKED UP AGAIN.
SO? WE ARE LOOKING FOR A SLASHER HERE?

MY GUT TELLS ME THIS NURSE CHICK IS STEW-ING IN *CRAZY SAUCE.*
ON THE OTHER HAND, WE'VE SEEN CRAZY-SOUNDING LEGENDS RUNNING AROUND BEFORE. I FIGURE, AT THE VERY LEAST, WE CAN TAKE ADVANTAGE OF THE HOSPITALITY.

WE'VE STILL GOT THE ***WEIRD BODILESS SKIN*** CASE TO WORK ON WHILE WE INVESTI-GATE THE KILLER LESBIAN GHOST.

I LIKE THIS IDEA.
NOW? PERHAPS WE CAN PLAY OUR "SLAP JACK"?

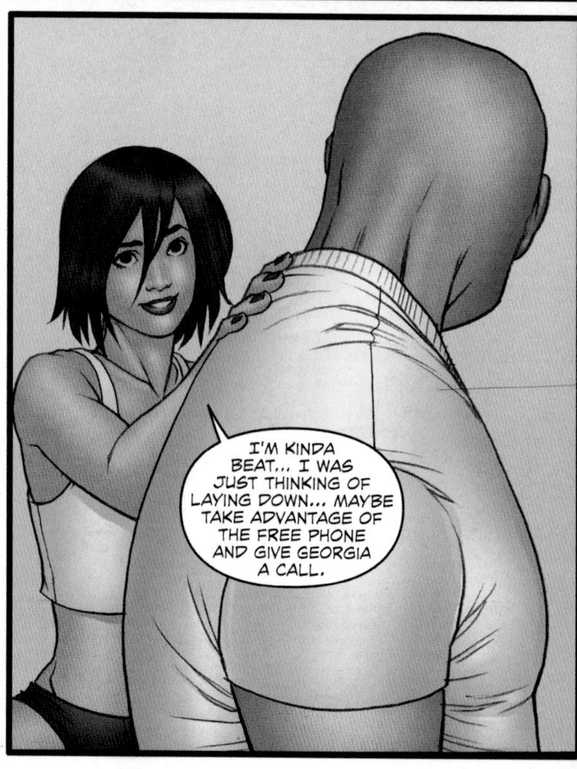
I'M KINDA BEAT... I WAS JUST THINKING OF LAYING DOWN... MAYBE TAKE ADVANTAGE OF THE FREE PHONE AND GIVE GEORGIA A CALL.

HURRRRRRMMMM.
OH VLAD... I'M SORRY. YOU'RE... ARE YOU JEALOUS?
NO. I ... HURRRMM.
VLAD..LOOK... YOU'RE MY BEST BUDDY, OKAY? BUT, GEORGIA... SHE'S A GIRL, Y'KNOW?
SHE'S MY AGE. THERE'S JUST CERTAIN THINGS I CAN TALK TO HER ABOUT THAT MAYBE YOU WOULDN'T UNDERSTAND. THATS' NOT YOUR FAULT, IT'S JUST...
YES. I KNOW. I WILL LEAVE YOU TO TALK TO GEORGIA. SHE IS A GOOD GIRL.
I WILL GO TO TAKE A LOOK AROUND...

ARE YOU SURE THAT'S A GOOD IDEA?
I KNOW HOW TO NOT BE SEEN...

AND HOW TO WALK ALONE.

GOOD AIR. CRISP. SMELL OF DYING LEAVES.
ENERGY IN THE AIR. ENERGY OF YOUNG PEOPLE WITH LIFE AHEAD.
NO CITY LIGHTS. SKY FULL OF STARS. IT IS BEAUTIFUL. CASSANDRA WOULD LIKE THIS VERY MUCH...
SOMEONE COMES.
HELLO? IS SOMEBODY HERE? IF YOU ARE, JUST COME OUT...
...OR I'LL CALL CAMPUS SECURITY!

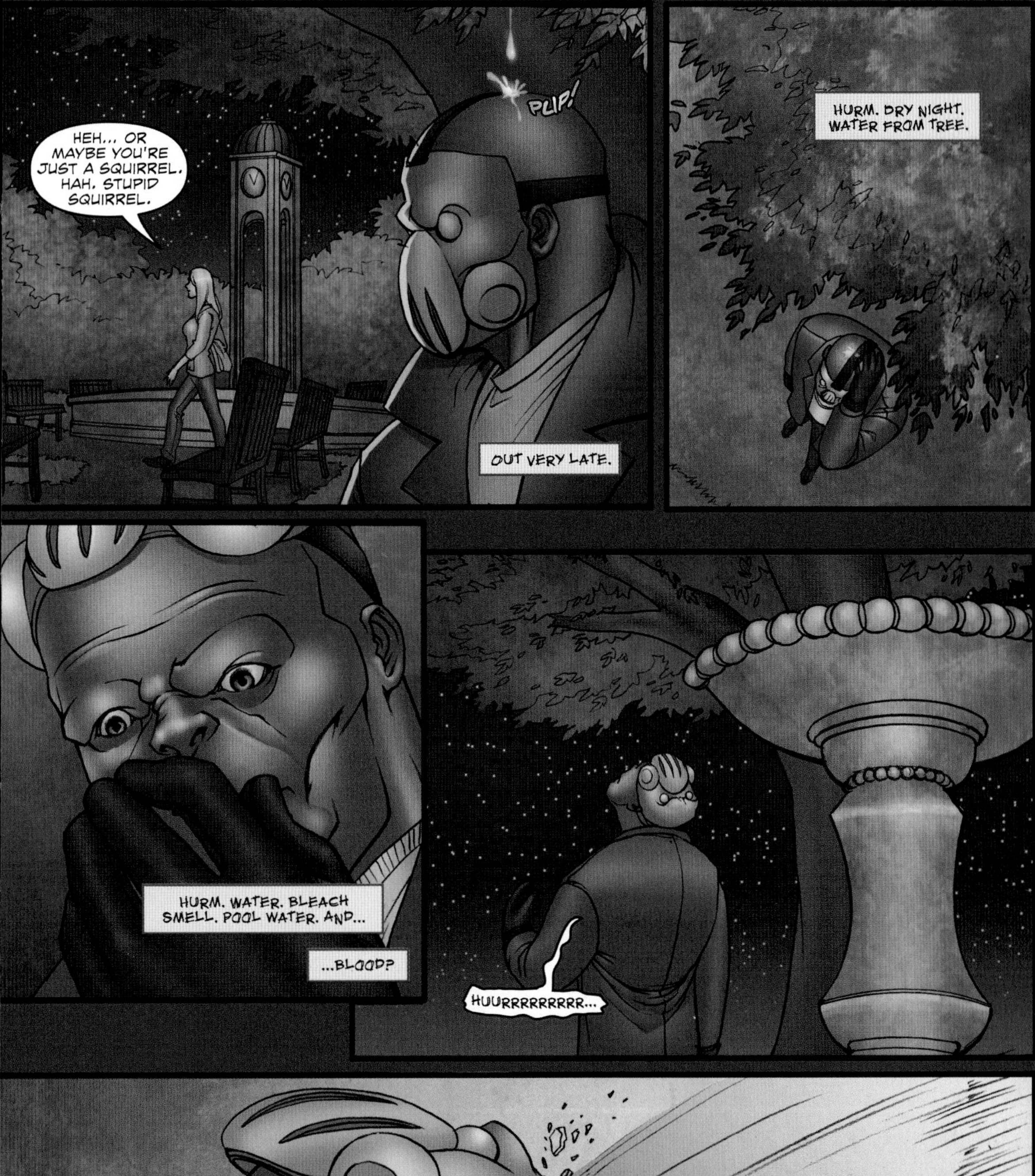
HEH... OR MAYBE YOU'RE JUST A SQUIRREL. HAH. STUPID SQUIRREL.
PLIP!
OUT VERY LATE.
HURM. DRY NIGHT. WATER FROM TREE.
HURM. WATER. BLEACH SMELL. POOL WATER. AND...
...BLOOD?
HUURRRRRRRRR...

UR!

MNNUHHH
VLAD?
TO BE CONTINUED...

VLAD. I AM. VLAD. WOMAN TALKS.

URR. HEAD HURTS. RINGS. SOUNDS LIKE ALARM CLOCK. **BIRDS** SINGING...

MOTHER?
NO. MOTHER LEFT ME. ALONE.
URR. HEAD IS WARM.

VLAD!
DAMN IT.
CASSIE.

HOLD IT RIGHT FUCKING THERE!!
YES.
OH GOD. VLAD! ARE YOU OKAY? JESUS FUCK...
URRM? WOMAN?
SHE HIT YOU WITH A FUCKING *BIRD BATH.*
YES, I HEAR THEM SINGING.
YOU SHOULD CHASE HER?
FUCK HER. FIRST WE TAKE CARE OF YOU.

SOON.
NURSE'S OFFICE
The Nurse is IN

IS HE OKAY?!
YES, I BELIEVE SO.

YOUR FRIEND IS BLESSED WITH THE GOOD KIND OF "THICK HEADEDNESS" THAT COMES IN VERY HANDY IN SITUATIONS LIKE THIS.
WISH IT WAS THE KIND MY HUSBAND HAD.
DID YOU GET A GOOD LOOK AT HIS ATTACKER?

NO. BUT WHEN I FIND HER, I'M GONNA SHOVE THAT BIRD BATH RIGHT UP HER ASS.
IN THE MEANTIME, VLAD MAY BE SUFFERING FROM A CONCUSSION, IN WHICH CASE, I DON'T RECOMMEND HE SLEEP.
SO, KEEP HIM AWAKE. THE MORE TALKING, THE BETTER.

I'M SURE THAT WON'T BE TOO HARD. OLD FRIENDS LIKE YOU TWO SHOULD BE ABLE TO GAB LIKE GIRLS AT A *SLUMBER PARTY*.

EMINENCE, INDIANA.
CHRIS, COME TO BED. PORN WILL STILL BE ON THE INTERNET TOMORROW.
ACTUALLY, I'M TRYING TO FIGURE OUT WHY WE HAVEN'T HEARD BACK FROM MY GUY IN IOWA...
WELL, KEEP IN MIND YOU MET THE GUY PLAYING WORLD OF WARCRAFT. MAYBE HE'S... I DUNNO... SACKING A VILLAGE OR WHATEVER.
YEAH, I GUESS.
NOW, COME TO BED...
ALBERT CITY POLICE DEPARTMENT, IOWA.
"LET HIM BURN AND PILLAGE..."

WEEEEOOOO
WEEEEOOOO
WEEEEOOOO
THERE ARE ASPECTS OF THIS JOB THAT I FIND DOWNRIGHT *UNSAVORY.*
WE'VE ACCOUNTED FOR ALL THE UNFORTUNATE WITNESSES. A "GAS LINE" EXPLOSION AT THE POLICE DEPARTMENT. HOW TRAGIC.
WHAT'S THE PROGRESS ON DR. GENUNG'S OUTGOING MAIL?
HE DELETED THE MESSAGES THEMSELVES, DR. WHITE. GEEK EVEN HAD THE SENSE TO USE A NETSHREDDER, BUT I TRACKED AN ISP TO A PROVIDER IN A SMALL TOWN IN INDIANA.
SWEET. SO WE'RE GONNA HAVE TO HAVE A COOKOUT IN INDY TOO.
HOLD ON...
...WE'VE GOT A REPORT OF A BREAK IN AT A MORGUE IN MARYLAND. REPORT INCLUDES A REFERENCE TO AN UNUSUAL BODY. JUST SKIN.
EAST COAST. HER FILE SAYS SHE GREW UP AROUND THE AREA. INDIANA WILL HAVE TO WAIT.
JUST WHERE ARE YOU HEADED MS. CRISTY?

9 HOURS LATER.
SWAP!

SLAPJACK! I WIN!
YEP, YOUR 381ST WIN IN FACT.

NOT BAD FOR A GUY WITH BRAIN DAMAGE.
I AM GOOD AT SLAPPING.
YEAH, WELL, IT HELPS THAT I'M AFRAID TO GO ANYWHERE NEAR YOUR GIANT MEAT HOOKS WHEN THEY START A-SWINGIN'.

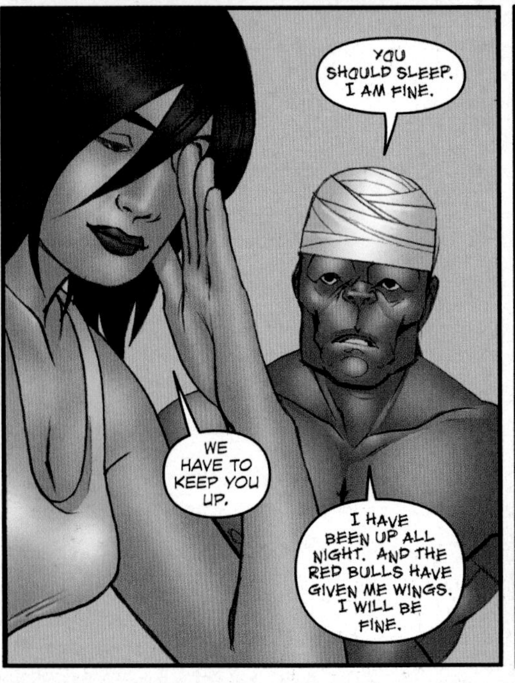
YOU SHOULD SLEEP. I AM FINE.
WE HAVE TO KEEP YOU UP.
I HAVE BEEN UP ALL NIGHT. AND THE RED BULLS HAVE GIVEN ME WINGS. I WILL BE FINE.

OKAY... BUT, I'M NOT GOING TO SLEEP. THE CHLORINATED WATER YOU NOTICED... I THINK MARSH IS RIGHT. THIS IS SOME KIND OF HOT TUB VERSION OF ELIZABETH BATHORY.
AND IT AIN'T MUCH, BUT I KNOW YOU SAID THE CHICK THAT HIT YOU HAD BROWN HAIR AND A SHELL NECKLACE.
YES. AND REMEMBER, I BELIEVE I HEARD MY NAME...
YEAH, THAT'S THE WEIRD PART. BUT, IT COULD'VE JUST BEEN HEAD DAMAGE TALKING.
GO. I WILL BE READY SOON.

VLAD... I'M... I'M SO SORRY. I SHOULDN'T HAVE LET YOU... I SHOULD HAVE TALKED TO YOU... INSTEAD.

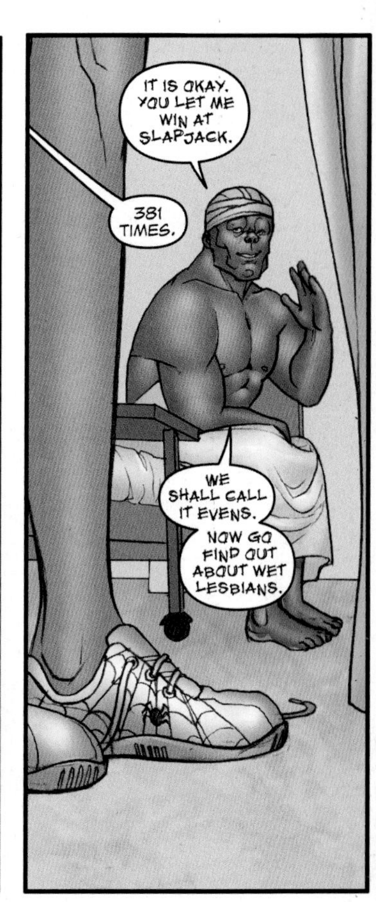
IT IS OKAY. YOU LET ME WIN AT SLAPJACK.
381 TIMES.
WE SHALL CALL IT EVENS.
NOW GO FIND OUT ABOUT WET LESBIANS.

BRRING
BRRING

FUCK.
GEORGIA

CASSIE! I KNOW YOU FELT BAD ABOUT VLAD WALKING OUT LAST NIGHT.
I JUST WANTED TO MAKE SURE EVERYTHING WAS OKAY.
NOT FROM CONCENTRATE NOW 12% JUICE!
Florida Made

NO... NO, IT'S NOT OKAY. VLAD GOT ATTACKED. I SHOULDN'T HAVE LET HIM GO OUT ALONE.
OH GOD! IS HE HURT?
HE'LL LIVE. BUT, I GOTTA REMEMBER THAT HE'S ALL I HAVE. I CAN'T HAVE OTHER FRIENDS.
IT WAS ME BEING ON THE PHONE WITH YOU ALL THE TIME THAT MADE HIM GO OUT AND DAMN NEAR GET HIS FUCKING SKULL CAVED IN.

IT'S REALLY NICE TO TALK TO YOU. IT'S NICE TO HAVE SOMEONE WHO SAYS THEY UNDER-STAND ME.
BUT, I'M A FREAK WHO HUNTS DOWN OTHER FREAKS. YOU'LL NEVER KNOW ME. AND, I'LL NEVER KNOW YOU.
FUCK, I DON'T EVEN KNOW YOUR REAL FUCKING NAME.
IT'S MARGARET. MARGARET CRUMP.
Nutrition Facts
Per 1 cup (250 g)
Amount
% Daily Valu
Calories 100

IT DOESN'T MATTER. THERE'S A REASON I DON'T HAVE ANY FRIENDS. I CAN'T TALK ABOUT YOUR PROBLEMS AND YOUR LIFE. I CAN'T LAUGH AND GIGGLE.
AT ANY MOMENT I COULD BE ELBOW DEEP IN BLOOD AND GORE. THAT'S MY LIFE. SO DON'T CALL ME UNLESS IT'S ABOUT A FREAK IN A MASK THAT NEEDS KILLING.
BIOLOGY
OKAY... SORRY CASSIE. I'M SORRY.
CLICK

DAMN.

GUNNISON HALL.

ELIZA?
HEY CHAS...

OH, NOW YOU'RE BACK. WHERE WERE YOU LAST NIGHT? I WAS WORRIED SICK! YOU DIDN'T PICK UP YOUR PHONE!
BUSY. I WAS BUSY WITH KATHY AND THE NEW INITIATE.

BUSY!? TOO BUSY TO CALL ME? I KNOW TONIGHT'S CEREMONY IS A BIG DEAL, BUT YOU COULD'VE BEEN DEAD OR... WHO KNOWS WHAT?!
WHAT'S BEEN UP WITH YOU THE PAST FEW DAYS? YOU'RE TOTALLY DIFFERENT! EVEN YOUR VOICE... AND... AND... WHAT'S WITH THE BLUE CONTACTS? I LOVED YOUR BIG BROWN EYES.

IT'S JUST... EVER SINCE WE JOINED THAT TUB CLUB... SOMETIMES I WISH WE HADN'T. I MISS WHEN IT WAS JUST... YOU AND I.

OH CHASTITY. SO YOUNG AND IDEALISTIC. SO BEAUTIFUL.
THE TUB CLUB IS IMPORTANT. IT'S THE MOST IMPORTANT THING WE DO. THIS LIFE IS A ONE-WAY STREET. EVERYTHING IN IT IS TEMPORARY.

IN TUB CLUB WE'RE FINDING THE PROCESS OF REBIRTH AND IMMORTALITY.

THE KEYS TO ETERNITY.

MMMHH. IT'S JUST... THE THINGS THEY WANT TO DO NOW... I DON'T WANT TO DO IT. I JUST WANT TO BE WITH YOU...

LIZA? WHAT'S... DID YOU HURT YOURSELF?

ELIZA, YOU NEED TO SEE THE NURSE.

DAMN IT. I'M SORRY CHASTITY.
FOR WHAT?

YOU HAVE REACHED THE END OF YOUR STREET.

MMMMPPH!

POOR CHASTITY. AS INNOCENT AS A DOVE, YES...

...BUT YOU LACK THE SHREWD-NESS OF THE SNAKE.

AND THOUGH YOUR BODY WILL BE UNABLE TO JOIN US IN THE FORM OF THE OUROBOROS...
...YOUR BLOOD WILL REPLENISH THIS SKIN...

THANKS CHRIS. YEAH, I KNOW HOW PAINFUL IT WAS FOR YOU TO LOOK UP GIRL SCHOOL LESBIANS ON FACE BOOK.
IF IT MAKES YOU FEEL BETTER I SPENT EIGHT HOURS HANGING OUT OUTSIDE THE HOT TUB.
Annalee & Becky
LUV U GIRLS!!
CALL ME! -SARAH
AUDREY HEPBURN
BREAKFAST AT TIFFANYS
LOVE

NAH, NONE OF THE GIRLS YOU SENT MATCH THE DESCRIPTION OF THE CHICK THAT COLDCOCKED VLAD.
OKAY. CASSIE OUT.

HI. WAITIN' FOR SOMEONE?
YEAH... ANNALEE. SHE'S... I NEED SOME NOTES FROM CHEM LECTURE.

I THINK ANNA IS IN HER ART STUDIO CLASS TODAY. SHE PROBABLY WON'T BE BACK FOR A WHILE.
OH. YAWWWWN! SHIT. OKAY... WELL...
LONG NIGHT? YOU LOOK EXHAUSTED.
YEAH. Y'KNOW... STUDYIN'.

YOU WANT TO COME IN FOR A WHILE? YOU CAN WAIT IN HERE. I'VE GOT NOTHING ELSE TO DO FOR THE DAY.

NO. I'LL JUST COME BACK...

ON SECOND THOUGHT... I SUPPOSE I COULD KILL SOME TIME.

NO ROOMIE?
NOPE. I'M THE R.A. I GET TO RULE OVER THE PEASANTS FROM MY OWN LONELY CASTLE.

THAT'S A LOT OF BOOKS. HISTORY BUFF?
YEAH... I'M THINKING ABOUT MAKING THAT MY MAJOR. I READ ALL THAT STUFF ANYWAY.

OH. WOW. I JUST SAW A THING ON HISTORY CHANNEL ABOUT THIS YESTERDAY...
YEAH? WHAT'S THAT?
ELIZABETH BATHORY.
ELIZABETH BATHORY

OUT OF ORDER

OUT OF ORDER

OUT OF ORDER

OUT OF ORDER

OUT OF ORDER

OH!

AAAIIIEEE!!

MR. VLAD? I'LL BE HEADING HOME NOW. GOTTA MAKE DINNER FOR MY LAZY HUSBAND, BUT I'LL COME BACK TONIGHT TO...

...CHECK ON YOU.
HNNNN...

SUCH A GENTLE SOUL.

PAIN-KILLER'S KNOCKED HIM RIGHT OUT.

HI NURSE MARSH. READY FOR *YOUR* INJECTION?
UGK?

WHAT A FREAK. AND I THOUGHT ANNE COULTER WAS A SICK BITCH.
HA! WELL, SOME ACCOUNTS SAY THAT BATHORY MIGHT HAVE BEEN FRAMED. YOU KNOW HOW IT WAS... NOTHING SCARIER THAN A WOMAN WITH POWER.
I SUPPOSE. THE CHICK MADE AN IMPACT, THAT'S FOR SURE. I HEAR THINGS AROUND CAMPUS...

WHAT KIND OF THINGS?
WOW, THAT IS A HELL OF A SCAR. WHAT HAPPENED?
DON'T...

JESUS. YOUR SHOULDERS ARE SO TIGHT!
I ... SLEPT FUNNY.
HERE, I GIVE REALLY GOOD SHOULDER MASSAGES. I CAN FIX THAT RIGHT UP.

YOU DON'T HAVE TO...
IT'S OKAY. JUST RELAX.

OHHH...
YOU CAN READ THE BOOK...

I'LL ATTEND TO OTHER THINGS...

MMMMMM...

MMMMM...
GEORGIA...

NO.

WHAT ARE YOU DOING?!

I'M... I'M SO SORRY. I THOUGHT. I THOUGHT YOU WERE *FLIRTING* WITH ME...

OH GOD. I'M SO STUPID. I NEVER HAD ANY PRACTICE. I DON'T KNOW THE SIGNALS, YOU KNOW?
I MEAN, THERE WERE NO OTHER GAY GIRLS IN MY TOWN AND... WELL... YOU WERE HINTING ABOUT THE CLUB AND YOU MENTIONED ANNALEE WHO *ALWAYS* SAYS SHE'S GOING TO GET ME LAID...

WAIT. THE CLUB. WHAT CLUB?!
THE *TUB CLUB...* I THOUGHT YOU KNEW ABOUT IT... *ELIZABETH BATHORY* AND ALL THAT...
ASSUME I DON'T, AND THAT I MIGHT GET REALLY MAD IF YOU *DON'T* TELL ME.

IT'S THIS CLUB WHERE THE GIRLS GET TOGETHER... ITS LESBIAN TANTRIC SEX... THEY SHARE BLOOD, LIKE IN THE SPIRITUAL WAY.
IT'S ALL ABOUT EMPOWERMENT AND SPIRITUALITY. THEY WEAR THE COWRIE SHELL NECKLACE... IT'S A SYMBOL OF FEMALE SACRED POWER.
I DON'T KNOW THAT MUCH. I JUST GOT INITIATED LAST NIGHT...

LAST NIGHT?! WAS THERE A GIRL THERE WITH LONG BROWN HAIR?
YES... THERE'S ELIZA. SHE'S THE NEW *YOGINI*. SHE... SHE INITIATED ME.

LOOK. THIS CLUB IS DANGEROUS. WHATEVER IT IS THEY'RE UP TO, IT'S CAUSED GIRLS TO DISAPPEAR IN THE PAST...
THOSE GIRLS *DIDN'T* DISAPPEAR. THEY GOT CAUGHT BEING DYKES AND QUIETLY EXPELLED FROM SCHOOL.
THERE'S NO CONSPIRACY... JUST A GROUP FOR GAY WOMEN TO LEARN ABOUT THEMSELVES, AND A WORLD THAT WASN'T READY FOR THEM.

TELL THAT TO MY FRIEND THAT GOT CREAMED WITH A BIRD BATH... OH... SHIT...

WHY DO YOU HAVE THIS PICTURE?!

THAT'S *EMILY CRISTY*. SHE WAS A MS. AMERICA. BUT SHE LOST THE CROWN WHEN SHE DID NUDE PHOTOS FOR A MEN'S MAGAZINE.
SHE BECAME ACTIVE IN WOMEN'S RIGHTS, STARTED A MAJOR COSMETIC'S FIRM. AN AMAZING WOMAN... SHE'S KIND OF AN IDOL OF MINE. SHE DISAPPEARED A FEW MONTHS AGO... SO SAD. SHE'S ACTUALLY ONE OF THE REASONS I CAME HERE.

SHE'S ONE OF FRANCO-BELLE'S MOST FAMOUS *ALUMNI*.

I TELL YA DR. WHITE, I TRAINED WITH NAVY S.E.A.L.S TO STAY UP FOR A WEEK AT A TIME IF I HAVE TO.
BUT DRIVING ACROSS THE *MIDWEST* IN EIGHTEEN HOURS IS GONNA KILL ME.
WE HAVE AN ESCAPED *REVENANT* ON THE LOOSE. IF ANYONE FINDS OUT, OUR DIVISION WILL BE CLOSED IN A HEARTBEAT.
AND YOU KNOW WHAT THEY DO WITH EX-EMPLOYEES WHO KNOW TOO MUCH. SO, SHUT UP, POP A NO DOZE AND DO THE JOB.
I JUST FOUND SOMETHING...
A POLICE CALL CONCERNING AN APPARENT SUICIDE IN A SHOWER. FRANCO-BELLE COLLEGE... MASSACHU-SETTS.
HER ALMA MATTER. INTERESTING.
WHINEY BOY! TO MASSACHU-SETTS!

MNUUUH...
SHE'S COMING TO...
MMMMMPPPH!
WELCOME, LINDA MARSH.
YOUR CURIOSITY ABOUT US HAS BROUGHT SOME UNWANTED ATTENTION...
BUT WE UNDERSTAND CURIOSITY.
SO TONIGHT WE ARE GOING TO GIVE YOU A CHANCE TO BEAR WITNESS...
...TO AN ASCENT INTO *DIVINITY*.
TO BE CONTUNUED... (LIKE YOU'D MISS THIS!!!)

FRANCO-BELLE UNIVERSITY.
BROOKLINE, MASSACHUSETTS.
AMBER BENNETT ♥ RA ♥
Hi Amber!
Lunch 2morrow?
Call Me!
B.F.F.
LIVE!

DON'T TOUCH ME!
AMBER BENNETT

YOU AREN'T GOING ANYWHERE.
TELL ME WHERE! WHERE IS THE TUB CLUB MEETING TONIGHT!?
I'M NOT SELLING OUT THOSE GIRLS JUST SO THEY CAN GET EXPELLED AND CHASTISED LIKE EVERY OTHER GAY GIRL BEFORE US!
NOW GET OFF ME, YOU CLOSET CASE!

UNGF
BEEE-YOTCH.

HELP! HEL--
WHAT THE--?!

WHERE'S EVERYONE GOING?
SOMEONE'S DEAD. IN THE SHOWER.

WHO IS IT?
OH MY GOD.
IS IT, LIKE, SUICIDE?
CHASTITY.

OH GOD. CHASTITY.

IF YOU DON'T TELL ME WHERE THAT MEETING IS...

...ALL YOUR FRIENDS ARE GOING TO END UP *JUST* LIKE THAT.

LATER.
STUDENT MEDICAL SERVICES
SCAN ALL THE MEDICAL FILES!

WE NEED ANY REFERENCES TO BLOOD LOSS OR SKIN ABNORMALITIES. IF CRISTY IS HERE, SHE MAY BE RESIDING IN THE SKIN OF ONE OF THE STUDENTS.
RUN THE NAME OF THE "SUICIDE VICTIM" ALSO. AS SOON AS LOCAL LAW ENFORCE-MENT--

SIR?
I'VE GOT BLOOD...

NOT ONLY IS IT BLOOD, IT APPEARS FRESH.
SHE WAS SO WHITE... LIKE ALL HER BLOOD WAS GONE...
NURSE'S OFFICE
HOURS
M-F 8-5
I KNOW. BUT I NEED YOU TO COME BACK TO REALITY. I NEED YOU IN THE GAME SO YOU CAN TAKE VLAD AND I TO THIS UNDERGROUND SPRING...
WHAT THE--?!
KA-KRASH!

AGGHH!!
RAAAAH!!!
VLAD!
SHOOT TO INJURE! IT'S CRISTY IN A NEW SKIN!
BLAM!
PWOK!
UNGF
WHO
THE
FUCK
ARE
YOU?

CASSIE HACK...

HOLD UP, FREAKS. OR I'LL SHOOT THIS LITTLE PIECE OF ASS RIGHT IN THE BRAINPAN.
BREAST HEALTH

TELL HIM TO DROP IT.
YOU DON'T UNDERSTAND. I KNOW YOU. I READ YOUR FILES FROM CEUTOTECH. AND, I WORKED WITH YOUR ***FATHER.***
MY FATHER? PLAY ME ANOTHER ONE. YOU THINK I'M FUCKING RETARDED? TELL HIM TO LET HER GO!

LET THE GIRL GO!
ARE YOU KIDDING ME?
SHE ISN'T OUR ENEMY!

NOW. WHAT'S GOING ON?!
I BELIEVE WE'RE LOOKING FOR THE SAME THING. EMILY CRISTY.
AND I WANT YOUR HELP BECAUSE--?
BECAUSE I KNOW THINGS. ABOUT YOUR MOTHER, ***DELILAH.*** ABOUT YOUR FATHER, ***JACK...***

...AND HOW TO ***FIND*** HIM.

BELOW.
YES. WE ARE NOW UNIFIED IN OUR ECSTASY... EACH YONI PULSING IN RHYTHM WITH THE ENERGIES OF ALL THAT IS.
AND NOW WE SHALL RELEASE THE BLOOD...

THE VERY BLOOD THAT KEEPS THESE BODIES ALIVE WILL NOW ACT AS THE MEDIUM BY WHICH WE SHALL ALL BE CLEANSED. CLEANSED OF OUR PAINS AND SINS, AND MADE NEW.
AND WITH EACH REBIRTH WE COME CLOSER TO DIVINITY.
WE ARE READY FOR THE FINAL ACT. WE ARE READY TO BE AS *ONE,* AND JOIN IN THE ETERNAL CIRCLE.
WE ARE READY TO FORM THE *OURO-BOUROS.*
OUROBOUROS...
OUROBOUROS...
OUROBOUROS...
OUROBOUROS...
OUROBOUROS...
OUROBOUROS...

OH YES. I CAN FEEL EVERY-THING. THE VIBRATIONS IN THE VERY FABRIC OF REALITY.
AND I FEEL THAT WE ARE NOT ALONE.
OHH! NOOOO!!!
SPLORCH!
OH YES. I LOVE YOU GIRLS. I LOVE YOU.
AHHH!
WHAT?!
SPLOOOT!
AAAAIIIEEEE!

AAAAIIIEEEE!!
AMBER SHOULDN'T BE HERE.
SHE MAY BE LEADING US INTO A TRAP. SHE MAY EVEN BE CRISTY. I'M NOT TAKING ANY CHANCES.
SHE'S NOT EMILY.
AND YOU SEE THINGS AS BLACK AND WHITE. JUST LIKE YOUR FATHER THAT WAY.
HERE... TO THE RIGHT... THE MAIN CAVERN IS JUST AROUND THE SECOND BEND.

GOOD. CAMPBELL, YOU'RE WITH ME. CONTAIN CRISTY AT ALL COSTS. WADZINKSI, REIS, YOU KNOW WHAT TO DO.
NNGH
FOONT!

OH GOD! AMBER!

WHO WANTS TO WATCH WHO GO? I'M ITCHIN' TO POP THE BIG GUY FIRST.
WHACK!
NUHN!
YOU MOTHER-FUCKERS!

I TRULY AM SORRY, MS. HACK. THIS CASE DEMANDS THERE BE NO WITNESSES.
BUT, I DO WANT YOU TO KNOW, YOUR FATHER TRULY WAS A GOOD AND HONORABLE. MAN.

EVEN IF THE WORK HE DID WAS NOT.

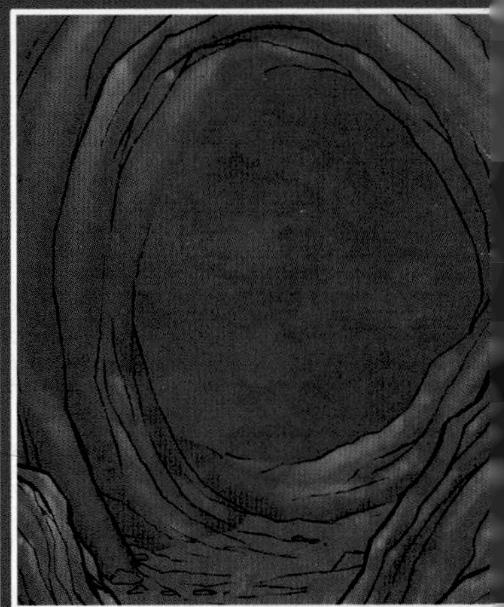

CAMPBELL! THERE'S--
CAMPBELL!
FOONT!
FOONT!
FOONT!
SPLUTCH!!!

AAAIIIIGHHH!!!...

AIIIGHH!!!
DR. WHITE!!
WHAT THE--!?
AGGHGH!
SPLOOPP!!
YESSSSSS...
FOONT!
FOONT!
FOONT!
FUCK!! REIS!!!

VLAD? ARE YOU OKAY?!
MURRRHHH

KLICK
KLICK
OH FUCK ME! FUCK ME!

MUH.
YOUR GUN IS EMPTY. LIKE YOUR SOUL. ALL YOU ARE IS SO MUCH FLESH.

I. AM. FINE.

WHOK!!!
UNGH!
EMILY. JESUS. WHAT... WHAT'S HAPPENED TO YOU?
Y-YOU STRIKE ME? I SAVED YOUR LIVES.
I MAY HAVE TRANSCENDED MY OLD LIFE. BUT I RE-MEMBER YOU AND VLAD. I REMEMBER YOU HELPED ME...

BUT, WE RE EVEN NOW. OLD LIFE FOR YOURS.
I WAS A FAILED BEAUTY QUEEN. NO MORE ADMIRERS. THE BEAUTY GONE. THE REPUTATION TARNISHED.
BUT NOW, I WILL HAVE WORSHIPPERS. I HAVE ATTAINED GODHOOD...
SQUARCH!!!
...AND GODS DO AS THEY WILL.
SPLAP!
UNG!
NOW LEAVE THESE SACRED GROUNDS. I WON'T SAVE YOU AGAIN.
BITCH, I'M UNSAVE-ABLE.
CASSANDRA!
NOOO... DON'T...

I-I OWE HER. AND... AND HER F-FATHER.
HERE... T-TAKE THIS...

GIVE THIS... TO CASSIE. HE WILL KNOW WHERE HER F-FATHER IS.
Howard Phillips
Hellgate Rd
Winnett

HURRM.
WAIT! WAIT!

P-PLEASE.
KILL ME.

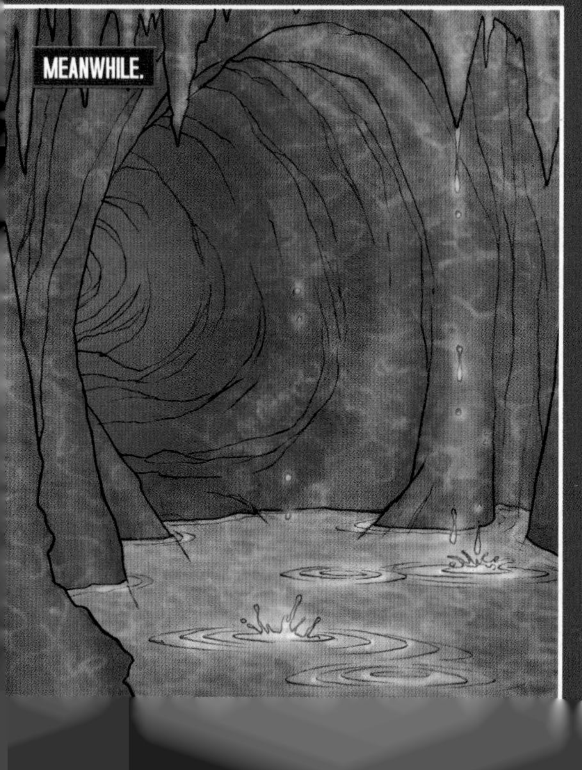
MEANWHILE.

FUUUCK!
SPLASH!

HUNGH!!

FUCKIN' A.

OH JESUS.
DAMN YOU. I DON'T WANT TO KILL *YOU.*
FWAK!
UNF!
W-WHY NOT, EMILY?! YOU KILLED ALL THOSE GIRLS. ALL THOSE POOR GIRLS WHO JUST WANTED TO--
COFF
--HUNH... JUST WANTED TO BE WITH PEOPLE LIKE THEM.
NO. THEY GAVE THEIR LIVES TO *CONTINUE* MINE. THEY HAVE BEEN MARTYRED, RISING TO A HIGHER STATE OF CONSCIOUS-NESS. THEY LIVE ON AS I LIVE ON.
WITH THEIR BODIES AND MINE JOINED, I HAVE ELIMINATED THOS THAT WOULD DESTROY ME.

IT'S UNFORTUNATE THAT ALL MY FOLLOWERS HAVE MOVED TO THE NEXT REALM, UNABLE TO COMMUNICATE WITH THOSE LIVING THEIR HALF-LIVES.
BUT IN RETURNING HERE, I WAS ABLE TO FULLY UNDERSTAND MY MESSAGE AND TO FULLY SHED THE REST OF MY HUMAN TRAPPINGS.
I SUPPOSE EVEN JESUS CHRIST HAD TO MAKE A FEW DRY RUNS.
COME, NURSE.
GIVE ME YOUR BODY SO THAT I MAY CONTINUE TO INHABIT THIS GARDEN OF EDEN.
NOO... MARSH...
COFF
GRAAAH!!!
SPLOOSH
NO MORE STUPID TALK. NO MORE FAKE FACES. YOU MUST BE STOPPED.
SHRRRIP!

ERRGH. YOU WERE THERE WHEN I WAS REBORN. YOU COULD HAVE BEEN A DISCIPLE. *A WITNESS.*
ARRRGGHGGH!
SPLOOPP!!
SPLOOOT!
NO. NO, I WON'T TAKE YOUR SKIN. I DENY YOUR OFFERING.

BUT NOT BECAUSE I OWE YOU. *NOT* BECAUSE YOU ARE SPECIAL.
BUT BECAUSE I OFFERED YOU A CHANCE TO BECOME BEAUTIFUL ONCE. TO FIX YOU. AND YOU DIDN'T TAKE IT. I DON'T *WANT* YOUR SKIN...
...BECAUSE YOU'RE TOO FUCKING...
...UGLY.

SPLUK!!
HURR. YES.
EEEIGH--
BUT, AT LEAST I AM COMFORT-ABLE...
...IN MY OWN SKIN.

LATER.
THERE YOU GO.

NOW YOU'VE GOT A MATCHING SET.
WHEE.

THANK YOU. I MEAN, FOR SAVING MY LIFE.
I WAS EXPECTING A POLTERGEIST, MAYBE A DARK APPARITION. BUT THIS...

IN ANY CASE. YOUR WORK HERE IS DONE. I'LL CALL MS. ELSTEN, AND MY HUSBAND AND I WILL GET ON SETTING UP SOME KIND OF... I DON'T KNOW... COVER-UP, I GUESS.
THE POLICE WILL HAVE TO BE NOTIFIED ABOUT THE GIRLS... BUT, THE STATE OF THOSE CORPSES AND THE GOVERNMENT MEN... WELL... WE'LL THINK OF SOMETHING.

JUST REMEMBER... WHEN IT COMES TO SLASHERS, FIRE IS YOUR FRIEND.
DON'T YOU WORRY ANY... YOU'RE TALKING TO THE WOMAN WHO PREVENTED PRYING EYES FROM DISCOVERING ***THE GREAT HOWLING APPARITION OF SPANISH COVE.***
YEAH, MUSTA WORKED, CUZ... UH... I'VE NEVER HEARD OF IT.

HOWLING APPARITION?
YEAH. AND HE WOULD HAVE GOTTEN AWAY WITH IT TOO, IF IT WASN'T FOR THAT PESKY NURSE.
DR. WHITE ASKED ME TO GIVE YOU THIS.
IT IS AN ADDRESS. FOR A MAN WHO KNOWS THE LOCATION OF YOUR FATHER.

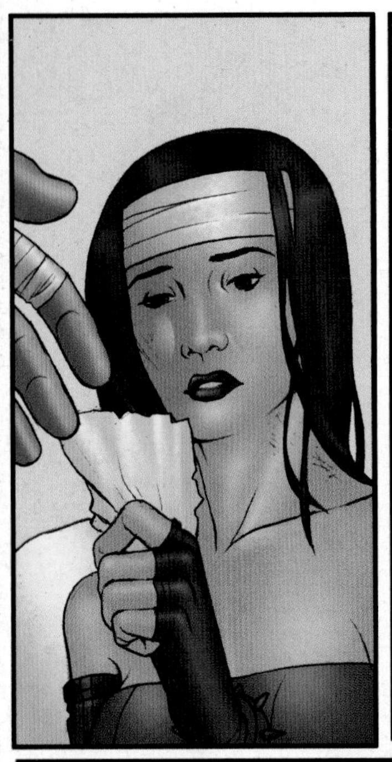

I... I ALSO KNEW THAT THIS WOULD BE DIFFICULT FOR YOU. THAT IT WOULD MAKE YOU CONFUSED. CONFLICTUATED.
SO... SO I WANT YOU TO CALL YOUR FRIEND. GEORGIA... SHE WILL UNDER-STAND.

NO. I DON'T NEED TO CALL HER.
BREAK OUT THE CARDS... I THINK IT'S TIME FOR A SLAPJACK REMATCH.
7:15

BUT THIS TIME, I'M NOT GOING EASY ON YOU.
FRANCO-BELL
COLLEGE FOR
WOMEN
est. 1873
F B
THE END.

LITTLE CHILDREN
#10A by TIM SEELEY & JEREMY ROBERTS

June 22.
This is it.
NO TRESPASSING
VIOLATORS WILL BE SHOT SURVIVORS WILL BE SHOT AGAIN

Any minute now I suspect I'll hear them.
Those sounds they make.
Somewhere in-between cries of pain and pleasure.

Terrible, guttural noises no human throat should be able to make.

HIGH VOLTAGE
Let them come. I'm ready for it. I deserve it. I've spent my whole life convincing myself that every experiment was for the greater good of humanity.
The bummer of it is, I wasn't even a very good God. I was guilty of hubris.
I created flawed beings.
Now, in my last moments, I can finally admit I just really got my rocks off playing God.
I created evil..
UEEEEEEEEEEE
And it's come back to bite me in the ass.
UEEEEEEEEE

NOW.
FUCK.
WE CAME ALL THE WAY TO MONTANA FOR NOTHING.
ALL WE'VE GOT IS GRIZZLY ADAM'S CABIN, A LINK TO SCARY GOVERNMENT SHIT, AND A BIG, GODDAMNED RED STAIN.
BUT THERE ARE SO MANY BOOKS. PERHAPS THE INFORMATIONS OF YOUR FATHER ARE SOMEWHERE IN HERE.

THAT'S JUST IT. I ACCEPTED MY DAD BEING GONE A LONG TIME AGO. I HAVEN'T EVEN THOUGHT ABOUT HIM IN YEARS.
YOUR MOTHER TAKES UP MUCH OF YOUR BRAINSPACE.
I'D FINALLY SETTLED INTO JUST BEING THE "SLASHER-HUNTER CHICK". THAT'S NICE AND SIMPLE, Y'KNOW?
FIND PSYCHO. BEAT PSYCHO WITH BAT. MOVE ON. DON'T ASK. NO QUESTION, SO NO STRESS.
BUT WITH THAT GOVERNMENT GUY, AND MY DAD, AND NOW THIS BACKWOODS MILITIA BIOLOGIST GUY... THAT RAISES A SHITLOAD OF QUESTIONS...
YEAH.
YOU DESERVE TO FIND ANSWERS. YOU DESERVE TO KNOW IF YOU HAVE A FAMILY. YOU DESERVE TO KNOW ABOUT YOUR FATHER.
BUT WHAT IF THAT MEANS FINDING OUT MY DAD IS AS BIG OF A MONSTER AS MY MOM?

NEARBY.
ANNA! TIME FOR BED!
I DON'T WANNA GO TO BED. THERE'S SCARY NOISES IN THE WOODS.
IT'S JUST ANIMALS, HONEY.
WHAT KIND OF ANIMALS? CUZ EVERYONE SAYS SOMETHING ATE WINNEY PYLE'S DAD.
NO ONE ATE MR. PYLE. HE... WELL... DON'T YOU WORRY... IT'S JUST DEER. SQUIRRELS. BUNNIES. LOTS OF BUNNIES.
IT'S NOT BUNNIES. BUNNIES DON'T SCREAM.
THEN IT'S PROBABLY OWLS, HONEY. OWLS SOMETIMES MAKE A NOISE LIKE A SCREAM.
NOW, GET SOME SLEEP, HONEY.
UEEEEEE

YEEEEEEEE
BUNNIES DO SCREAM.
MOMMY...
RRRRRRMMMMMMMM

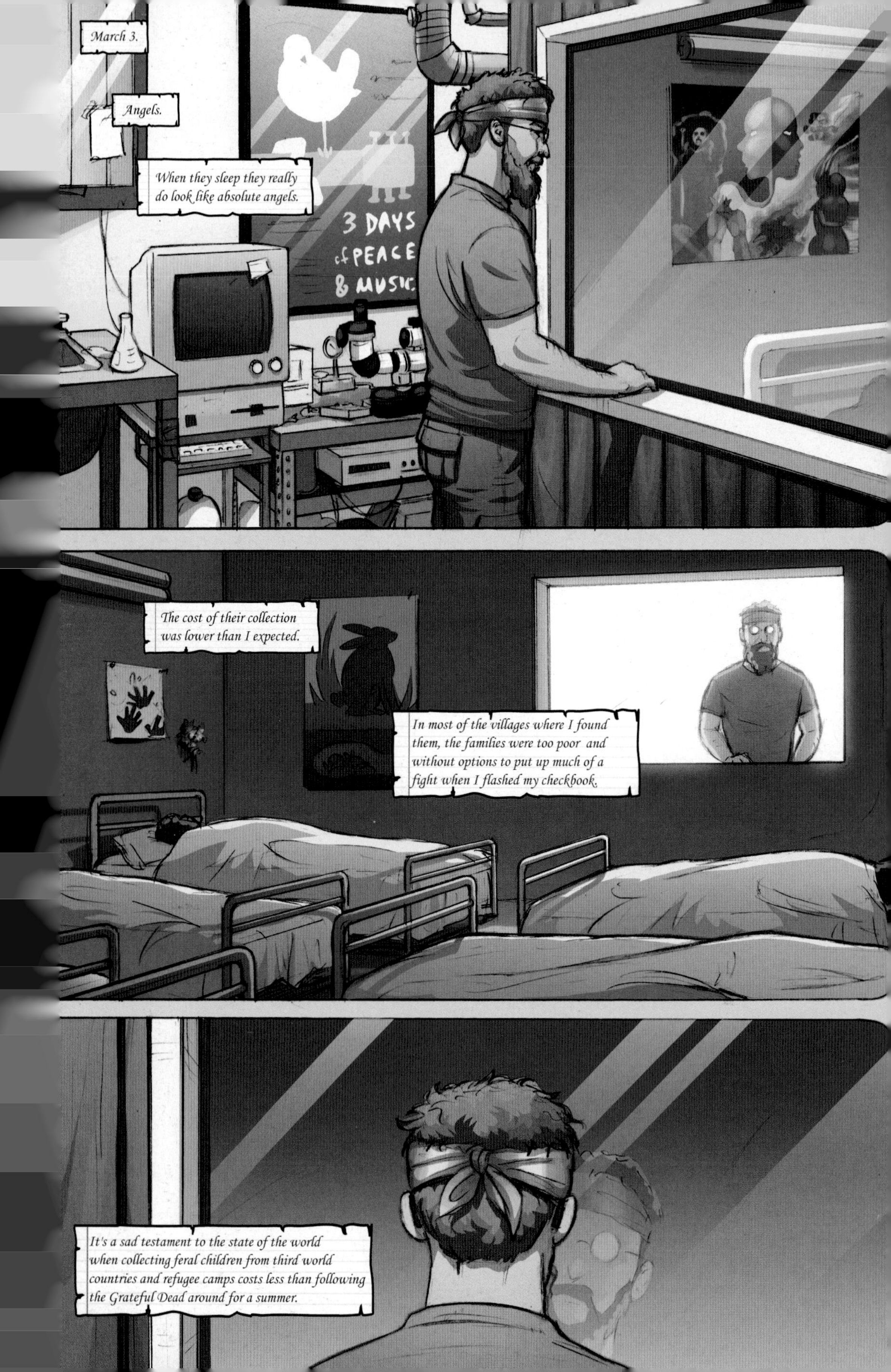
March 3.
Angels.
When they sleep they really do look like absolute angels.
3 DAYS of PEACE & MUSIC
The cost of their collection was lower than I expected.
In most of the villages where I found them, the families were too poor and without options to put up much of a fight when I flashed my checkbook.
It's a sad testament to the state of the world when collecting feral children from third world countries and refugee camps costs less than following the Grateful Dead around for a summer.

The children, whether they were raised by animals or learned to survive on war torn streets, remain at their core, children.
And though they lack in communicative and social skills, they more than make up for it with their wide-eyed wonder.

I'm finally beginning to understand why so many of my colleagues decided to start families. The bond I'm forming with them is strong...
...almost fatherly.
WOLF

And though my original intent of this study was not to integrate feral kids back into the world, if I can help them in any way, I'll consider the experiment a personal success.

March 15.
CAT
CDE
AEOU
Romulus has quickly become the fastest learner.
He also appears to be the leader of the children, and they defer to him in a manner not unlike that of dogs or wolves. Hence the name.
Though I first believed he was far past the stage of being able to learn language, he has picked up one word...

DAAAD.

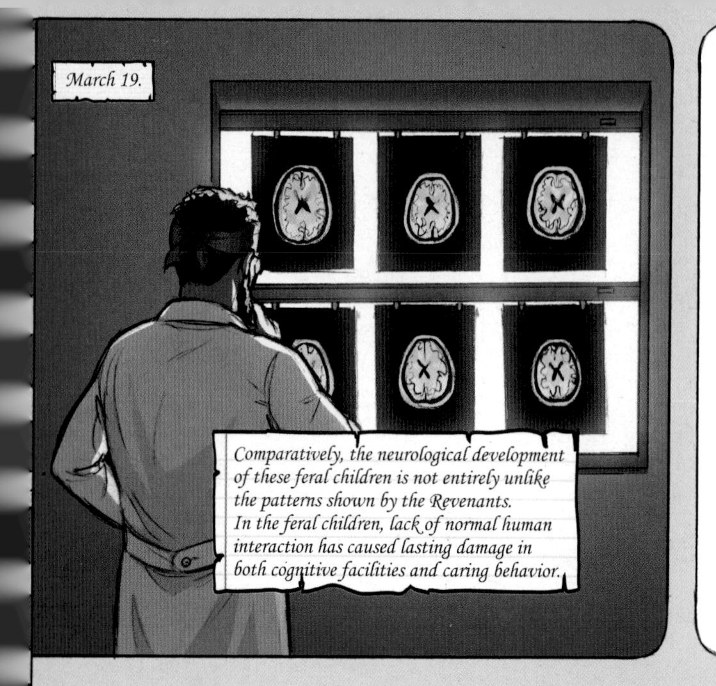
March 19.
Comparatively, the neurological development of these feral children is not entirely unlike the patterns shown by the Revenants.
In the feral children, lack of normal human interaction has caused lasting damage in both cognitive facilities and caring behavior.

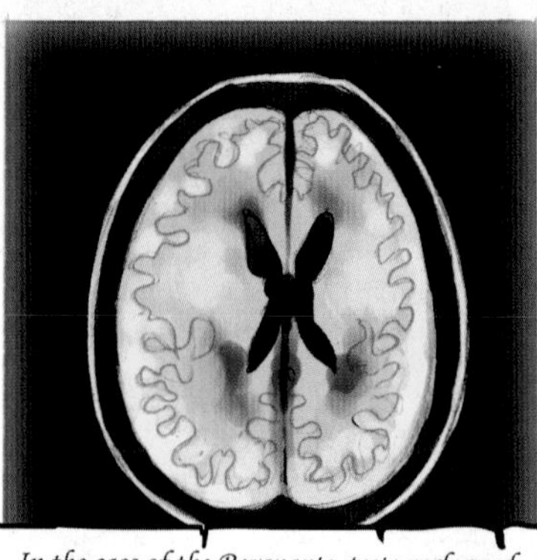
In the case of the Revenants, tests performed after a post-mortem reactivation show a lack of regenerative biology in the brain, whereas the rest of the body has undergone a major metamorphosis.
The brain, especially parts known to deal with moral and social interaction, has actually seemed to degrade.
Within the week, I will be ready to test my Rev-D, which I believe may be able to reverse the downward curve of the children's development, and provide answers regarding Revenants.

April 1.

I let my guard down.
The children had been progressing so well. I decided to relax. In the time it took me to listen to side A of Bitch's Brew and smoke one joint, a massive social upheaval had befallen the kids.

Apparently, Romulus felt Remus had challenged him for his role as leader.

Romulus tore out his throat with his teeth.
I believe the Rev-D has increased his feral urges rather than restrained them.

April 8.
Separating the girls from Romulus has caused them to regress farther into their feral states. Without him to act as their social leader, they are resistant to any of my studies.
And, by being the one to remove him, they now believe me to be the enemy.
My attempt this morning to separate Phoebe from the group...
...resulted in an impromptu amputation.
The scans show a small, but noticeable degeneration in their brains, likely responsible for their more aggressive behavior.
Maybe it's time to admit that the Revenant-derived cells cannot, for all practical purposes, be reverse-engineered. Maybe they really are some kind of black magic mumbo-jumbo that man was never meant to fuck with.
Maybe my old friend Jack was right all along.

JESUS... MY DAD'S NAME WAS JACK.
GODDAMMIT.
WHAT THE HELL IS GOING ON HERE? REVENANTS AND FERAL KIDS?
I DON'T HAVE TIME FOR THIS DETECTIVE SHIT!
SWOK!

HRM. WHY DOES A PERSON NEED A CERTIFICATE TO DIE?
WHAT ARE YOU TALKING ABOUT?
THIS.

BUNCH OF OLD MAIL... BIRTH CERTIFICATES AND DEATH CERTIFICATES... MOSTLY KIDS WHO DIED IN THE 60s...
WHEN I WAS AT THE HALFWAY HOUSE, THERE WAS THIS KID THERE WHO GOT IN DEEP SHIT FOR STEALING IDENTITIES AND MAKING FAKES...
HE WAS A TOTAL DOUCHE, BUT I REMEMBER HIM SAYING THAT ALL YOU NEEDED WAS A BIRTH CERTIFICATE AND A DEATH CERTIFICATE TO BECOME SOMEONE ELSE.
YOUR FATHER DISAPPEARED, YES? JUST GONE.
PERHAPS HE TURNED INTO SOMEONE ELSE?

UeEeEEEeEe!
Aoooooooow!
WOLVES?
NO...

KIDS.

CRASH!
YeEeEEEEEe!
TAKE THESE! WE CAN'T LET THIS PLACE BURN!
WHAT IS GOING ON HERE?!
THE KIDS ARE HO-- OW!
AOOOW!
UCK!
YEEeEe!

GODDAMMIT! GOT SO INVOLVED WITH FINDING DAD...
YAAAH!
DAAAAD?
DAADD.
DDEDD.

VLAD! WE CAN'T LET THIS PLACE GO UP! TAKE THOSE FUCKING KIDS OUT!
IF I HIT THEM, I WILL BREAK THEM! THEY ARE CHILDREN!
THEY'RE WILD, VLAD! ABANDONED!
WINTER IS COMING... HE'S TRYING TO FEED HIS PACK...
URF
PLEASE. DO NOT.
I HAVE BEEN ABANDONED. I KNOW...
RAAAAAAA...

THWAK!
AIIIGH!
AIEEE!
RRG
WHOK!
EIGHGHEGHGH!

RAUGH?
EEEEEiiiiiii!
NOW! GRAB THE BOOKS!
IT'S TOO LATE!
I AM SORRY. I COULD NOT HIT THE GIRLS. THEY ARE SO SMALL.
I KNOW, VLAD.
JACK HACK

EEEEI. EEEI.
HERE THEY ARE.
WHERE WILL WE TAKE THEM? TO LISA?
NO.
I'M SORRY.
WHAT?! BUT...
IN THE NOTEBOOK, PHILLIPS TALKED ABOUT STUDYING THEIR BRAINS. HE WAS INJECTING THESE KIDS WITH CELLS FROM REVENANTS.
REVENANT? WHAT IS THAT?

IT'S AN OLD TIME WORD FOR A CORPSE THAT RETURNS FROM THE GRAVE TO GET REVENGE.
IT'S JUST A FANCY WAY TO SAY "SLASHER".
YOU AND I BOTH SAW WHAT HAPPENED TO EMILY AFTER SHE INJECTED HERSELF WITH THAT COSMETIC COMPANY'S DESIGNER SLASHER-POTION.
BUT--!
NO. THEY'RE CANNIBALS. THEY'RE UNTREATABLE. NO TIME TO DEBATE THE ETHICS OR POSSIBILITIES.
THIS IS A COMMAND DECISION.
KRAK! KRAK! KRAK!

YOU HAVE TOLD ME BEFORE, THAT IF YOU SHOULD EVER GO OVER THE EDGE... GO BAD... I SHOULD STOP YOU.
TODAY, I FEEL... CONFUSED. MY STOMACH FEELS BAD.
WHAT WE DID TODAY...
I ALMOST THOUGHT I HAD TO STOP YOU. MAYBE THIS IS TOO FAR.
NO. WE DID WHAT HAD TO BE DONE.
SLASHERS AREN'T SOME RANDOM EVENT. PEOPLE HAVE TRIED TO USE THEM FOR THEIR OWN ENDS. SOMEONE KNOWS HOW THIS STARTED. SOMEONE KNOWS HOW TO STOP IT.
IF THAT PERSON IS MY DAD, WE'LL FIND HIM.
THAT'S WHAT WE DO. WE HUNT MONSTERS.

LATER...
JESUS CHRIST. FIVE BODIES. ALL KIDS. WHAT THE HELL WAS GOING ON HERE?
WE'RE NOT SURE. FORENSICS SAYS THEY JUST FOUND SOME KIND OF ELABORATE BASEMENT LEVEL. MIGHT'VE BEEN SOME OF MILITIA. WHO THE HELL KNOWS WHAT.
I HATE TO ADMIT IT, BUT I THINK IT MIGHT BE THAT TIME. PEOPLE ARE GONNA WANT ANSWERS.
UNDERSTOOD, SIR. I'LL CALL IN THE SECRET WEAPON.
HELLO? HELLO?
OH, DEAR. I'M SORRY. SOMETIMES I PICK UP THE PHONE BEFORE IT RINGS. YES, THIS IS THAT MUFFY JOWORSKI.
A CASE?
WHY, OF COURSE I'M INTERESTED!

YBOR CITY, FLORIDA.
BEEP BEEP BEEP
ON MELTAN
CASSIE?!
HEY, GIRL. DIDN'T EXPECT TO... Y'KNOW... HEAR FROM YOU.
AL'S KWIK STOP
NO. IS EVERYTHING OKAY? YOU SOUND ROUGH. IS VLAD OKAY?
SORRY. YOU'RE NOT BUSY, OR... WITH SOMEONE?
YEAH. HE'S ASLEEP.
WHAT CAN I DO FOR YA? IS THIS ONE OF THOSE "HACK SLASH, INC." CALLS?

...
NO... I JUST...
AL'S KWIK STOP
...I JUST NEED TO TALK.
TO BE CONTINUED...

THE COLDEST DISH
#11 A by TIM SEELEY & JEREMY ROBERTS

PORTLAND, OREGON.
THURSDAY. 10:38 AM.
FUCK. I HATE THIS GUY. HE'S ALWAYS LATE...
DO NOT FEED PIGEONS
WELL, IF HE IS, REMIND HIM TO HURRY NEXT TIME. FOR HIS SAKE...
...HE BETTER BE RUNNIN' HIS ASS OFF.
AHHHH!!!
FUCK, MAN! LEAVE ME ALONE! WASN'T ME, MAN!

SERIOUSLY, MAN! YOU'RE CHASIN' THE WRONG DUDE! I WAS JUST THERE. I DIDN'T DO NOTHIN'. MOST FUCKED UP THING I EVER SAW...
VEHIC
SHE
#3
UNGF
WHOMPH
HICLE
SHED

SHOULD HAVE CLOSED YOUR EYES.
CITY OF PORTLA
AAAAAH!
STILL NO FUCKIN' KID.
WAIT... GONNA LET YA GO, SHAWN. HEAR SOMETHIN'...
WHAT THE HELL? WHAT'S THAT ASSHOLE DOIN'?
CLICK
HEY MAN, TURN THAT FUCKIN' THING AROUND!

FUCK!
OH FUCK!
IT'S YOU! IT'S--
IT IS.
I WANT YOU TO LOOK INTO MY EYE.
WHAT DO YOU SEE?!
N-NOTHIN'! BLACK!
DO NOT FEED PIGEONS
YES.
AND THAT'S WHAT YOU'LL SEE FOREVERMORE.

EAU CLAIRE, WISCONSIN.
FRIDAY. 12:45 AM.
GOODWILL
WAY TO GO. YOU GET US T'ROWN OUTTA MARGE'S, NOW WE GOTTA WALK TO THE DOWNHILL PUB. AN' IT'S COLD.
QUIT WHININ'! IF IT'LL HELP, I'LL WARM YOUR BEER IN MY ARMPIT 'FORE YOU DRINK IT.
WHATEVER, AS LONG AS FIRST ROUND'S ON *YOU...*
HEY... DO YOU SEE SOMETHING... OVER IN FRONT OF THE *GOODWILL?*
YEAH... I THINK SO. LIKE A DOG OR SOMETHING?

I will save you master!

I will not let these earth ones keep you trapped on that fuzzy plate!

I will save you!

FWAM!

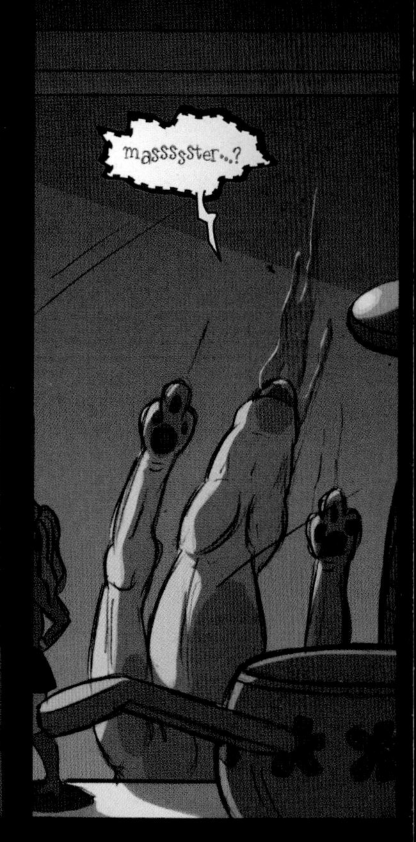
massssster...?

D'YOU SEE THAT? CRAZY DOG RUNNED RIGHT INTO THE GLASS!
YEAH, GOT IT ON MY PHONE...

WAIT'LL THE GUYS AT WORK SEE THIS...

BAKER CITY, OREGON.
Ronald Morrison - Blackfoot, I
Colin DeMatteis - Kennewick, W
Michael Palahnink - Bake
Fred Moore - San Franci
Bud Shaw - Potts Camp, Mis
Asa Turnipseed - Huntsville, A
Müenster Speckmann - Bonn, Ge
MICHAEL PALAHNINK. CONGRATULATIONS, YOU ARE NOT MY FATHER.
THREE DAYS DRIVING AROUND THE NORTHWEST, CHECKING OUT NAMES FROM A LIST WE PULLED OUT OF A LAB THAT MADE THE ISLAND OF DR. MOREAU LOOK LIKE MR. WIZARD'S WORLD.
ALL THE NAMES ARE ASSUMED IDENTITIES. PLACEHOLDER LIVES FOR SOMEONE TO STEP INTO. A NEW STORY WHEN YOUR ORIGINAL TALE WENT TO SHIT.
GAMBLING DEBTS? FUCK THE WRONG GUY'S WIFE? GET INVOLVED WITH SECRET GOVERNMENT EXPERIMENTS INVOLVING UNDEAD, VICIOUS SLASHERS? STEP RIGHT UP AND PICK ONE OUR NEW LIVES, COMPLETE WITH REFRIGERATOR AND COMFY RECLINER...
DID I JUST...?
I DID.
I TOTALLY JUST STARED THAT GUY DOWN. I LOOKED HIM UP AND DOWN. LIKE PEOPLE DO WHEN THEY WONDER WHAT SOMEONE LOOKS LIKE WITHOUT CLOTHES. WHAT THEIR "OH GOD!" FACE LOOKS LIKE.
OKAY. STOP.

WHAT DOES THAT MAKE ME?
HUMAN, I GUESS.
HORNY IS HUMAN. HORNY IS NORMAL. IT'S THE "FALLING IN LOVE" I CAN'T DO.
NOT THAT I WOULD EVEN KNOW IF I WAS "FALLING FOR SOMEONE". I BARELY KNOW WHAT A CRUSH FEELS LIKE, MUCH LESS...
Georgia
GHYAAH! STOP THINKING.
LOOKING FOR MY DAD IS MESSING WITH ME. SEARCHING FOR SLASHERS KEEPS ME FOCUSED. KEEPS ME FROM FEELING ANYTHING BUT ANGER. CRUISING AROUND, TRYING TO FIND SOME ASSHOLE WHO ABANDONED ME, DOES NOT.
C'MON, LISA. GIMME AN EMAIL. GIMME SOMETHING TO KILL. SOMETHING WITH AN AXE AND A BAD ATTITUDE.
INBOX
Cassie--
This is going around YouTube. Chris thought it looked like the creature you described in that Nef place. The weird dog. Give it a look and let us know what you think.
--Lisa
YouTube
OH, HELL.
POOCH.

VLAD... LET'S MOVE.

THESE ARE COOL, YES?
NOT EVEN CLOSE.
C'MON. WE GOT A DEVIL DOG IN WISCONSIN.
DONATE
OTHES
ERE

HRRRM. I FOUND THIS. IT IS CLOSE BY.

IT IS IN PORTLAND. ONLY A FEW HOURS DRIVE. I KNOW WE ARE STILL LOOKING FOR YOUR FATHER?
Britney's baby an alien?
EXCLUSIVE
MASKED MAN: RESPONSIBLE FOR DEATHS?

NO... THIS IS *PERFECT.*
BUSTED!

EMINENCE, INDIANA.
ELSTEN ANIMAL SHELTER. THIS IS CHRIS. HOW CAN I HELP YOU?
OOOOH. NOW YOU'RE HER SECRETARY, TOO? IT'S GETTING SERIOUS.
FUNNY, HACK. I'M JUST HELPING OUT. THE DOC'S UP TO HER ELBOWS IN CAT AND DOG ASS THIS WEEK. LITERALLY.
WHAT'S UP? DID YOU GET THAT VID WE SENT YOU?
YEAH. AND I'M PRETTY SURE THAT'S POOCH. I DON'T KNOW WHAT HE'S DOING HERE, BUT IF HE'S IN EAU CLAIRE, I HAVE A FEELING THE NEFLORDS SENT HIM AFTER ME TO GET REVENGE.
NEFLORDS? I THINK THEY WERE IN AN EPISODE OF DR. WHO.
VLAD AND I ARE ON THE OTHER SIDE OF THE COUNTRY CHECKING ON A MASKED KILLER. SO, I'M GOING TO NEED YOU TO GO LOOK FOR THE LOST DOGGIE.
YOU MEAN... LIKE, WITHOUT YOU?
EXACTLY. VLAD AND I TALKED IT OUT. EAU CLAIRE IS A LOT CLOSER TO EMINENCE THAN PORTLAND. POOCH IS PRETTY HARMLESS, BUT WE CAN'T HAVE HIM RUNNING AROUND UNCHECKED, ESPECIALLY IF HE'S UP TO SOMETHING.
SO, CONSIDER IT THE FIRST HACK/SLASH, INC. SOLO MISSION...
I HATE YOU.

MONTANA.
NO TRESPASSING
ANY SECOND NOW, MUFF'LL GET STRUCK, LIKE AS IF BY SOME BOLT OUTTA THE BLUE. SHE'LL SHAKE AROUND ALL CRAZY, AND ALL OF A SUDDEN WE'RE GONNA HAVE A WHOLE SHITLOAD O' EVIDENCE.
IMAGES, NAMES AND A WHOLE BUNCH OF STUFF WE WOULD NEVER FOUND BY OURSELVES.
NO TRESPASSING
ANY SECOND NOW.
NO TRESPASSING
WHATCHA GOT, MUFFY? USE YOUR PSYCHIC POWERS TO FIGURE OUT OUR CRIME?
COULDJA FIND OUT WHERE ELVIS IS WHILE YOU'RE AT IT?
I HAVEN'T GOTTEN A THING FROM THIS PLACE. TAKE ME HOME. PERHAPS I'LL TRY AGAIN TOMORROW.
WH--?! W-WHATEVER YOU SAY, MA'AM.
SO YA REALLY DIDN'T SEE NOTHING', MRS. JOWORSKI?
NOT A THING.
NOT A THING...

PORTLAND, OREGON.
CLICK
ESTER?

MORNINGS ARE THE WORST, ESTER. I NEVER DREAM ABOUT ANYTHING BEFORE THE... INCIDENT. MY MIND IS STALLED OUT, LIVING IN THE PAST. WITH YOU.
THEN I WAKE UP, AND I'M IN THE WORLD WHERE YOU'VE BEEN MURDERED, AND I'M JUST A SHADOW OF A MAN.
SOMEONE LOOKING FOR YOU. ASKING AROUND. TEENAGE GIRL AND BIG GUY.
BE CAREFUL

NOT ENOUGH OF A SHADOW, APPARENTLY.
YOU MAY BE GONE, ESTER, BUT YOU MADE A LOT OF FRIENDS. AND NOW YOUR FRIENDS ARE MY FRIENDS. THEY SET ME ON THE RIGHT PATH, AND WARN ME OF DANGERS ON THE ROAD AHEAD.

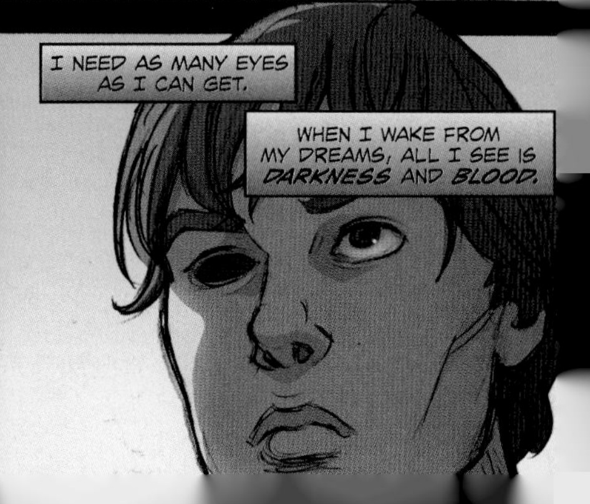
I NEED AS MANY EYES AS I CAN GET.
WHEN I WAKE FROM MY DREAMS, ALL I SEE IS DARKNESS AND BLOOD.

PINELLAS PARK, FLORIDA
GOOD WORK, CLASS. WE'LL TAKE A FIFTEEN MINUTE BREAK, AND WE'LL RECONVENE TO GO OVER OUR MONOLOGUES.
WHAT'S ALL THE HUB-BUB WITH THE REST OF THE CLASS?
THE USUAL. WHO'S DATING WHO, WHO'S THE NEXT ANGELINA, AND WHAT HAPPENED ON THAT MOVIE SET OVER IN TEXAS...
WHAT HAPPENED?
WELL, IF YOU ASK ME, IT SERVES THEM RIGHT. APPARENTLY THERE WAS AN INCIDENT ON THE SET OF THE WIZARD OF OZ REMAKE... A MASKED MURDERER OR SOMETHING.
A MASKED MURDERER?

EAU CLAIRE, WISCONSIN.
THIS IS RETARDED.
I DRIVE 12 HOURS BY MYSELF, TO BUMBLEFUCK, WISCONSIN. A PLACE THAT'S COLDER THAN INDIANA, MIGHT I ADD.
NOW, I'M CRUISING AROUND AIMLESSLY, WITH PANTIES STUCK TO THE CAR.
THAT'S ALL STUFF CASSIE HAS USED, BORROWED OR LEFT BEHIND. IF THIS THING REALLY IS SOME KIND OF DOG, HE MIGHT BE ABLE TO SMELL HER ON THEM.
STEEL MAGNOLIAS
I KNOW, I KNOW... YOU'RE THE ANIMAL DOCTOR. I'M GONNA PULL OVER AND TAKE A LITTLE BREAK. I'VE GOT TWO CANS OF MONSTER AND SOME GENUINE WISCONSIN BEEF STICKS CALLING MY NAME.
DANZIG-MOTHER
BEEF STIX
OKAY. G'NIGHT, CHRIS.
HAPPY HUNTING.

PORTLAND.
THIS IS WHERE OUR MASKED MAN HAS BEEN SPOTTED MOST. SOME OF HIS VICTIMS WERE KILLED USING SOME PRETTY HEAVY GEAR. IT'S LIKE HE HAD ACCESS TO THE MUNICIPAL STORAGE.
A PUBLIC WORKS SLASHER.
DID YOU NOTICE? EVERYONE WE ASKED WAS ALMOST PROTECTIVE OF THIS GUY. HE'S KILLING OFF CROOKS AND SCUM, AND THEY LIKE IT.
TRIMET BUS YARD
YES, I NOTICED. ARE THERE SLASHERS WHO KILL ONLY BAD PEOPLE?
I GUESS THAT DEPENDS ON YOUR DEFINITION OF BAD. WE'VE DEFINITELY RUN INTO A BUNCH THAT DICED UP PEOPLE WHO THEY THOUGHT WERE EVIL FOR HAVING TEEN SEX.
BUT THAT GOES AGAINST THE STANDARD SOCIETAL DEFINITION OF "A CRIME WORTHY OF A GRISLY MURDER". THUS, THE SLASHER EQUALS BAD.
BUT IF THE SLASHER KILLS ONLY MURDERERS AND DRUG PUSHERS??
NOW WE'RE JUST COMPLICATING THINGS. LET'S HOPE THIS GUY IS JUST YOUR GARDEN VARIETY NUT, AND HE'S ACED ENOUGH SLUTTY TEENAGERS TO WARRANT US FUCKING HIM UP.
USUALLY WE DISCUSS THESE THINGS BEFORE WE GO. BUT WE DID NOT ASK MANY QUESTIONS ABOUT THIS KILLER. YOU SAW WORDS "MASK" AND "KILL" AND WE JUST GO.
BLAM!
YEAH, SO... I WAS...
AIEEEE!

THAT CAME FROM INSIDE THE BUS YARD!
YES. A GUNSHOT.
JESUS.
SIGH SPLIT UP?
I'M LEFT, YOU'RE RIGHT, WE MEET IN THE MIDDLE.
FUCK. FUCK. GHYAAAH!
ARE... ARE YOU ALRIGHT?
HELP... ME....

HELLO?
ANYONE HERE?
ARE YOU HURT?

HURR?

UNGHF

NO!

YOU... YOU, AND A GIRL. YOU'RE LOOKING FOR ME.

WHY?

NAAAAAATHAAAN!!!

NAATHAN! SHOW YOURSELF, MAN! I'VE GOT SOMETHING FOR YOU. ANOTHER BITCH FOR YOU TO WATCH ME BEAT TO DEATH!
YOU MOTHERFUCKER.
OH! AND SHE'S A REAL FIRECRACKER.

WHAK!
UNGF

NOW GET OVER HERE SO I CAN FINISH WHAT I STARTED, OR I'LL PERFORATE THIS LITTLE PIECE OF ASS!

HE'S NOT COMING. I ALREADY SHOT THE BASTARD IN THE STOMACH.
HE'S PROBABLY BLEEDING TO DEATH IN ONE OF THE BUSES, CRYING JUST LIKE THE NIGHT WE BEAT HIS 'SPIC COP WIFE TO DEATH.
ISN'T THAT RIGHT, NATHAN?!
IS THIS ALL SOME STUPID "EYE FOR AN EYE" THING, NATE? I MEAN, YEAH, WE DID BEAT YOUR EYE RIGHT OUT OF YOUR HEAD.
BUT, REALLY, YOU THINK ALL THE GUYS WHO WORKED FOR ME DESERVED TO DIE FOR THAT? I MEAN, COME ON, MAN! HOW FUCKED UP YOU GOTTA BE TO PUT MY GUYS THROUGH WOOD CHIPPERS?
THEY DIDN'T KILL YOUR WIFE. I DID. THEY WERE JUST THERE, PROVIDIN' THE MUSCLE, SO I COULD DO THAT BITCH FOR SENDING ME TO THE JOINT. WHAT'D YOU WANT 'EM TO DO?
SQUUIRRRT
THEY WATCHED.
THEY WATCHED HER DIE. THEY WATCHED YOU TAKE HER FROM MY LIFE, AND FROM THIS CITY.
WEED

THEY SHOULD HAVE CLOSED THEIR EYES.
VRRRRRMMMM!
INSTEAD, THEY CHOSE TO SEE OBLIVION.
VRRRRRMMMM!
AIEEEE

RRRRRIIIING
CHRIS! ARE YOU OKAY?
NO. I'M NOT.
NOW I'M 12 HOURS FROM HOME, IN THE COLD, WITH THE UGLIEST FUCKING DOG I HAVE EVER SEEN.
THE CASSIE-SMELL WORKED JUST LIKE YOU SAID. BUT THE MISERABLE FUCKING THING WAS SO COLD AND HUNGRY, HE JUST WALKED UP THE DOOR AND ASKED FOR HELP.
HE'S FROM HELL. GOT HIS ASS DROPPED IN WISCONSIN. TOO COLD, EVEN FOR HIM.
GUESS THESE NEFLORD GUYS COULD DETECT CASSIE'S ENERGY IN THIS AREA, SO THEY SENT BALD LASSIE HERE TO AVENGE THEM.
WAIT... HE ASKED FOR HELP?!
YEAH. FREAKY THING SPEAKS ENGLISH. GUESS HIS MASTER TAUGHT HIM, WHOEVER THAT IS.
ANYWAY, I'M COMING HOME NOW.
SO CLEAN OUT A KENNEL. YOU'VE GOT A NEW PET.

VRRRRRMMM
MY FRIEND. THE BIG GUY... WHERE IS HE?!
UNHURT. NEARBY. I WRAPPED HIM IN A TIRE.
WHY WERE YOU LOOKING FOR ME?
I THOUGHT YOU WERE SOMETHING... BUT... YOU AREN'T.
NO. I'M NOTHING. JUST A TOOL TO MAKE THINGS RIGHT. EVERYONE TURNED A BLIND EYE... LET ME USE THE CITY TO AVENGE ONE OF ITS FAVORITE DAUGHTERS. AND NOW IT'S ALL OVER.
I HAVE TO CHECK ON MY FRIEND. CAN I GET AN AMBULANCE FOR YOU?
NO. I'LL BE DEAD SOON. FIVE MINUTES AT THE MOST.
FIVE MINUTES AND I'LL SEE MY BEAUTIFUL ESTER AGAIN.
I'LL LOOK ON HER WITH BOTH EYES AT LAST.

GOOD BYE, NATHAN.
GOOD BYE.
YOU... YOU MUST HAVE *REALLY* LOVED HER.
YES.
HOW...
...HOW DID YOU KNOW YOU WERE IN LOVE?

THE END.

MURDER/SUICIDE
0 123456 789005
ANNUAL A by TIM SEELEY & JEREMY ROBERTS

NOW.
I HAVE DONE SOME PRETTY SCARY SHIT IN MY SHORT LIFE.

I'VE HAD A ROTTING SAINT BERNARD, DEAD EYES LOCKED ON MINE, JUMP FOR MY THROAT.
I'VE FELT IT'S COLD, DAMP BREATH ON MY FACE JUST BEFORE I WATCHED ITS HEAD DISAPPEAR IN A FINE, RED MIST.

I'VE BEEN TRAPPED IN THE DARK WITH A HOMICIDAL HOLY MAN.
I'VE FELT THE TENSION IN THE AIR AROUND HIM, AS EVERY FIBER OF HIS BEING FOUGHT TO BE FREE OF HIS RESTRAINTS SO HE COULD DO THE ONE THING HE WANTED MORE THAN ANYTHING:
TO WRAP HIS HANDS AROUND MY THROAT AND SQUEEZE.

I'VE BEEN HELD UNDER SIX INCHES OF STAGNANT SWAMP WATER BY AN ANIMATE DOLL, WONDERING IF THE LAST THING I WOULD EVER SEE WAS HIS PLASTIC SMILE.
YEAH, I'VE BEEN IN SOME FUCKING SCARY SITUATIONS.

BUT I THINK **THIS MOMENT** TRUMPS THEM ALL.
46
FAKE

THEN.
LOS ANGELES, CALIFORNIA.
THIS IS IT, SEXY WOMAN. THIS IS THE MOMENT.
I WROTE IT LAST NIGHT, RIGHT AFTER I DID IT. IT'S THE BEST FUCKING THING I'VE EVER WRITTEN.
MAYBE THE BEST THING ANYONE HAS WRITTEN. AND I PUT IT ON U.S. BOBA FETT SO WE COULD UPLOAD IT TO MY BLOG TOGETHER.
FUCK, IAN.
NIXON? AREN'T YOU EXCITED? MY DIABOLIQ BLOG IS HUGE. GOD'S TITS HUGE. IT'S THE INTERNET NEW TESTAMENT!
YOU AND I BOTH KNOW THIS IS THE NEXT STEP IN CYBERLUTION. THE OLD LAWS ARE FOR THE MEAT MONKEYS AND THEIR BROKEN, DEAD SOCIETY.
IAN... I-I THOUGHT THIS WAS ABOUT CULTURE... AND, LIKE, ENTERTAINMENT. YOU STARTED THIS THING AS A MUSIC BLOG FOR FUCK'S SAKE.
ALL THOSE PEOPLE AT SUICIDEGIRLS LOVE YOU BECAUSE YOU WRITE A MEAN NICK CAVE REVIEW. I WANTED TO SCREW YOUR BRAINS OUT BECAUSE OF WHAT YOU SAID ABOUT GUITAR WOLF.
I'M A MODEL, IAN... NOT AN INTERNET MESSIAH. THIS REVOLUTION, ALL THIS OTHER STUFF... IT'S TOO FAR.
TOO FAR?!
THAT'S WHAT I'M FIGHTING AGAINST!
LIMITATIONS WRITTEN IN BOOKS BY CANDLELIGHT AND PRINTED ON A PRESS, ONE WORD AT A TIME.
OUTDATED DETRITUS THAT HAS NO MEANING IN A WORLD WHERE EVERY THOUGHT CAN BE SHOWN ON GLOWING GLASS FROM L.A. TO TOKYO INSTANTLY!
IAN, YOU KILLED SOMEONE.

I *DID.* AND WHEN I POST *THIS,* EVERYONE WHO READS IT WILL KNOW EXACTLY WHAT IT'S LIKE TO FIND A LOWER FORM OF HUMAN LIFE AND END HIS MISERABLE EXISTENCE.
MURDER BY PROXY. EVERY ONE OF US A VOYEUR TO THE GREATEST...
...

WHAT DID YOU DO, NIXON?!

WHAT DID YOU DO?!
I'M SORRY, IAN.
WHO PUT YOU UP TO THIS?! WAS IT THOSE OTHER SLUTS ON *SUICIDEGIRLS?* WERE YOU ALL IN YOUR LITTLE CHAT ROOM, PLANNING ON TURNING ME OVER TO JOHNNY LAW?
I'M GOING TO EAT UP ALL KINDS OF BANDWIDTH DESCRIBING WHAT I'M ABOUT TO DO TO YOU!

CRASH!
FREEZE!
GRRRRRRRRRR

YIPE!
GAH!

GLARF!
GLARF!
HOLD IT, DIRTBAG! FREEZE!
NO. PERPETUAL MOTION IS THE WAY FOR ME.

KRISSH!
GLARF!
GLARF!

WHERE'D HE GO?!
YOU MEAN THE CRAZY-LOOKING WHITE BOY WITH THE BAD HAIRCUT?

HE WENT IN THERE.

COME ON OUT, MR. MATHESON. YOU'RE OUTNUMBERED, AND WE'VE GOT BACK UP ON THE WAY.
ELECTRICAL HAZARD
JUST COME OUT PEACEFULLY. IT'S OVER.
IT'S NEVER OVER FOR ME. I'M FROM THE INTERNET.
GHAUK!
AHHHHHHH!
PKOW!
GLUH. GODDAMIT! WHY--?
STUPID, STUPID MEAT MONKEY.
COMIN' SOON. WWW... DOT... BLOODY HOT STINKY REVENGE... DOT... COM.

IAN! NO!
GKKHGHH.
FRRRZKKKK!
IAN!
STAY BACK, MISS!
YOU ASSHOLE!! YOU STUPID--!
I'M SO SORRY.
IT'S OVER... COME ON... IT'S OVER...

SPARKS, NEVADA.
MORENO
Café
MOVIES ON THE BIG SCREEN. I AM VERY EXCITED! WILL IT BLOW MY MIND?

I DON'T KNOW IF A CHEAP MIDNIGHT SHOWING OF BIKINI CARWASH WILL BLOW YOUR MIND...
HERE'S YOUR TICKET MONEY.

YOU AND I SERIOUSLY DESERVE SOME R & R AND A FUCKING LAUGH OR TWO. SO, A BAD MOVIE FESTIVAL SHOULD BE JUST THE TICKET.
CHANGE FOR THE HOMELESS?
SORRY, MAN.

HEH. KINDA FUNNY THAT GUY ASKING US FOR MONEY FOR THE HOMEL--
VLAD?

HARD WARE
GODDAMMIT, VLAD!
THANK YA' SIR! EVERY LITTLE BIT HELPS!

VLAD, DON'T GIVE THIS GUY YOUR MONEY.
HE SAID HE IS HUNGRY. THAT IS MORE IMPORTANT THAN A LAUGH, YES?
WE'RE HUNGRY, TOO! DUDE, GIVE HIM BACK HIS MONEY.
HE GAVE IT TO ME!

LOOK, HE DOESN'T KNOW BETTER, AND HE'S TOO NICE FOR HIS OWN GOOD...
NO! INDIAN GIVER!

THAT WAS THE ONLY MONEY WE HAD *NOT* BUDGETED ON GAS OR FOOD!
BUT... HE NEEDED IT.
OH SURE, MOTHER TERESA, BUT NOW WE CAN'T *BOTH* SEE THE MOVIES.

YOU... YOU SHOULD SEE THE MOVIE WITHOUT ME. I WILL WAIT IN THE VAN.
I HAVE WAITED MY WHOLE LIFE FOR A MOVIE THEATRE. I CAN WAIT SOME MORE.

OH, JEEZ. *HERE.* GO SEE 'EM. *GOD.*

THANK YOU, CASSIE! MUCH THANKS YOUS! I WILL TELL YOU ALL ABOUT IT.
GODDAMN RIGHT YOU WILL. JUST PAY ATTENTION SO YOU DON'T MESS UP THE FUNNY PARTS.

LOS ANGELES, CALIFORNIA.

...STILL NEED TO GET HER STATEMENT.
WE'LL TAKE HER DOWN TO THE STATION IN A FEW.

CAN I... CHECK MY EMAIL BEFORE WE GO?
SURE. WE'LL LEAVE IN JUST A FEW MINUTES.

VIVID: NIXON! ARE U OKAY?! WHAT HAPPENED??
NIXON: I'M HERE. I'M FINE.
NIXON: IAN'S DEAD.

DETROIT. VIVID SUICIDE.
VIVID: OH GOD. SO SORRY.
KYRA: GLAD YUR OKAY. WE LOVE YOU.
SALOME: YES. WE'RE HERE FOR YOU.

MASSACHUSETTS. KYRA SUICIDE.
KYRA: YEAH. ANYTHING WE CAN DO, JUST SAY IT.
NIXON: I KNOW YOU GUYS WERE RIGHT. THAT HE WAS CRAZY. BUT, I CAN'T STOP THINKING THAT I WAS WRONG TO CALL THE POLICE.
NIXON: I HAVE HIS LAST BLOG. THE MURDER ONE.

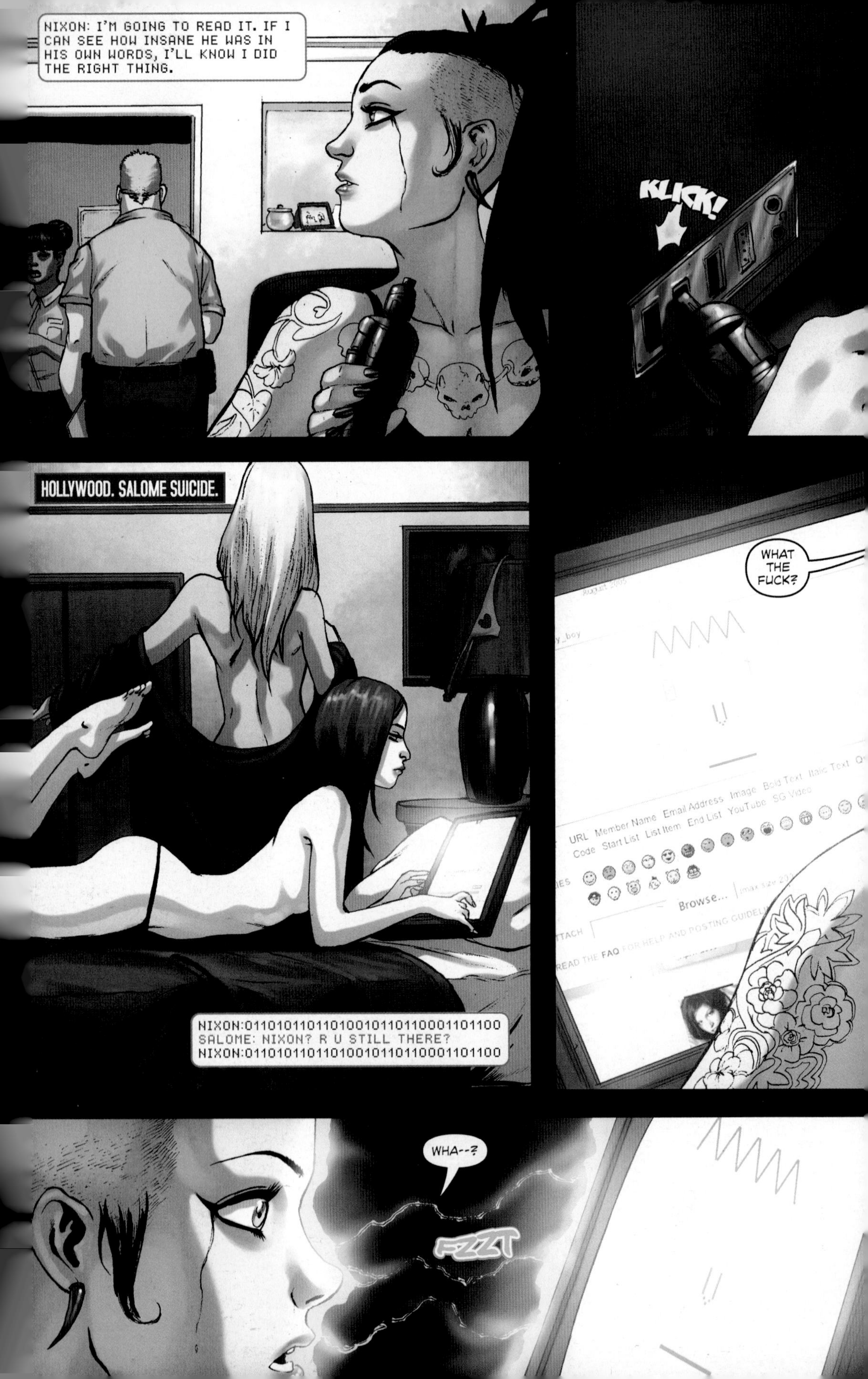
NIXON: I'M GOING TO READ IT. IF I CAN SEE HOW INSANE HE WAS IN HIS OWN WORDS, I'LL KNOW I DID THE RIGHT THING.
KLICK!
HOLLYWOOD. SALOME SUICIDE.
NIXON:01101011011010010110110001101100
SALOME: NIXON? R U STILL THERE?
NIXON:01101011011010010110110001101100
WHAT THE FUCK?
WHA--?
FZZT

YEAH, I'LL BRING HER IN NOW. SHE SEEMS OKAY.
READY TO GO, MISS?
HEY... ARE YOU OKAY?

WHAT ARE YOU--?! DON'T!

DON'T!
BLAM!

FRRRZKKKK!
HEY HON, ARE YOU MAKING BACON?
WHAT ARE YOU DOING, BABY?
FZAAARK!!!...

SPARKS, NEVADA.
HUR. AND THEN THEY INSTALL A TWO-WAY MIRROR IN THE TRAINING ROOM. HUR.
BOOBIES. AND FUNNY HIJINKS.

THAT'S IT? THAT DOESN'T SOUND VERY FUNNY.
THEN, THERE IS A RAID FOR PANTIES. BECAUSE MAYBE THE MEN WERE OUT OF THEM.
FORGET IT. YOU'RE THE WORST SUMMARIZER EVER.
BEEP BEEP BEEP

CHRIS. TELL ME ABOUT BIKINI CARWASH.
LOST MY 'SPANK VIRGINITY' TO IT. NOW, READY FOR THE BEST NEWS EVER?

WELL, I MEAN... BAD NEWS FOR THEM, BUT GOOD NEWS FOR US. OR... WELL... FOR ME. BAD FOR THE VICTIMS, BUT GOOD FOR...
ENGLISH, PLEASE.
SUICIDEGIRLS!!
DO YOU WANNA CALL BACK AFTER THE COCOA PUFFS HAVE WORN OFF?

SUICIDEGIRLS.COM. IT'S A WEBSITE... SUPER-HOT-PUNK-ROCK-GOTH-EMO-GIRLS (LIKE YOURSELF) GETTING NAKED.
I DON'T LIKE WHERE THIS IS GOING.
THEY CALLED THIS MORNING. APPARENTLY, SEVERAL OF THEIR GIRLS COMMITTED SUICIDE LAST NIGHT. THE COPS WERE WILLING TO LET IT GO AT THAT, BUT THE GIRLS THINK THERE MIGHT BE SOMETHING HINKY GOING ON.
JUST SO HAPPENS THEY HAD RECENTLY INTERVIEWED OUR OWN SKOTTIE YOUNG, AND HE GAVE MISSY SUICIDE OUR INFO!

OKAY. WHERE?
LOS ANGELES.
SIGH. I HATE L.A. YOU CAN SUM UP THE WHOLE PLACE JUST BY STROLLING DOWN HOLLYWOOD BLVD: A RITZY VENEER COVERING UP AN UNDERBELLY OF BROKEN DREAMS AND SLEAZE.
UH HUH. YEAH. SO...

I'LL TEXT YOU THE OFFICE ADDRESS AND ALL THE INFO I HAVE WHEN I GET OFF THE PHONE.
MAN! JUST THINKING OF ALL THOSE HOT GIRLS LOUNGING AROUND THAT OFFICE IN THEIR TORN LINGERIE AND THEIR BAUHAUS T-SHIRTS IS GIVING ME A MAJOR RAGER.
THANKS, CHRIS. I'M GONNA GO SEE IF ANYONE'S INVENTED "MIND BLEACH". CASSIE OUT.

available
in the SG SHOP
DIABOLIQ BLOG. POST #4713 BY DIABOLIQ IN BINARY DREAMS.
NEWS SHOP LIVE
$4/MONTH BOARDS GROUPS ARMY LOCAL MODEL CHAT IPOD RADIO
CHECK IT: Buy SG magazine Issue 1 & 2, save $$$
NEWEST PICS HOPEFULS' PICS VIDEOS CLASSIC PICS WE REDEFINE BEAUTY WITH NEW

Lucca
EASTER EGGS
2 hours ago
48 Photos
231 comments
MANKO
14 hours ago
1 day ago

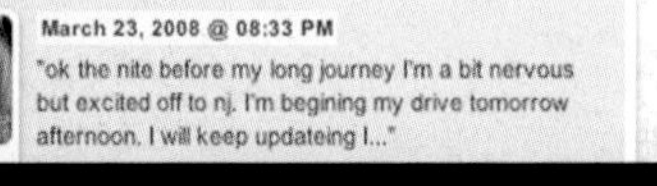
SUICIDEGIRLS' BLOGS
MEMBERS' BLOGS
ALL
March 23, 2008 @ 08:33 PM
"ok the nite before my long journey I'm a bit nervous but excited off to nj. I'm begining my drive tomorrow afternoon. I will keep updateing I..."

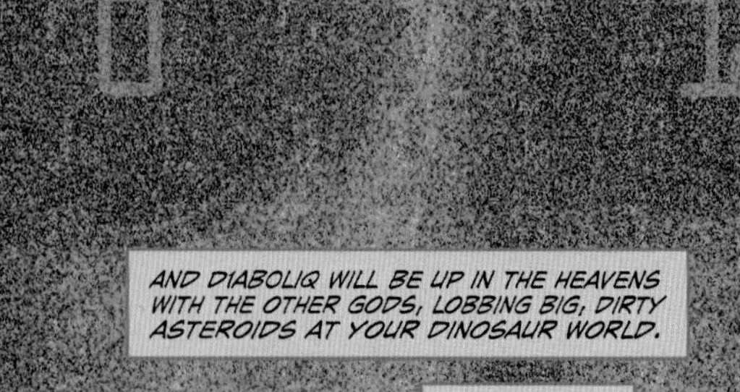
THE MEAT MONKEYS ARE CAPTIVATED BY DEATH.
WHEN THEY AREN'T COUNTING DOWN THE MINUTES, WAITING FOR THEIR LABOR SENTENCE TO BE UP FOR THE DAY, THEY'RE WRINGING THEIR MONKEY HANDS ABOUT THEIR MORTALITY.
THEN THEY GO HOME, INGEST SOME RECONSTITUTED ANIMAL FATS, AND FLIP ON A SHINY BOX WHERE THEIR DEATH OBSESSION CAN BE LIVED OUT THROUGH SOME QUIRKY SCIENCE POLICE WHO SOLVE MURDERS WITH QUICK THINKING AND SUNGLASSES.
DIABOLIQ WELCOMES DEATH. IT'S JUST A CHANGE IN STATES.
AN EXCHANGE OF ENERGIES.
BUT BEFORE THAT ENERGY MOVES TO A HIGHER LEVEL, IT MUST BE REFINED. PURIFIED, LEVELED UP IN VOLTAGE.
SO BEFORE I GO, I MUST STEAL THE ENERGIES OF OTHERS. MAKE THEM MINE. USE THEM TO JUMPSTART CYBERLUTION.
AND DIABOLIQ WILL BE UP IN THE HEAVENS WITH THE OTHER GODS, LOBBING BIG, DIRTY ASTEROIDS AT YOUR DINOSAUR WORLD.
DIABOLIQ OUT.
SUIIZZZIDDE GIRLZZZZ!!!1!!!!!

SUICIDEGIRLS HQ.
LOS ANGELES, CALIFORNIA.
HI. I'M HERE ABOUT THE... UH... DEAD GIRLS?
SG
suicidegirls.c
OH HI... YEAH, LET ME GET MISSY.
BEEP BEEP BEEP
WHAT, CHRIS?!
JUST MAKING SURE YOU FOUND IT.
I DID.
OKAY, ARE THERE NAKED GIRLS LOUNGING AROUND, AND IF SO, DOES YOUR PHONE HAVE CAMERA CAPABILITIES?
THERE IS SOMETHING SO WRONG WITH YOU.
MS. HACK?
I'M MISSY. IF YOU AND YOUR... UH... FRIEND WOULD LIKE TO COME INTO MY OFFICE, SOME OF THE GIRLS AND I ARE HAVING A SMALL MEMORIAL FOR OUR LOST FRIENDS.
WE'VE GOTTA FIGURE OUT HOW TO FIND THAT SONOVABITCH AND GIVE HIM A GARDEN WEASEL RIM JOB!
HOW? HE'S DEAD!
HOW COULD HE POSSIBLY HAVE KILLED NIXON? OR KYRA AND VIVID WHO WERE THOUSANDS OF MILES AWAY?!
THEN WHO SENT THAT DIABOLIQ EMOTICON TO EVERY SINGLE SG'S MAIL ACCOUNT THIS MORNING?
IT WAS HIM. THE COPS SAID IT WAS PTSD.** THAT I DREAMED IT...
...BUT SOMEHOW THAT PRETENTIOUS PRICK WAS IN MY HEAD.
** POST TRAUMATIC STRESS DISORDER.

YOU WERE ONE OF THE GIRLS TALKING TO THIS NIXON GIRL?
YEAH. I KNOW HE MADE NIXON SHOOT HERSELF, AND I KNOW THOSE OTHER GIRLS WOULDN'T KILL THEMSELVES.
IT WAS IAN. IT'S LIKE HE JUMPED FROM THE COMPUTER AND MADE ME STICK THAT SCREWDRIVER INTO THE OUTLET.
BUT YOU SURVIVED?
LUCKILY I WAS STANDING ON A RUBBER... WELL... OBJECT THAT SORT OF GOT THROWN ON THE FLOOR... UM... EARLIER.
OH.
...I'VE SEEN THIS KIND OF SHIT BEFORE.
AND YEAH, IT SOUNDS FUCKED UP AND IMPOSSIBLE. IT IS FUCKED UP. BUT IT ISN'T IMPOSSIBLE.
SO, THE QUESTION ISN'T WHY SOME ASSHOLE WANTS YOU DEAD OR HOW HE CAN DO IT THROUGH THE COMPUTER.
THE QUESTION IS: HOW DO WE MAKE A PLAN TO RE-KILL THIS BASTARD?
ACTUALLY, WE REALLY LIKED THE PLAN YOUR FRIEND CHRIS CAME UP WITH...
OH, NO.
HE SUGGESTED WE CLOSE DOWN THE SITE FOR A DAY, KEEP ALL THE GIRLS OFF THE COMPUTERS. AND THEN WE REOPEN TONIGHT, WITH A NEW SET OF PICTURES. ONE THAT WILL HOPEFULLY DRAW IAN INTO A TRAP...
YEAH, CHRIS WAS RIGHT...
...YOU'LL MAKE A GREAT SUICIDEGIRL.

NOW.
COIN LAUNDRY
LAVANDERIA
PARKING IN REAR
HEY, CASSIE. YOU ALRIGHT?
STELLAR.
2606
CLOSED SORRY!
RIGHT. Y'KNOW I'VE SEEN THE LOOK BEFORE. THE "OH GOD, I'M GONNA BE NAKED ON THE INTERNET" FACE.
I... I'VE DONE WORSE THINGS. I'LL BE FINE. *SOMEDAY.*
WELL, I'VE HEARD EVERY CRITICISM AND ARGUMENT AGAINST BEING A SUICIDEGIRL. "YOU'RE BEING OBJECTIFIED. YOU'RE RUINING YEARS OF FEMINIST PROGRESS. YOU'RE TOO YOUNG AND DUMB TO KNOW BETTER."
BULLSHIT.
EVERYONE'S MISSING THE BIG PICTURE. YOU GOTTA ENJOY EVERY GODDAMN MOMENT YOU CAN.
CELEBRATE. GET A HAIRCUT THAT SCARES YOUR GRANDMA. DRAW ON YOUR BODY WITH A NEEDLE AND *BLEED* FOR THE THINGS YOU LOVE.
TAKE OFF YOUR CLOTHES AND SHOW EVERYONE IT'S FUCKING SEXY JUST TO BE *ALIVE.*
THAT'S WHAT IT *ALL* COMES DOWN TO. *NO ONE* LIVES FOREVER.
HEH.
NOT A BAD PHILOSOPHY.
NOW. EXCUSE ME. I HAVE TO GO GET READY TO BE *BAIT* FOR A *PSYCHOTIC KILLER.*

THAT NIGHT.
DRAKE SUICIDE'S APARTMENT.
SG SHOP
INTERVIEWS NEWS SHOP
Cassie
SPIN PSYCHO
33 PHOTO
OKAY... THE SITE IS BACK UP, AND THE SET IS LIVE.
GOOD. VLAD... YOU READY?
CAN I SEE YOUR PICTURES?
NO.
THEN I AM READY.
DRAKE. OPEN THE CHAT ROOM... AND THEN GET THE HELL OUT OF HERE. I'LL CALL YOU WHEN THIS GEEK IS THOROUGHLY SPANKED.
THANKS CASSIE. YOU'RE MUCH BETTER THAN THOSE CSI GUYS.
HEY DRAKE. WE'RE HERE FOR THE FUCK UP IAN PARTY.
SO EASY TO LOVE. SO HARD TO KILL.

NO WAY. GET THE FUCK OUT. WE WORK ALONE.
IAN KILLED OUR FRIENDS. AND NO ONE FUCKS WITH THE SUICIDEGIRLS.
WE'RE GONNA GET ALL KINDS OF JACK HILL ON HIS SKINNY ASS.
LOOK, WE DON'T EVEN KNOW HOW IAN WORKS. THE MORE UNKNOWNS WE HAVE, THE TOUGHER IT'S GONNA BE TO FIGURE OUT HOW TO KILL HIM.
YES. WE DO NOT EVEN KNOW IF HE WILL...
BEEP
MEN'S & WOMEN'S HOODIES available in the SG SHOP
YOU'VE GOT MAIL.
SHIT. THAT'S IAN.
VLAD! SHUT OFF THE INTERNET... WE'VE GOTTA TRAP HIM IN THIS...
UNHH...

SHIT! HE CAN SENSE SALOME!
HURM. RESIDUAL HAUNTING-NESS.
MOVE AWAY!
MNUUHNN
SUIIIZZZZIIIDDDE--
0101 D1E MEAT MONKEY SLUT!!100
DON'T TOUCH HER! I DO NOT WANT TO HAVE TO FIGHT YOU! WE'LL HAVE A CHUCKY SITUATION ALL OVER AGAIN.
OKIES.
CHEW COUCH, BLOG BOY!

DOGPILE HER! BUT DON'T LET HER TOUCH YOU!

VLAD! I NEED YOUR BIG OL' ASS--
FZZT

FRAKRASSH..!!!

AHHH!
FUCK!

BLOODY HOT ST1NK1NG REVENGE!!

NUHH

WHAP!
FRACTAL. N1XON IS DEAD, YOU JUDAS MONKEY. NOW, YOU D1E TOO.
HURM.
THANK YOU.
FZZK!
RAAAHHH010101010101!!!!

OH GOD. EVERYONE OKAY?
SHK!
OR SOMETHING. SALOME. IS SHE...?
SHE'S ALIVE. WHERE'S FRACTAL?
SHIT. IAN HIJACKED HER AND LEFT WHILE THE LIGHTS WERE OUT.
DRAKE. YOU STAY WITH SALOME.
VLAD AND I NEED RUBBER STUFF... GLOVES, BOOTS, WHATEVER YOU HAVE.
I FEEL SILLY.
YEAH? STAND AROUND IN A LAUNDROMAT WITH YOUR DRAWERS AT YOUR KNEES AND GET BACK TO ME.
W-WILL THAT EVEN WORK?
RUBBER INSULATES, SO EVERY LITTLE BIT WILL HELP KEEP US FROM GETTING OUR ASSES FRIED.
I THINK.
SMASH!

KNOK! KNOK!
YAAAAWNN. JUST A SECOND...
WELL, HELLO THERE.
PRETTY LOUD UP THERE. YOU HAVING SOME KIND OF SEXY PARTY? WHAT CAN I DO FOR--
I NEED TO USE YOUR INTERNET, HAMBURGER APE.
CHUK!!

GRAH!
OOOOOF!

WHAT'S WRONG, FREAK? DON'T WANT TO GET TOO NEAR?

FZAK!
THAT IS A BIG, MEAN BODY. IT'S TRUE.
BUT I FIND THIS ONE A LOT MORE ATTRACTIVE. LOL.
GHUH!
K-TING!
THUNK!
HURRY UP AND DIE. I'VE ALREADY KILLED A WORTHLESS, HOMELESS FREAK. TIME TO MOVE ON TO BIGGER AND BETTER PLACES.
LIKE HELL, MAYBE?
FZAK!
RAAAHHHH!
FOOL ME ONCE, BITCH...
SZK!

FZAKRAK!!
MNUHZZ. 0101...UNHAPPY BZZTWITH SIZE OF YOU PENIS01010?/I HAS A CHEESEBURGER 010101
TRASH
LEAVE HER BODY...
010FAAAD 1019999
GHYAHN!
TRASH

SMA-KK-SH!
THE BASEMENT. WE CAN CORNER HIM THERE.
AND THEN WHAT?
AS SOON AS HE FINDS INTERNET, WE'LL LOSE HIM. I'LL HAVE TO FORCE HIM INTO ME. KEEP HIM LONG ENOUGH...
AND YOU CAN PUT US BOTH OUT OF OUR MISERY I GUESS.
NO.
YEAH, IT'S A SHIT IDEA... YOU GOT ANOTHER ONE, STUD?
VLAD... YOU'VE... YOU'VE GOT A KNIFE STICKING FROM YOUR WRIST.
YES. IF I TAKE IT OUT ALL THE BLOOD WILL COME.
SO... YOU'RE LEAVING IT IN.
YES. ALREADY THIS GLOVE IS HALF FULL OF BLOOD.
A DISHWASHING GLOVE FULL OF BLOOD.
THAT IS SO METAL.
THE TASER IS SHOT.
YOU MAY BORROW ONE OF MY KNIVES.
SWEET. LET'S GO GET THIS FUCKER.
NO WAY I SHOWED MY ASS FOR NOTHING.

BASEMENT.
COME ON OUT, FUCKER. THIS ISN'T THE INTERNET. YOU CAN'T HIDE BEHIND FAKE SCREEN NAMES OR BLURRY PHOTOS HERE.
ZZZKTT!
YOU'RE JUST LIKE ALL THE REST. SHOWING YOUR HAM FLAPS TO EVERYONE ELSE, ALL THE WHILE SCHEMING BEHIND MY BACK.
I'VE EVOLVED BEYOND THE FLESH WHILE YOU'RE STILL SHAKING YOUR MEAT PILLOWS FOR MONE--
WASHSONIC
CHUK!
YOU CAN'T TURN ME OFF THAT EASILY, FLESH SACK!
FLESH. ALL THIS SOFT, WARM FLESH. HOW FAR I COULDA GONE, IF I HADN'T BEEN SO DISTRACTED BY SKIN.
IF I HAD NEVER MET NIXON, I'D HAVE REACHED SOME FORM OF TECHNOLOGICAL ENLIGHTENMENT SO FAR BEYOND ALL THAT SWEATY RUTTING.

THE WHOLE INTERNET. ALL OF CYBERLUTION. HALTED. WHY? SO WE CAN LOOK AT SUICIDEGIRLS.
AMATEUR TEENS. MILFS. TWINKS AND BEARS.
WE COULD BE EXPERIENCING NEW LEVELS OF FEELING. ADVANCING SOCIETY. CREATING NEW RULES AND MORALITY. INSTEAD, WE'RE STILL CHOKING THE CHICKEN TO BARELY LEGALS.
I KNOW MY NEW MISSION...
I HAVE TO SCOUR THE INTERNET CLEAN.
I'LL BURN OFF ALL THE BARE FLESH AND BODILY FLUIDS. EVERY CAM GIRL. EVERY PORN STAR. THE TERRIBLE WEIGHT OF SHAME WILL DRIVE THEM TO SUICIDE...
AND BY SHAME, I MEAN ME.

HM... I CAN SMELL THE WI-FI SOMEWHERE. PROBABLY A STARBUCKS NEARBY. HAH... WHO'M I KIDDIN'?
THERE'S ALWAYS A STARBUCKS NEARBY. THIS IS L.A.
I'M OUT. DON'T WORRY, I'LL FIND THE TWO OF YOU AGAIN. SO DON'T FORGET ABOUT ME.
BEFORE I LEAVE, LET FRACTAL SHOW YOU WHY SHE'S SUCH A PERFECT FIT FOR SUICIDEGIRLS...
LAME ONE-LINER, BITCH.
PWOK!
VLAD! FIREHOSE!
HURM. BIKINI CARWASH.

YOU SHOULD NOT DIS INTERNET BOOBIES. YES?
SPLOOSH
FZZZZZZZATT!
GRRUNH!
VLAD!
FUCK! SHOULDA PAID BETTER ATTENTION IN SCIENCE CLASS.
FUH... FZZT00101...
GET OUT OF MY HEAD! GET...
FZKK! SHUT. UP.
THAT'S ENOUGH. WATER MESSED YOU UP, EH? HERE'S THE DEAL, IAN.
GHUH?!

THERE. NO WI-FI FLOATING AROUND OVER HERE IS THERE?
IS THERE?!
N-NO!
NOW, I DON'T WANT TO DO THIS. BUT I'LL KILL HER. AND YOU'LL BE STUCK INSIDE TO DIE, TOO.
THAT'S OPTION ONE.
OPTION TWO: YOU GET YOUR ELECTRO-GHOST ASS INTO ME.
MAYBE YOU CAN CONTROL ME LONG ENOUGH TO GET SOMEWHERE AND JUMP OUT. OR MAYBE, I KILL MYSELF, AND TRAP YOU IN ME SO WE DIE TOGETHER.
PICK QUICK, MOTHER-FUCKER.
CASSIE??!
FRACTAL?
PLEASE... I DON'T WANNA DIE...
HA HA! WEAK SAUCE! I LET FRACTAL OUT JUST LONG ENOUGH FOR YOU TO LOOSEN THE BLADE. D1PSHIT!
KHOK!
OOF!

LOL. I AM GONNA PHOTOGRAPH ALL THE THINGS I DO TO YOU AND THE BALD FREAK. AND THEN, WHEN YOU TYPE "H1DEOUS INSANE MURDER SCENE" INTO GOOGLE, MY PAGE WILL...
ERK...
UHGN... CASSIE...
FRACTAL... YOU GOTTA GET HIM OUT!
I DUNNO IF I CAN. HE FUCKED UP BY LETTING ME THROUGH TO DISTRACT YOU. HE...
010101 BITCH 0101...
NUH!
I'M YOUR L-LAST VICTIM... DIE!
D1ABOLIQ LIVES FORE-000110
AAHHH!!
AHHH01HHH!!

JESUS. I'M SO SORRY. YOU OKAY?
IT IS LIKE PEEING ON THE ELECTRIC FENCE.
OH GOD. IS IT OVER. IS IT...?
OH...
IT...
IT WAS THE *ONLY* WAY...

SO DID WE GET IAN MATHESON, THE DOUCHE BAG, AKA DIABOLIQ?
WE'RE NOT SURE. BUT HE HASN'T SHOWN UP, AND SUICIDEGIRLS.COM IS BACK UP FOR BUSINESS.
Kodak THEATRE
MISSY ASKED ME IF I WANTED HER TO TAKE MY SET DOWN. I THOUGHT LONG AND HARD ABOUT IT... THEN I SAID FUCK IT. LEAVE IT UP.
SO MISSY PAID ME FOR THE SET. I THINK SHE THREW IN A LITTLE BONUS FOR SAVING THE REST OF THE GIRLS.
WE SHOULD PROBABLY HAVE SAVED THE MONEY. USED IT FOR A ROUGH NIGHT ON THE ROAD, OR TO BUY BETTER FOOD THAN WE NORMALLY EAT.
INSTEAD, WE CAME DOWN TO HOLLYWOOD BLVD, WHERE ALL THE OTHER POOR HOMELESS BASTARDS COME TO HANG OUT.
YOU KNOW, WHERE THE TOURISTS SNAP PICTURES OF SOME LONG-DEAD, GLAMOROUS ACTRESS' STAR ON THE WALK OF FAME.
WE BOUGHT 20 MOVIE TICKETS FOR THE KODAK THEATRE AND 20 GIFT CERTIFICATES FOR THE HOLLYWOOD GRILL, AND THEN GAVE 'EM OUT TO ALL THE OUTCAST AND FREAKS HOLLYWOOD GLAMOUR LEFT BEHIND.
HOLLYWOOD
SURE, IT'S NOT THE OSCARS, BUT EVERYONE DESERVES SOME R & R EVERY ONCE IN A WHILE. MAYBE EVEN A LAUGH OR TWO.
YOU GOTTA ENJOY EVERY MOMENT YOU CAN.
EL CUCUY
DIABOL1Q WUZ RIGHT
NO ONE LIVES FOREVER.
THE END.

INTERLUDE

#12 B by **JOE QUINONES**

ELSEWHERE.
NOW.
ALL I CAN DO IS RUN.
RUN... AND HOPE THAT THEY DON'T CATCH ME. HOPE THAT SOMEONE ELSE INCITES THEIR ETERNAL RAGE, GIVING ME THAT EXTRA SECOND I NEED TO GET AWAY.
I CAN HEAR THE SCREAMS. THE BREAKING GLASS. THE BREAKING BONES.
THEY ARE THE LIVING EMBODIMENTS OF HATE. UNSTOPPABLE. UNSWERVING.
THEY'RE GAINING ON ME. I CAN HEAR THEM YELLING NOW. INCOHERENT SPITE-FILLED BABBLE. FOLLOWED BY A DULL, WET THUD.
WHAT KEEPS THEM GOING? WHAT FUELS THEIR RAGE? WHA--
UNF
NO...
JACKALS OF BOTSWANA! A DAMSEL IN DISTRESS!
STAND BACK! THIS LOOKS LIKE A JOB FOR VIOLENCE!

BONE-SEWER, MADEMOISELLE VICTIM LADY! I'M MILK!
AND I'M CHEESE!
AND WE'LL BE YOUR DRUNKEN, PSYCHOTIC KILLERS THIS EVENING!
OUR SPECIAL TONIGHT IS A PROLONGED BEATING UGLY ENOUGH TO MAKE A CORONER VOMIT.
THIS WILL BE ACCOMPANIED BY A LUSTY RENDITION OF THE BUGALOOS' THEME SONG.
IN HALF-ASSED GERMAN ACCENTS, OF COURSE.
SO, HERR CHEESE? DISSECTION, VIVISECTION, OR HUMOR SECTION?
I SAY WHATEVER'S ICKIEST!
BY THE WAY, LADY, YOU CAN START SCREAMING NOW!
NOOO!!!!

WHUNNGH
DAIRY MEN DREAM AGAIN?
YEAH.
YOU'RE RIGHT... THERE'S DEFINITELY A CORRELATION BETWEEN EATING EZ-RITOS, AND DREAMING OF THE MILK AND CHEESE WHO WANT TO KILL ME.
BETTER THAN THE LUNCH LADY DREAMS ANY DAY. THANK YOU PROCESSED MEXICAN FOOD.
SO IS THE VAN FIXABLE OR ARE WE STRANDED?
THE VAN IS, AS YOU SAY, AN ISLAND OF SHIT IN THE TURD SEA.
THAT'S WHAT WE GET, I GUESS. THE VAN HAS BEEN GOING FOR A WHILE, AND IT'S A LONG WAY FROM PORTLAND TO... WHEREVER THE HELL WE'RE HEADING.
FOR ONLY ONE DOLLAR, I HAVE BEEN GIVEN A CHANCE AT MEGA-MILLIONS... OH.
WHAT?
MEGA CASH
I HAVE A WAY TO GET OUR SHIT MOVING AGAIN.
MEGA CASH
$800 $800 $800

LAUREL, MONTANA.
MUFFY? MUFFY?
C'MON, MUFF. YOU'VE BEEN WORKING ON THAT CRAZY CASE ALL DAY.
DESPERATE HOUSEWIVES IS ON. DONCHA WANNA WATCH WITH ME?
MUFF?
THE THINGS... THE THINGS I SAW, FRANK. I'VE BEEN LOOKING ON THE INTERNET... I CAN FEEL IT... I KNOW WHAT SHE IS...
WHO, MUFF? WHO ARE YOU TALKING ABOUT?
THE PERSON WHO KILLED ALL THOSE PEOPLE UP AT THE COMPOUND.
I THINK I MAY HAVE FOUND THE MOST PROLIFIC SERIAL KILLER IN THE WORLD.

EMINENCE, INDIANA.
AROOOO! AOOW!
BOW! ARF ARF ARF!
BOW BOW BOW!
≈SIGH≈
WHAT'S WRONG?
I CAN'T CONCENTRATE.
I *GOTTA* BRING POOCH IN THE HOUSE, LISA. THE OTHER DOGS HATE HIM, THEY'RE JUST GONNA BARK AT HIM ALL NIGHT.
THE OTHER DOGS WILL GET USED TO HIM. I GAVE HIM THE NICEST KENNEL IN THE WHOLE PLACE.
HE CAN'T BE IN THE HOUSE WHEN WE HAVE SEX. HE SPIES... AND IT CREEPS ME OUT.
I KNOW. BUT I CAN'T GET INTO IT... WITH... Y'KNOW, THE BARKING.
FINE. BUT HE STAYS IN THE BASEMENT.
GODDAMN ALIEN DOG...
BOW BOW BOW!
AROOOO! AOOW!
BOW! ARF ARF ARF!

AROOOO! AOOW!
BOW! ARF ARF ARF!
C'MON, POOCH. WE'RE GOING INSIDE.
Oh, thank you, Master, thank you! They make noises at me! They hate me!
I CAN'T IMAGINE WHY.
BOW BOW BOW!
Oh poorest Pooch. Trapped on world where his lower brethren hate him. Especially the one called "Goblin"! So much hate. So much.
GOBLIN?
YAP YAP YAP!
Into the cold! Oh, it is cold here! Lords of Nef, why did you send me to this hell?!
HEY, KEEP IT DOWN. WE'RE GOING INSIDE, YOU BIG BABY.
NOW, STAY HERE. LISA DOESN'T WANT YOU IN OUR ROOM, OKAY?
Yes, Master. Anything you wish.
HEY! WHAT ARE YOU DOING DRESSED? I PUT POOCH IN THE BASEMENT!
YEAH... I KINDA LOST THE MOOD, MYSELF. WANT SOME PIZZA ROLLS?
PIZZA ROLLS

SOON...
YOU AREN'T COMING TO BED?
NAH, I KNOW YOU WANT TO GET TO SLEEP, AND I... WELL, TOO MANY PIZZA ROLLS, SO I'M GONNA HIT THE--
ENOUGH INFO. GOOD NIGHT, CHRIS.
HEH HEH.
TEENS PORKATHON 4
PAY PER VIEW
AH, YES... THE BEST CURE FOR *COITUS INTERRUPTUS*.

MMMMMM BABY... YEAH, RIGHT THERE. HARDER.
OOOOH, YEAH. NAUGHTY TEEN...
Hello Master. Your pink thing likes to be pet too?
YEEEAAARRRRGHHHH!!!

CHIPPEWA FALLS, WISCONSIN.
HOPE HILLS CEMETERY
CAREFUL NOW.
GOTTA MAKE IT LOOK NICE...
THIS NEW SNOW WILL COVER UP ALL THE TURNED OVER SOIL 'TIL SPRING. LUCKY US.
GHAH. GROSS MAN. WHAT'S THIS GUY WANT WITH A COFFIN ANYWAY?
SNAP!
I DON'T WANT TO KNOW. THE GUY HAD THE MONEY. GOOD ENOUGH FOR ME.
I KNOW, I KNOW. BUT, DON'T YOU EVER WONDER WHAT PEOPLE DO AFTER WE DO THEIR LITTLE SHADOWY DIRTY WORK?
HM... NOPE... CAN'T SAY THAT I DO...
YOU DON'T KNOW THE NAME ON THE TOMBSTONE, DO YA?
WELL, IF YOU DID...
DELILAH HACK
BELOVED MOTHER AND WIFE
1965-2004
...YOU'D WANT TO KNOW EVEN LESS.

LAUREL, MONTANA.
GRANT. GET ME SOME COFFEE, WOULD YA?
OF COURSE, SHERIFF STRAY CALF. I KNOW HOW ORNERY YOU INJUNS GET IF YOU DON'T HAVE YOUR COFFEE IN THE MORNING.
HAR HAR.
SORRY. "COFFEE" IS A WHITE MAN WORD. I MEANT "JUICE WHICH INVIGORATES BRAI--
GHUH!
MAN... I JUST HAD THE WEIRDEST FEELING. HAIRS ON MY NECK ARE STANDING UP AN' EVERYTHING...
LIKE DEATH HERSELF JUST WALKED IN.
GOOD MORNING, OFFICER HAZLEWOOD.

WOAH! MRS. JOWORSKI! DIDN'T HEAR YOU COME IN!
YOU'RE UP EARLY. I HAVEN'T SEEN YOU SINCE THE PHILLIPS COMPOUND...
YES. I-I TOLD YOU I DIDN'T SEE ANYTHING THEN. I... WELL, I LIED. I SAW SOMETHING.
AND I NEED YOUR HELP.
SO... SO I CAN STOP SEEING IT...
TO BE CONTINUED...

OVER THE RAINBOW
#14 A by TIM SEELEY & WES DZIOBA

AUNTIE EM!
AUNTIE EM!
SIXTY. SIXTY ONE. DAMN, THAT'S A LOT OF POTATOES.
AUNTIE EM! UNCLE HENRY!
MISS GULCH DID SOMETHING TERRIBLE TO TOTO!
DOROTHY, PLEASE. CAN'T YOU SEE WE'RE BUSY?
BUT... MISS GULCH! SHE TRIED TO TASE TOTO! MEAN OL' HAG!
MAYBE WE CAN HELP, HONEY.
MAYBE I'LL HAVE TO PUT SOME SCARE INTO THAT OL' CROW.

DEL VALLE, TEXAS.
7 MILES SOUTHWEST OF AUSTIN.
9 DAYS AGO.
PRODUCTION THE WONDERFUL WIZARD OF OZ
DIRECTOR DONNIE P.
DATE SCENE 1 TAKE 5
CLACK!
CUT!
RICK ROSS, YOU ARE A SUPERSTAR!
I KNOW. I KNOW.
THE REST OF YOU... WE'RE REMAKING A CLASSIC HERE. A REALLY OLD CLASSIC. LET'S TRY TO ELEVATE THE MATERIAL. SNAPPIER! MODERN! THIS IS THE FACEBOOK GENERATION OF OZ! I WANNA HEAR IT POP!
FUCK, TEXAS IS HOT! WHY CAN'T WE FILM IN CANADA LIKE EVERYONE ELSE?!
WELL... IT'S SUPPOSED TO BE A DUST BOWL ERA HOME.
WHATEVER! RUN OVER AND GET JESSE READY FOR SOME SECOND UNIT MUNCHKIN SHIT. WE'RE WRAPPING THIS SCENE IN 20!
YESSIR.
AND TELL THOSE MUNCHKINS THEY BETTER KNOW THE GODDAMN "LOLLIPOP RAP"!
"LOLLIPOP RAP". JESUS. WHAT KIND OF ASSHOLE TRIES TO REMAKE WIZARD OF OZ?
Crew Restroom
THE ASSHOLE WHO DIRECTED "EPIC MOVIE 2" AND "4 FAST 4 FURIOUS" I GUESS.
CREEEEK

AAAAHHHH!!!
OH GOD... SORRY... T-THE DOOR WASN'T LOCKED...
GET OUT!!

Crew Restroom

I'M REALLY SORRY.
HMPPH.

CAN'T BELIEVE I WALKED IN ON A LULLABY LEAGUE MUNCHKIN PEEING.
HA.
HAH HA!

HA. ≈SIGH≈ WHAT A DAY.
CLANK!

DEL VALLE, TEXAS.
NOW.
COME ON SARAH! WE HAVE TO KEEP MOVING!
EASY FOR YOU TO SAY, GAZELLE LEGS! FUCK!
HERE!
OH GOD, THANK YOU.
SHIT! THEY'RE BOLTED SHUT FROM THE OUTSIDE!
GOD-DAMMIT! I KNEW I SHOULDN'T HAVE COME BACK HERE.
I AM SO SORRY I GOT YOU INVOLVED IN THIS.
WE'RE NOT DEAD YET. COME ON. WE CAN BARRICADE OURSELVES IN. GIVE HIM ONLY ONE ENTRANCE.
FIGHT BACK.
HERE.
POLICE LINE DO NOT CROSS
THIS IS WHERE THEY FOUND THE FIRST VICTIM... HE MUST HAVE THOUGHT IT WAS ME IN THERE...

WHO? WHO THOUGHT...
IT... IT DOESN'T MATTER. HE DIDN'T GET YOU *THEN*, AND HE ISN'T GONNA GET YOU *NOW*.

43 TIMES. THE NEWS SAID HE WAS HIT 43 TIMES WITH A SHARP OBJECT.

YEAH... AND SLIPPING AND FALLING ON MY ASS *ONE* TIME WAS GOOD ENOUGH TO WRECK MY PHONE.
HE'S COMING. HE'S GONNA KILL US BOTH. AND IT'S ALL MY FAULT.
NO... IT'S NOT YOUR FAULT.
IT'S *MINE*.

I SHOULD HAVE WAITED FOR CASSIE BEFORE I CAME DOWN HERE. BUT ALL I COULD THINK WAS HOW IMPRESSED SHE'D BE IF I CAME DOWN HERE AND FIGURED OUT SOME STUFF FOR HER.
FIGURE OUT IF WE WERE DEALING WITH THE RIGHT KIND OF KILLER. SURPRISE HER, Y'KNOW?

IS YOUR FRIEND SOME KIND OF *BUFFY* OR SOMETHING?
HER NAME IS CASSIE. AND SHE'S THE SCARIEST, BADDEST ASS CHICK IN THE WHOLE DAMN WORLD.

I-35.
NEAR TEMPLE, TEXAS.

WOAH. DID YOU JUST FART?
NO. I DID NOT.

OH. CUZ I JUST DID.

HRRM. HOW FAR TO OZ? I WOULD LIKE TO BE OUT OF RANGE OF YOUR BUTT VERY SOON.
WE'RE NOT EXACTLY GOING TO OZ. JUST THE SET OF SOME REMAKE.
FIVE MEMBERS OF THE PRODUCTION GOT AXED LAST WEEK, AND MR. BIG-TIME-MOVIE-STAR RICK ROSS IS MISSING.
COPS HAVE ALREADY BEEN THERE. EVEN IF IT WAS A SLASHER, I'M SURE HE'S LONG GONE. BUT, GEORGIA IS GOING TO MEET US...
SO, THIS IS A GOOD EXCUSE TO SEE YOUR GOOD FRIEND, THEN.
OH, COME ON... I HAVEN'T TALKED TO HER THAT MUCH LATELY. NOT TO MENTION THAT SHE'S *YOUR* FRIEND TOO.
BESIDES, A FEW OF THE NAMES OF POSSIBLE CANDIDATES FOR MY DEADBEAT DAD LIVE AROUND HERE.
SO, WE ARE LOOKING FOR YOUR FATHER AGAIN?
I GUESS. I JUST TRY NOT TO THINK ABOUT IT TOO MUCH. IT'S LIKE WHEN I FIRST SAW THE WIZARD OF OZ, Y'KNOW.
THERE WAS ALL THIS HYPE ABOUT THE WIZARD... HOW HE WAS GONNA BE THE ANSWER TO ALL THOSE WISHES.
TURNS OUT HE WAS JUST A LITTLE WEIRDO HIDING BEHIND A CURTAIN.
AUSTIN
48 MILES

ELSEWHERE.
AT LEAST YOU PUT SOME EFFORT INTO IT.
MORE THAN HALF THE GUYS HERE THINK IT'S GOOD ENOUGH JUST TO OFFER ME PLASTIC BEADS THAT I CAN GET FOR 99 CENTS AT A PARTY STORE.
OH YEAAAHHHH...
HEY, LOOK OUT!
SINNER. FORNICATOR.
OH GOD!!
WOK!
HELP! OH GOD, HELP!
AH! MY LEG! SHIT!
WHORE.

ABOMINATION.
AAAAAHHHHHHH!
KRUNCH!
GHUUUHHH!

LAUREL, MONTANA.
MUNNNH... TWO MORE. MID-MARCH. BOY AND A GIRL. FLORIDA... RESORT TOWN... PANAMA OR SOMETHING...
I'LL PUT IN A CALL TO PANAMA CITY BEACH PD AND SEE IF THERE'S ANY MURDER CASES INVOLVING A BOY AND A GIRL IN THAT TIME PERIOD.
MUFF... YOU OKAY?
YES... YES, FRANK. I'M FINE, IT'S JUST... VIOLENT, YOU KNOW. A LITTLE MUCH TO SEE FOR AN OLD WOMAN LIKE ME.
YOU CAN'T KEEP THIS UP, HONEY. I KNOW YOU'VE DONE THIS STUFF BEFORE... BUT THIS...
IT DOESN'T MATTER. I HAVE TO DO THIS.
MY VISIONS CAN HELP THESE POLICEMEN. I GIVE THEM LOCATIONS AND SIGHTS, AND THEY'LL KNOW WHAT TO LOOK FOR. WE CAN PUT THESE CASES TO BED...
POLICE
...AND STOP CASSANDRA HACK BEFORE SHE KILLS AGAIN.

I/WE HAVE NO RESULTS FROM THE EARTHBOUND ASSASSIN? **
**TRANSLATED FROM THE PSYCHIC NON-SPEAK OF THE LORDS OF NEF.
NO. THE LOW-BEAST REPORTS NO DEATH OF THE HATED CASSANDRA HACK.
PERHAPS THE LOW-BEAST HAS EXPIRED. LET US REACH ACROSS THE DEPTH AND SEE THROUGH HIS MIND-EYE.
THERE. THE LOW-BEAST RESIDES IN THE OTHERWORLD, IN THE ORIGIN-LAND OF THE HATED CASSANDRA HACK, KNOWN AS WISCONSIN.
YES. HIS LOCATION IS CORRECT, BUT I DO NOT SEE THE FESTERING, ROTTING CORPSE OF THE HATED.
WHAT IS THIS? IT APPEARS THE LOW-BEAST IS ENTRAPPED, AT THE MERCY OF TWO OTHER-WORLDERS.
NOT SAYING...
JUST...
HELP...
ONCE IN A...
FOOLISH, WASTED THING. I/WE SUGGESTED THIS CREATURE WAS ILL-FIT TO BE A PROPER ASSASSIN.
YES. I/WE WERE CORRECT. USELESS FLESH LOW-BEAST. IT HAS FAILED. LET US ABANDON IT TO ITS CAPTORS.
LOOK, THIS IS A SHIT TOWN. THE ONLY JOBS AROUND ARE GAS STATION ATTENDANT AND FUCKING PRE-SCHOOL JANITOR!
I'VE BEEN PATIENT CHRIS. WHAT DO I HAVE TO DO? HOLD OFF SEX UNTIL YOU DO SOMETHING WITH YOURSELF?
OH NICE. THAT'S WHAT YOU THINK OF ME?
PERHAPS THEY WILL FIND SOME USE FOR IT.
I/WE HAVE A BETTER IDEA. THE LOW-BEAST SHOULD BE TAUGHT THE PRICE FOR SUCH FAILURE.

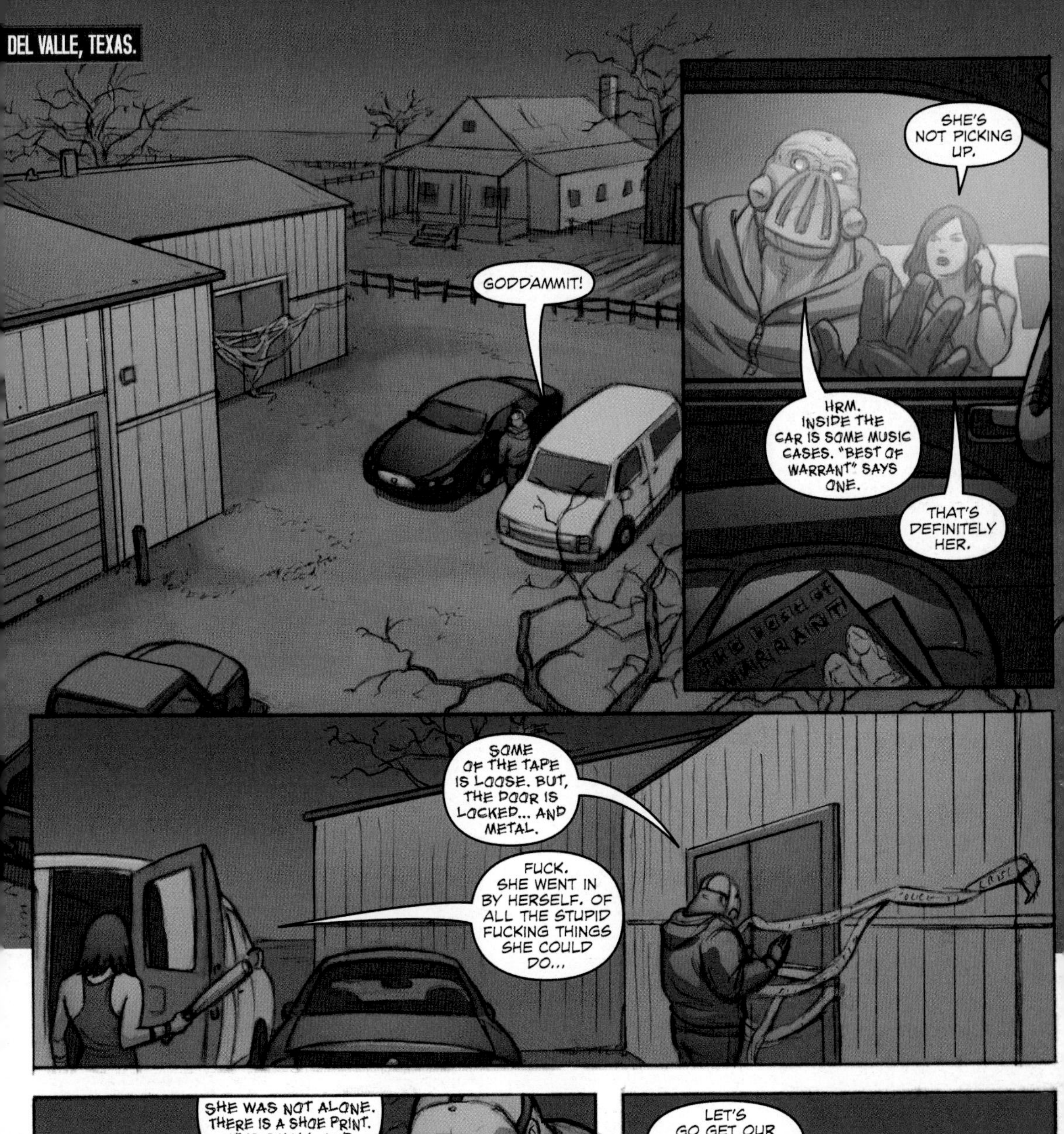
DEL VALLE, TEXAS.
GODDAMMIT!
SHE'S NOT PICKING UP.
HRM. INSIDE THE CAR IS SOME MUSIC CASES. "BEST OF WARRANT" SAYS ONE.
THAT'S DEFINITELY HER.
SOME OF THE TAPE IS LOOSE. BUT, THE DOOR IS LOCKED... AND METAL.
FUCK. SHE WENT IN BY HERSELF. OF ALL THE STUPID FUCKING THINGS SHE COULD DO...

SHE WAS NOT ALONE. THERE IS A SHOE PRINT. IT IS SMALL AND LIGHT. A CHILD PERHAPS.
JESUS. NOW GEORGIA'S GOT A SIDEKICK... MOVE ASIDE, VLAD.

LET'S GO GET OUR "PRETTY", AND HER LITTLE "DOG" TOO.
WHRRRRRRR!

CHK
CHK
CHK
OH GOD! DO YOU HEAR THAT? SOMEONE IS COMING!
YEAH... YEAH I HEAR IT. JUST... DON'T MOVE.

CHK
CHK
CHK
CHK
CHK

OH GOD! IT'S RIGHT OUTSIDE THE DOOR.
SHHH. I-I'LL PROTECT YOU. JUST LIKE CASSIE WOULD.

CREEEEK
MNUUUUHHHHH!
AAAAGHGH!

MNUUUUUH!
RICK?
TICK.
SUUURRUUUUHHHHH!
CLAK!
SQWIT!
SPLORCH!

HUH HUH HUH HUH.
OH GOD...

ALL RIGHT, GIRL. I DIDN'T ASK ANY QUESTIONS WHEN I FOUND YOU HERE, RUNNING FOR YOUR LIFE. BUT, NOW, IT'S TIME TO TALK.
A HUNH

I-I WAS WORKING ON THIS MOVIE. A MUNCHKIN. I WAS A MUNCHKIN. AND, I MET RICK ROSS. HE CAME ON TO ME... WANTED ME... SO... I MEAN HE WAS A BIG MOVIE STAR. AND HE WANTED *ME*.

BUT... I WAS ALREADY SEEING SOMEONE. HIS NAME WAS KENT... HE WAS A MUNCHKIN TOO. I MET HIM ON THE SET.
BUT... HE WAS UNSTABLE... SO JEALOUS. SO INSECURE.

TING
TING
TING
WHEN HE FOUND OUT ABOUT RICK... HE THREATENED ME. TOLD ME HE'D KILL ME. I CALLED THE POLICE... BUT... HE HUNG HIMSELF. IN HIS A-APARTMENT, BEFORE THEY GOT THERE.

BUT, WHEN THE MURDERS STARTED... IT ALWAYS SEEMED LIKE IT WAS MEANT TO BE ME... I THOUGHT IT MIGHT BE KENT. BUT... THAT'S CRAZY!
TING
TING
TING
TING

TING
YOU AIN'T WHISTLING DIXIE.

IF I ONLY HAD A HEART. IF I ONLY HAD A HEART.
MOVE!
GIVE ME BACK MY HEART, SARAH.
CHOK!
OH GOD! KENT!
I'D BE TENDER... I'D BE GENTLE. AWFUL SENTIMENTAL.

UNGH
NO!
I HEAR A BEAT. HOW SWEET.

UNNGH. AH... FUCK!
AND YET... I AM TORN APART.
SSHWTT!

WHAU!
NUUNGH!
CHUK!!

B-BLOOD. SO MUCH.
EVERY ATOM IN MY BODY IS TELLING ME RUN RUN RUN.
TELLING ME "YOU DON'T KNOW THIS CHICK... SAVE YOURSELF. PUSH HER IN FRONT, LET HER TAKE THE AXE, RUN RUN RUN."

BUT CASSIE WOULDN'T RUN.

KENT... I'M SO SORRY... I REALLY LIKED YOU... I DID.
WHEREFORE...
ART THOU...
WHIRRRRRRRRRRRRRRRRRRRRRR
ROMEO.
WHIRRRRRRRRRRRRRRRRRRRRRRRRR
THIS IS WHAT I GET FOR ASKING FOR A MIDGET SLASHER.*
WHIRRRRRR
*SEE HACK/SLASH: EUTHANIZED. --MICRO MIKE

HURM. I MAY NEED A BIGGER HANDKER-CHIEF...
IT'S... IT'S OKAY, VLAD. THANKS THOUGH.

VLAD. CHECK THE BLONDE.
YES.

I'M SORRY.

YOU'RE SORRY?! YOU TOLD ME YOU'D MEET ME OUTSIDE. YOU NEVER SAID ANYTHING ABOUT GOING IN, MUCH LESS ABOUT GETTING CHASED BY A FUCKING ARMORED DWARF!
I WAS! I WAS GOING TO WAIT. BUT, SARAH CAME, AND SHE KNEW SOMETHING, I JUST DIDN'T KNOW WHAT, AND...

NO EXCUSE! JUST BECAUSE WE'RE FRIENDS DOESN'T MEAN YOU GET TO DO MY JOB! I CAN'T KNOW PEOPLE WHO RISK THEIR LIVES! I'M SO PISSED I CAN BARELY LOOK AT YOU.

I'M GONNA MAKE A RUN THROUGH... MAKE SURE THERE ISN'T SOME GODDAMN FLYING MONKEY SLASHERS WAITING ANYWHERE.
VLAD. MEET ME OUTSIDE.

INNER LIFE
Meditation Circle 10 AM!
ER... UH... EXCUSE ME, I'M LOOKING FOR MR. LAZARUS?
DOWN IN THE BASEMENT.
MR. LAZARUS? IT'S GORDON. GORDON STUART.
MR. STUART! A PLEASURE TO HAVE YOU HERE!
DID YOU DO IT? DID YOU GET THE BODY?
OF COURSE I DID, MR. HACK.
IT'S STUART--
NOW, NOW JACK. WE'RE ALL FRIENDS HERE. LET'S BE HONEST. BE OURSELVES.
AND IN THE SPIRIT OF FRIENDSHIP, YOU MAY DROP MY RIDICULOUS ADOPTED BIBLICAL ALIAS...

AND CALL ME
DR. WEST.

DEL VALLE, TEXAS.
WE ARE READY. WE WILL TAKE SARAH HOME.
VLAD SAYS YOU'RE GOING TO LOOK UP SOME GUYS AROUND HERE... SEE IF THEY'RE YOUR DAD. THAT'S... UH... COOL. MAYBE YOU... Y'KNOW, WANT SOME COMPANY?
I'M... I'M REALLY SORRY.
DON'T... DON'T DO ANYTHING LIKE THIS AGAIN, OKAY, MARGARET? DON'T... JUST...
JUST DON'T DIE ON ME. PLEASE.
I... I WON'T.

GOOD. THERE'S TOO MUCH DEATH IN MY LIFE ALREADY.
THE END.

CASSIE & VLAD MEET THE RE-ANIMATOR

#15 A by **TIM SEELEY & WES DZIOBA**

"That is not dead which can eternal lie, and with strange aeons even death may die"
Passage from the Necronomicon by Abdul Alhazred
HIGHWAY 25.
14 MILES OUTSIDE OF SANTA FE, NEW MEXICO.
THE AMERICAN SOUTHWEST. DRY. LIFELESS. A RELIEF FROM THE FESTERING HUMIDITY OF AN ARKHAM SUMMER.
BREATHING FREE AIR AT ALL IS SOMEWHAT OF A GIFT FOR A MAN LIKE ME, GIVEN THE PUBLIC'S TYPICAL REACTION TO MY WORK.
POK
HMM.
PERHAPS IF THE PUBLIC KNEW HOW CLOSE I'VE COME TO CURING THAT ACCURSED DISEASE -- DEATH -- FOREVER, THEY'D TREAT ME AS A GOD RATHER THAN A MONSTER THEY'D PREFER TO SEE BEHIND BARS.
IF THEY ONLY KNEW THE POWER THESE HANDS WIELD... THESE HANDS THAT GIVE LIFE!
YES, THERE HAVE BEEN SETBACKS, BUT, AS ALWAYS, THE EVOLUTION IN SCIENCE THAT I HAVE PERSONALLY ACHIEVED HAS BEEN WORTH THOSE MINOR, SHALL WE SAY, 'DIFFICULTIES'.
SEE THE MOVIES RE-ANIMATOR, BRIDE OF RE-ANIMATOR, AND BEYOND RE-ANIMATOR! RENT 'EM ALL! -- BLOCKBUSTER MIKE.

FASCINATING HOW THE DRY AIR AND SUNLIGHT HAVE AFFECTED DECOMPOSITION. THE MUSCLES AND TENDONS, LACKING MOISTURE ARE ALMOST MUMMIFIED. ALMOST LIKE...

'DILLO-JERKY.
I BELIEVE WE HAVE ENOUGH FOR NOW, DR. HACK.

THERE ARE PROBABLY SOME LOCALS WHO'D BE PRETTY PISSED IF THEY KNEW WE WERE COLLECTING ALL THE GOOD ROAD KILL.
MET A GUY ONCE IN FLORIDA WHO CONSIDERED HIMSELF THE WORLD'S FORE-MOST GOURMET CHEF OF TIRE TRACK ARMADILLO.

CHARMING. WE'VE PICKED THIS STRETCH PRETTY WELL CLEAN. LET'S MOVE OFF THE HIGHWAY BEFORE WE ALERT ANY LOCAL AUTHORITIES.
YOU'RE THE BOSS, WEST.

POLICEMEN?

NAH. JUST SOME LOCALS PICKING UP DEAD SHIT FOR STEW.
IN ANY CASE, THEY'RE GONE, SO LET'S WORK ON YOUR SHOOTIN', TEX.
YEAH, YEAH, THAT'S JUST BECAUSE YOU COULDN'T HIT KIM KARDASHIAN'S ASS FROM SIX PACES.
HURM. I DO NOT LIKE GUNS.
NOW, ALL YOU GOTTA DO...
PWASSH!
GHUH!
...IS AIM.
OH, AND MAYBE WORK ON THAT GULLIBILITY THING, TOO.
SUCKER.
HURR. I WILL WASH THE SMUG OFF YOU WITH YOUR OWN WATER BALLOON, YES?
HA HAH!

AHHH!

HURR?

THERE IS ONLY FOUR MEN LEFT ON YOUR LIST!
YEAH. I KNOW.
WE SHOULD GO LOOK FOR THEM NOW! ONE OF THESE MEN MAY BE YOUR FATHER. WHY DID YOU NOT SAY YOU WERE SO CLOSE?
I DUNNO. AFTER THE WHOLE 'KIDS' THING, YOU WERE KINDA MAD AT ME, AND THEN THERE WAS THE KILLER MIDGET...

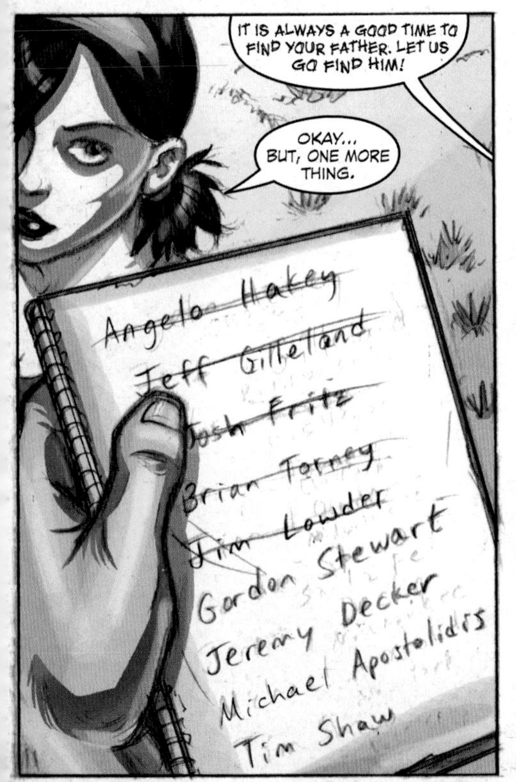
IT IS ALWAYS A GOOD TIME TO FIND YOUR FATHER. LET US GO FIND HIM!
OKAY... BUT, ONE MORE THING.
Angelo Hakey
Jeff Gilleland
Josh Fritz
Brian Torney
Jim Lowder
Gordon Stewart
Jeremy Decker
Michael Apostolidis
Tim Shaw

GOD, SOMETIMES IT'S LIKE STEALING CANDY FROM KIDS ON THE SHORT BUS.

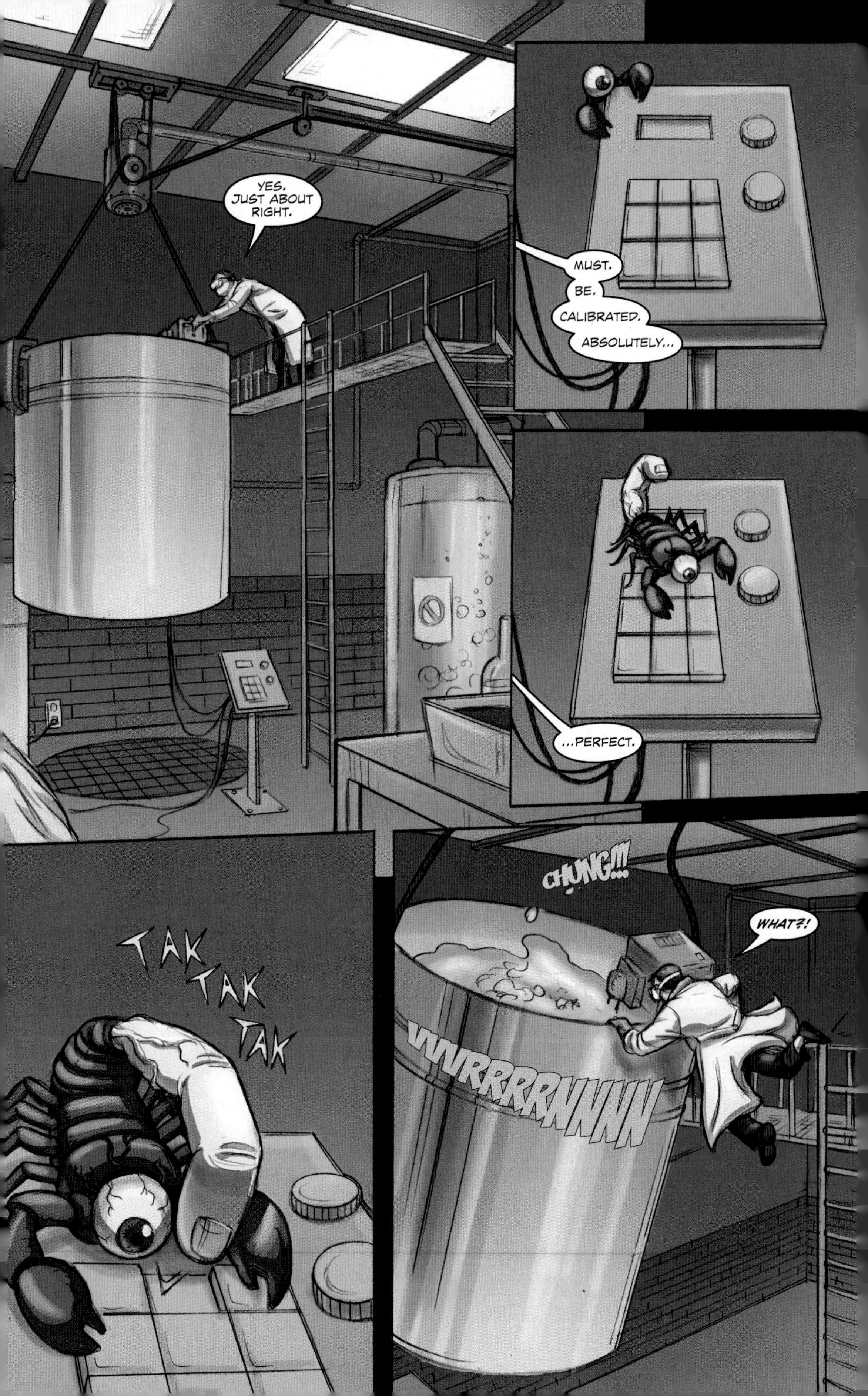
YES. JUST ABOUT RIGHT.
MUST.
BE.
CALIBRATED.
ABSOLUTELY...
...PERFECT.
TAK
TAK
TAK
CHUNG!!!
WHAT?!
VVVRRRRRNNNNN

OH NO. NO!
NRRGHHH
JACK!
JAAAACK!
HERBERT? JESUS CHRIST!
HOLD ON, WEST!
SWAK!
YIEEH!
THANK YOU. THANK YOU.
WE COULD HAVE LOST WEEKS OF IMPORTANT WORK AND RESEARCH.
NOT TO MENTION SOME OF YOUR VALUABLE SKIN.
WHAT WAS THAT THING ON THE PANEL?
OH... JUST A... DOODLE. MY THANKS.

NO PROBL-- OH.
THAT'S... THAT'S *HER*, ISN'T IT?

YES. *DELILAH HACK.* NEE DELILAH CORDERO. AKA "THE LUNCH LADY." SELF-REANIMATING BODY. SHE'S REALLY QUITE SOMETHING, ACTUALLY.
MY *WIFE.*

AH. YES.
I-I WOULDN'T REMOVE THE SHEET. THE BODY IS MIRACULOUS IN ITS SELF-PRESERVATION BUT THERE HAS BEEN SOME... *DECAY*, AND A BIT...
...WELL, QUITE A BIT OF *PRE-DEMISE TRAUMA.* NOT HER FINEST HOUR, I'D SAY.

AHEM YES... I'LL LEAVE YOU ALONE FOR A MOMENT.

NEF.
WELCOME NEF SPAWN!*
*TRANSLATED FROM THE PSYCHIC NON-SPEAK OF THE LORDS OF NEF. -- MOUTHFUL MIKE.
THOSE GATHERED HERE THIS DAY REPRESENT THE FINEST OF MY/OUR SPAWN.
THOSE WHO HAVE MADE MY/OUR WRETCHED COPULATION WITH THE LOWLY ALIENS TOLERABLE. SOME OF YOU HAVE EVEN MADE ME/US PROUD TO HAVE INSEMINATED THOSE WRETCHED BEASTS.
I/WE RECENTLY SENT AN ASSASSIN TO DESTROY THE HATED-ONE-CASSANDRA-HACK.
BUT THE LOW-BEAST HAS FAILED. HAS BECOME TRAITOR!
GONE NATIVE!!
FOR THE HONOR OF TRAVELING TO THE OTHERWORLD TO ASSASSINATE THIS LOW BEAST AND THE HATED...
I/WE HAVE COLLECTED YOU, THE MOST LOVED. THE GREATEST. OUR PROUD SEED.
BUT WE HAVE THE POWER TO SEND ONLY ONE OF YOU. SO LET THERE BE A GREAT CONTEST TO DETERMINE WHOM I/WE CAN TRUST WITH THIS GREAT DEED!
BEGIN KILLING EACH OTHER MY/OUR BELOVED CHILDREN FOR THE HONOR OF NEF!

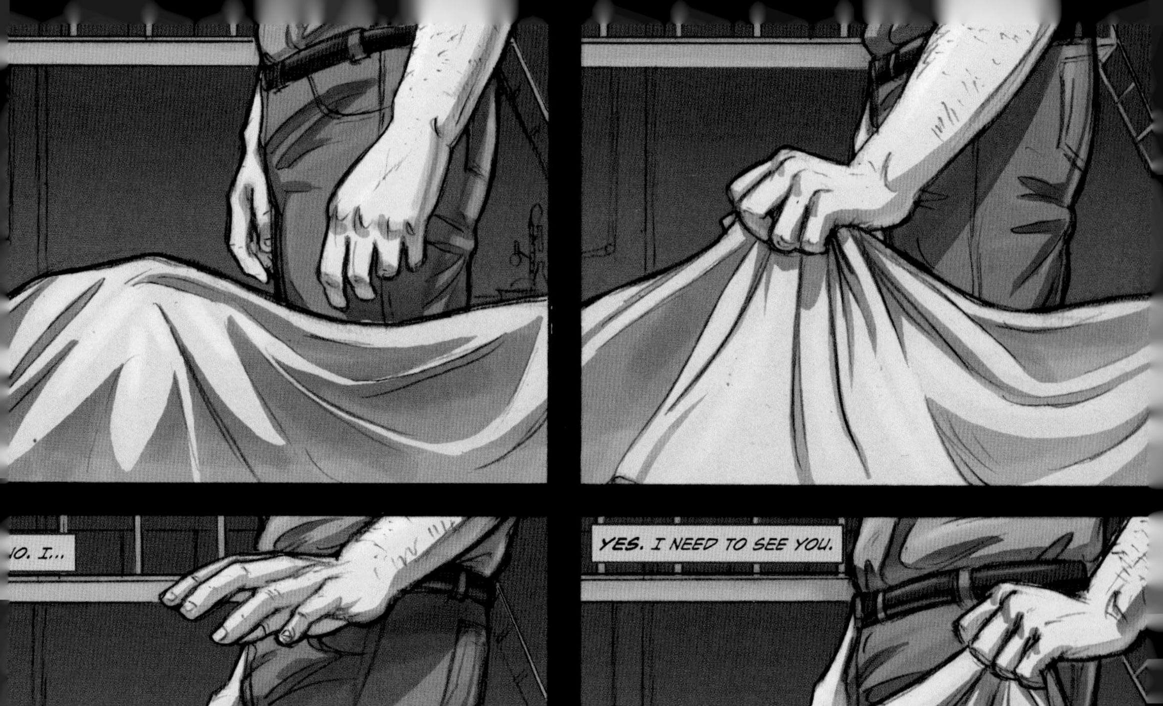

O. I...

YES. I NEED TO SEE YOU.

GOD...

DELILAH...

MY DELILAH...
MY NAME'S DELILAH.
I'M JACK. ER... WELL... DR. HACK.
A PLEASURE. SO... TELL ME, DOC, WHY ARE YOU SO INTERESTED IN ME?
EXCUSE ME?
I'M JUST TRYIN' TO FIGURE OUT WHAT'S SO SPECIAL ABOUT ME THAT Y'ALL WOULD BE WILLING TO DRIVE ME ALL THE WAY DOWN FROM KENTUCKY AND PAY ME JUST TO TALK.
IT'S A STUDY, MS. CORDERO. YOUR PROFILE FITS THE PARAMETERS.
THAT'S IT? YOU LOOK AT MY FILE, DETERMINE I'M JUST CRAZY ENOUGH, AND ALL OF A SUDDEN I DON'T HAVE TO WORK AT PIGGLY WIGGLY FOR A SUMMER?
HA. THAT'S ONE WAY TO THINK OF IT.
JACK HACK
AHEM. I'M SORRY... IS SOMETHING... UH... WRONG?
HA. NO... I WAS JUST LOOKING AT YOU.

HOW'S IT GOING WITH THE PSYCH EVALUATIONS?
GOOD. I'VE GOT SOME... UH... REALLY INTERESTING SUBJECTS. THIS ONE... SHE'S REALLY FUNNY. KINDA ECCENTRIC.
YEAH? IS SHE HOT?
WELL, IT'S NOT REALLY LIKE THAT, OF COURSE...
I SUPPOSE NOT. GUESS I'M JUST JEALOUS. MUST BE NICE TO WORK WITH LIVE PEOPLE, EVEN IF THEY ARE GONNA GO NUTS SOME--
MOVE ASIDE!
ONE MORE X! JUST ONE MORE AND THE GAME CAN BE PLAYED AGAIN!
I NEED THE GAME! THE GAME NEEDS ME!
POK!
AHHHHH!
X'S FOR MEN! ONE MORE!!

GODDAMMIT! I TOLD YOU TO MOVE ASIDE!
KRAK!
MHUUNNN...
DR. PHILLIPS! I NEED TECHS IN RECEPTION BAY FOR REV-SUBJECT KARL VOX ASAP!
THE GAME NEEDS MEEEEEE!
JUST ANOTHER DAY ON THE JOB. YOU OKAY, DR. HACK?
AHEM YEAH... THANKS, DR. WHITE.
SURE, KID. MAYBE YOU SHOULD STAY OVER ON YOUR SIDE OF THE CITADEL. I'M GUESSING THE SUBJECTS ARE A BIT FRIENDLIER.
OH, GOD... YEAH!
YESSSSSS.
AHUNH... UHN... OH!
GOD... GOD, I NEEDED THAT.
ME TOO.
IT'S JUST... SOMETIMES... WHEN YOU SEE THE LOOK IN THEIR EYES... IT'S JUST... IT MAKES YOU FEEL LIKE YOU NEED TO FEEL SOMETHING GOOD.
YOU KNOW?

THAT'S WHY I'M HERE, ISN'T IT?
THAT'S WHY I'M NOT BAGGING GROCERIES THIS SUMMER.
WHAT ARE YOU TALKING ABOUT, DEE?
ALL THOSE MEN IN LAB COATS... THEY WANTED YOU TO STUDY *ME*. THEY SAW MY FILE.
THEY KNOW ABOUT WHAT I'VE *DONE*. AND THEY THINK I MIGHT BECOME ONE OF THOSE "THINGS."
THAT SOMEDAY I'LL KILL, AND I WON'T STOP, EVEN WHEN I DIE.
YOU'LL NEVER BE ONE OF THEM, DEE.
BESIDES, IT DOESN'T MATTER WHAT *THEY* THINK. IT ONLY MATTERS WHAT *I* THINK.
JACK, I'M PREGNANT.

LEAVING?
HEADING HOME FOR THE DAY. I'LL BE BACK IN THE MORNING.
BUT... I THOUGHT TONIGHT WE WOULD...

I'M... I'M NOT READY YET HERBERT. SEEING *HER*...

BUT, WE ARE ON A SCHEDULE HERE. THIS IS IMPORTANT WORK!
EVEN IF YOU *DON'T* SHARE MY QUEST TO DESTROY DEATH, CONSIDER THE POTENTIAL MONETARY COMPENSATION FOR THE APPLICATIONS OF OUR WORK! ISN'T THAT ENOUGH MOTIVATION--
NOT TONIGHT, HERBERT!

=HMPH=

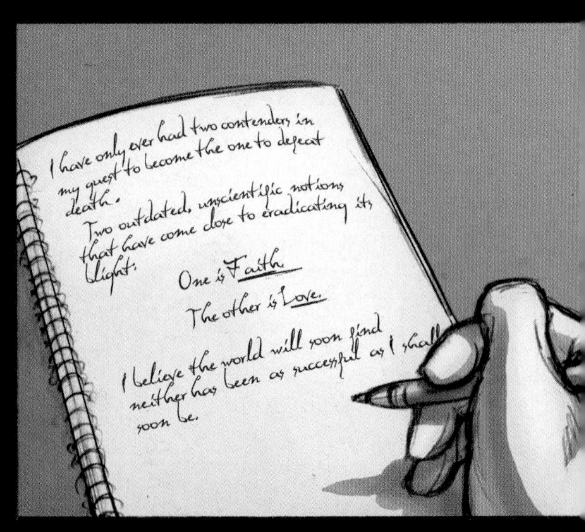
I have only ever had two contenders in
my quest to become the one to defeat
death.
Two outdated, unscientific notions
that have come close to eradicating its
blight.
One is Faith
The other is Love.
I believe the world will soon find
neither has been as successful as I shall
soon be.

NIIIICE NEIGHBORHOOD, MR. GORDON STUART.
MANY PAWN SHOPS. THAT IS NEVER A GOOD SIGN.
WELL, THIS IS THE ADDRESS.
OKAY, LET'S POP IN ON THIS LOSER. FIVE BUCKS SAYS HE'S IN HIS TIGHTY-WHITIES AND THERE'S A TV ON IN THE BACKGROUND PLAYING THE GAME SHOW NETWORK. NO! PEOPLE'S COURT.
THERE ARE ONLY FOUR MEN LEFT ON THIS LIST. ONE OF THESE MUST BE YOUR DAD YES? ARE YOU NOT EXCITED?
NO.
NO, I'M ***NOT***.
WE NEVER KNEW IF ANY OF THESE NAMES BELONGED TO MY DAD IN THE FIRST PLACE. AND IN THAT TIME HE COULDA GOTTEN ***KILLED*** OR HAD A ***SEX CHANGE***... MAYBE EVEN CHANGED HIS NAME AGAIN.
THEN THERE'S HIS CONNECTION TO THAT DR. WHITE ASSHOLE... AND MAYBE TO THE KIDS IN MONTANA. I MEAN, IT SEEMS LIKELY THAT IF I DO FIND HIM, I'LL HAVE TO PUT A BULLET IN HIS BRAIN, JUST LIKE I DID TO MY MOM.
ONCE YOU ARE ALONE, IT IS EASIER TO THINK IT WILL ALWAYS BE THAT WAY THAN TO BELIEVE YOU MAY HAVE TO ACCEPT NEW PEOPLE INTO YOUR LIFE.
YEAH.
THAT, TOO.

WHAT THE FUCK'RE ***THEY*** DOIN'?
PROBABLY WAITIN' FOR STEWART, SAME AS ***US.***
JEEZ... ***THAT'D*** BE AWKWARD.
YA' THINK HE OWES ENOUGH PEOPLE MONEY TO GET ***TWO CREWS*** SENT FOR HIS ASS ON THE SAME DAY?
EJS 608

YEAH... LIKE... WOULD WE JUST TAKE TURNS THEN?
I MEAN, YA' WANNA MAKE SURE THE GUY GETS THE PROPER MESSAGE. THIS IS NOT ***ONE*** ASS KICKING. IT IS TWO ***SEPARATE*** ASS KICKINGS.
YOU GUYS ARE GAY.

OUR BOY GORDON IS COMIN' RIGHT NOW.
I GOT IT.

WHOOF!
WHOMP!!!

MR. STEWART. WE RECOMMEND YOU GET INTO THE CAR WITH US.
WE'D LIKE TO DISCUSS YOUR RELATIONSHIP WITH OUR EMPLOYER, ***LEON LOMAKEMA.***

TELL LEON... I'M GONNA... I'M GONNA HAVE THE MONEY SOON. I'LL BE ABLE TO PAY HIM... DOUBLE WHAT I OWE.

MR. LOMAKEMA SAID YOU'D SAY THAT.
MR. LOMAKEMA SAID IF YOU SAID THAT, I SHOULD TELL YOU *THIS*.
KRAK!
AND THIS.
GHNUH!
WHOOMP!
WHADDYA THINK, STEWART? HOW MANY MORE TIMES I GOTTA TELL YA'?
KLIK
VLAD.

THE FUCK?!
HURR.
HURR.
HURR HURR.
IF I WERE YOU, I'D THINK REAL HARD ABOUT WHAT I TELL MR. STEWART NEXT.

SLASHER.
WHAT A CRUDE AND PROFOUNDLY SILLY TERM FOR SUCH AN AMAZING BEING.
OF COURSE, NO LAYMAN COULD EVER UNDERSTAND THE COMPLEXITY OF THE PROCESS WHICH REVITALIZES THESE FORMERLY DEAD BODIES. IT IS PERHAPS BEST THEY CHOOSE TO STICK TO CAMPFIRES AND SLUMBER PARTIES TO DISCUSS THESE "SLASHERS."
DR. HACK'S TERM "REVENANTS' SEEMS LESS "B-MOVIE" BUT CERTAINLY RETAINS ITS FEARFUL AND SUPERSTITIOUS CONNOTATIONS.

AS WITH MY OWN EXPERIMENTS INTO REANIMATION, THE UNUSUAL CHEMICAL COMPOUND WHICH RESURRECTS THESE REVENANTS SEEMS TO ALSO CONCENTRATE ON THE BASEST OF EMOTIONS AND DRIVES.

RAGE.

RAGE WHICH LEADS TO REVENGE. DESTRUCTION. MURDER.

UNLIKE MY OWN REANIMATES, THE REVENANTS HAVE AN INCREDIBLE ABILITY TO REGENERATE AND RE-GROW DAMAGED OR LOST TISSUE, AND IN SOME CASES ARE APPARENTLY ABLE TO HEAL FROM MASSIVE TISSUE LOSS. UTILIZING THIS INCREDIBLE ABILITY, I HAVE BEEN ABLE TO INVENT A TWO STEP PROCESS WHICH WILL ENABLE ME TO BOTH RESTORE THE BODY TO ITS PRE-DEATH STATE, AS WELL AS TO REVERSE THE EMOTION AND INTELLECT-LIMITING BRAIN DAMAGE.

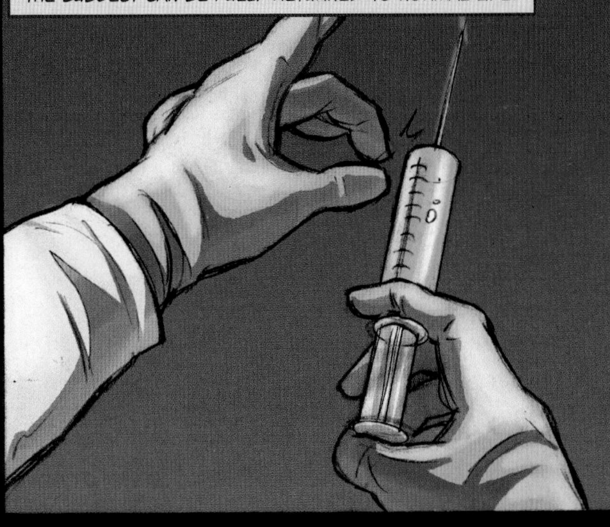

TO TREAT THE BRAIN, I HAVE CREATED A NEW SOLUTION, ONE THAT COMBINES FEATURES OF MY RE-AGENT WITH A CHEMICALS FOUND IN THE BODIES OF THE REVENANTS. SENEX-REV 5. BY INJECTING THIS INTO THE SUBJECT REVENANT'S BRAINSTEM, I SHOULD BE ABLE TO "NORMALIZE" BRAIN ACTIVITY AND REGENERATE MOST LOST CONNECTIONS. EVENTUALLY, THIS WILL CAUSE A RETURN OF MEMORY AND, WITH TREATMENT, THE SUBJECT CAN BE FULLY RETURNED TO NORMAL LIFE.

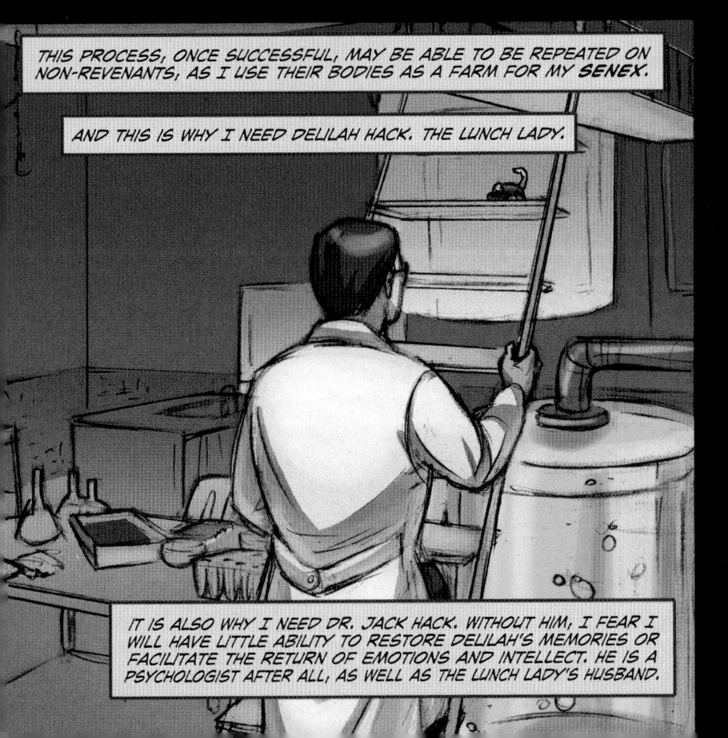

THIS PROCESS, ONCE SUCCESSFUL, MAY BE ABLE TO BE REPEATED ON NON-REVENANTS, AS I USE THEIR BODIES AS A FARM FOR MY SENEX.
AND THIS IS WHY I NEED DELILAH HACK. THE LUNCH LADY.
IT IS ALSO WHY I NEED DR. JACK HACK. WITHOUT HIM, I FEAR I WILL HAVE LITTLE ABILITY TO RESTORE DELILAH'S MEMORIES OR FACILITATE THE RETURN OF EMOTIONS AND INTELLECT. HE IS A PSYCHOLOGIST AFTER ALL, AS WELL AS THE LUNCH LADY'S HUSBAND.

YIIEH!

DR. HACK SEEMED HESITANT THIS AFTERNOON. NERVOUS.
THUS, I BELIEVE IT IS TIME TO INSTITUTE THE SECOND PART OF MY RESTORATION PROCESS.
BY COMBINING A SMALL AMOUNT OF MY RE-AGENT WITH A BIO-CHEMICAL STEW MADE UP OF A VARIETY OF ORGANIC TISSUES, I HAVE CREATED THE ULTIMATE RESTORATIVE BATH, THAT STIMULATES THE REVENANT ALCHEMICAL PROCESS FAR BEYOND IT'S "NORMAL" LEVELS.
A VERITABLE FOUNTAIN OF YOUTH.
YIIEH!
VVVRRRRNNNN
KLICK!
I NEED TO GIVE A FACE TO THIS PROCESS...
...ONE WHICH DR HACK KNOWS.

ONE HE HAS LONG LOVED.

AFTER ALL, HOW COULD HE SAY NO TO SUCH A PRETTY FACE?
WWRRRRRNNNNNNNNNNNNNNN

SIR? MR. STUART?
UNNGH...
OH GOD. ONE OF THEM...
REV'NANT...

CASSANDRA. YOU MUST COME NOW.
NUNH... CASSANDRA?

HE SAID "REVENANT." LIKE DOCTOR IN WOODS. THIS MAN IS YOUR...

CASSANDRA?
MY CASSIE?

DAD?

EMINENCE, INDIANA.
LEY AV
TOP
LIIIIISA!
WHY, HOW ARE YOU?
OH... HI, MRS. CALLAWAY... JUST, Y'KNOW... WALKING ONE OF THE DOGS.
OH, HOW CUTE! HIM'S ALL BUNDLED UP!
WHO'S IS HE? I JUST WANT TO SEE HIS LITTLE FACE...
ERR... I WOULDN'T... HE'S GOT... UM... MANGE.
Yessss... pet meee...
OH. WELL... THAT SOUNDS... UNPLEASANT. NOW WHAT'S THIS I HEAR ABOUT YOU SHACKING UP WITH SOME LITTLE ASIAN MAN?
OH... NO, HE'S A... JUST A TENANT...
BEEP BEEP
Sigh
OH! YOU'LL HAVE TO EXCUSE ME. BUSINESS, Y'KNOW. COULD BE IMPORTANT... MANGE INFORMATION...
CHRIS, THE ONLY REASON I EVEN PICKED UP THE PHONE IS TO GET OUT OF TALKING TO MRS. CALLAWAY, SO DON'T THINK I'M NOT STILL PISSED THAT YOU MISSED THAT JOB INTERVIEW...
LISA. SHUT UP. FOR JUST ONE SECOND.
I JUST READ AN ARTICLE FROM THE EAU CLAIRE LEADER TELEGRAM WEBSITE...
SOME-ONE STOLE THE LUNCH LADY'S BODY.

SANTA FE, NEW MEXICO.
INNER LIFE
AAAIIIIEGGHHHH!
ESSENTIAL OILS
CDs
WHAT'S GOING ON DOWN THERE? SHOULD WE CALL THE POLICE?
NO WAY, MAN. I GOT ENOUGH WEED STASHED IN THIS PLACE TO LAST AN ENTIRE PHISH TOUR.
I WOULD SAY THIS ANSWERS THE QUESTION OF WHETHER OR NOT I COULD PROPERLY RESTORE MRS. HACK'S "LIFE".
GRAAAAHHH!
AAAHHH!
NOW NOW. BE A DEAR AND LET DR. WEST HAVE A LOOK AT THE BACK OF YOUR HEAD.
IF YOU WANT TO TRULY LIVE AGAIN... YOU'LL HAVE TO TAKE YOUR MEDICINE.

ARE YOU SURE THIS IS SUCH A GOOD IDEA?
YOU'LL BE FINE. VLAD KNOWS HOW TO STITCH A CUT. HE HAD TO LEARN ALL KINDS OF THINGS LIKE THAT...
...AFTER HIS PARENTS ABANDONED HIM.
AFTER YOU LEFT US, I TRIED EVERYTHING A LITTLE KID CAN THINK OF TO MAKE YOU COME BACK.
I FIGURED IF I DID THE SAME THING I WAS DOING THE LAST TIME I SAW YOU, EVERYTHING WOULD GO BACK TO THE WAY IT WAS...
I SPENT A WHOLE SPRING SITTING IN THE RECLINER WITH MY STUFFED RABBIT REPEATING "DADDY COME BACK, DADDY COME BACK" OVER AND OVER IN MY HEAD.

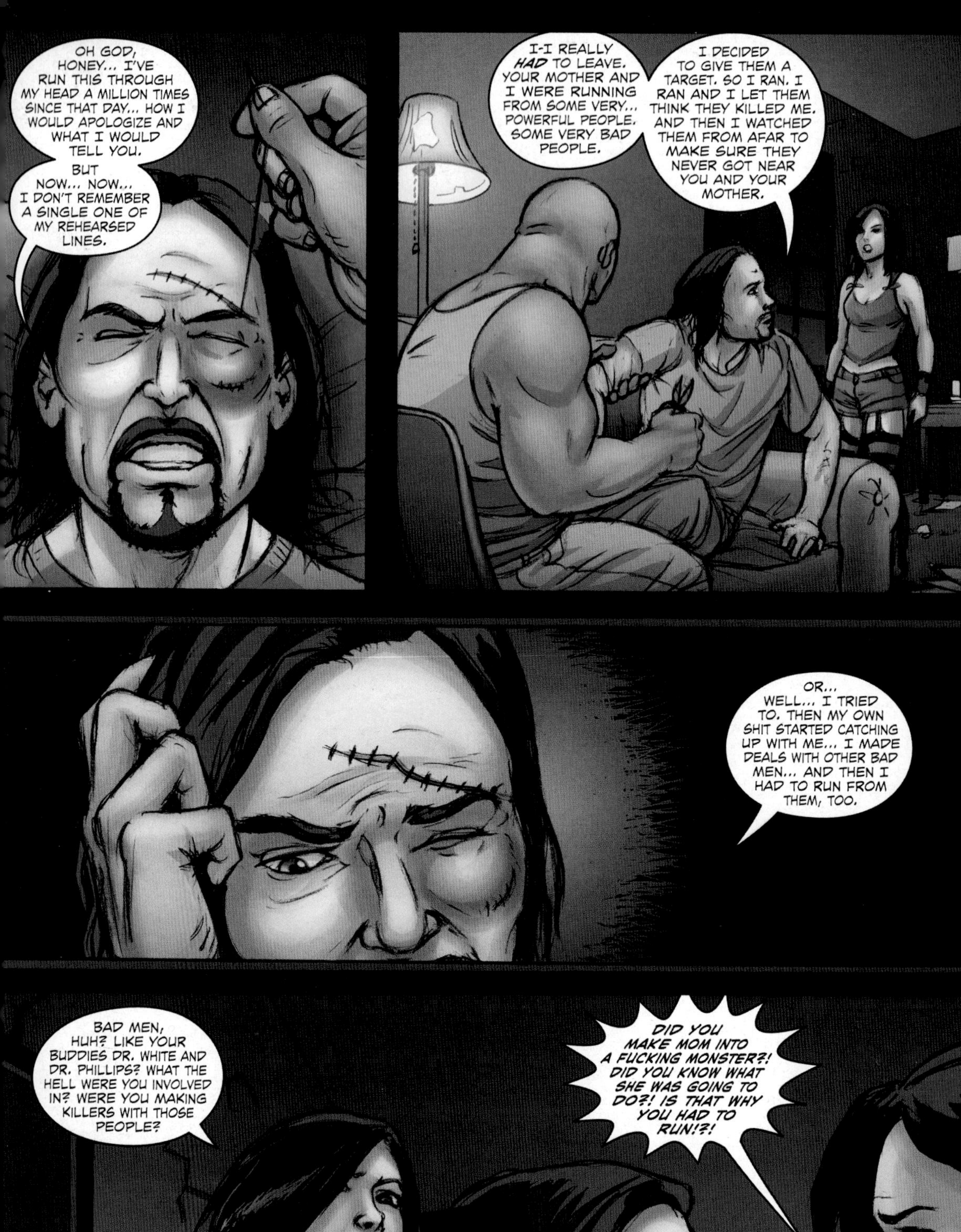
OH GOD, HONEY... I'VE RUN THIS THROUGH MY HEAD A MILLION TIMES SINCE THAT DAY... HOW I WOULD APOLOGIZE AND WHAT I WOULD TELL YOU.
BUT NOW... NOW... I DON'T REMEMBER A SINGLE ONE OF MY REHEARSED LINES.
I-I REALLY *HAD* TO LEAVE. YOUR MOTHER AND I WERE RUNNING FROM SOME VERY... POWERFUL PEOPLE. SOME VERY BAD PEOPLE.
I DECIDED TO GIVE THEM A TARGET. SO I RAN. I RAN AND I LET THEM THINK THEY KILLED ME. AND THEN I WATCHED THEM FROM AFAR TO MAKE SURE THEY NEVER GOT NEAR YOU AND YOUR MOTHER.
OR... WELL... I TRIED TO. THEN MY OWN SHIT STARTED CATCHING UP WITH ME... I MADE DEALS WITH OTHER BAD MEN... AND THEN I HAD TO RUN FROM THEM, TOO.

BAD MEN, HUH? LIKE YOUR BUDDIES DR. WHITE AND DR. PHILLIPS? WHAT THE HELL WERE YOU INVOLVED IN? WERE YOU MAKING KILLERS WITH THOSE PEOPLE?
DID YOU MAKE MOM INTO A FUCKING MONSTER?! DID YOU KNOW WHAT SHE WAS GOING TO DO?! IS THAT WHY YOU HAD TO RUN!?!

NO.
WE DIDN'T MAKE THEM. IF THERE'S ONE WAY I'VE BEEN ABLE TO LIVE WITH MYSELF AFTER ALL THIS, IT'S THE FACT THAT WE DIDN'T CREATE THEM.
"WE NEVER KNEW EXACTLY WHEN THEY BEGAN SHOWING UP, BUT WE HAD RECORDS OF THEM GOING BACK AT LEAST A FEW HUNDRED YEARS.
"WE DIDN'T KNOW ANYTHING ABOUT THEM REALLY. JUST THAT THEY KILLED, WOULDN'T STAY DEAD, AND THAT THEY'D BEGUN TO APPEAR MORE REGULARLY IN THE 80s.
"THE EARLIEST EDICT FROM LAW ENFORCEMENT AGENCIES WAS THAT THE REVENANTS WERE TO BE DESTROYED WHEN FOUND. BUT THAT ALL CHANGED WHEN THE REAGAN ADMINISTRATION WANTED NEW WEAPONS AND NEW WAYS TO WIN WARS.
"THE PROJECT MANAGED TO CAPTURE A FEW SUBJECTS, AND SET UP SEVERAL DIVISIONS TASKED WITH STUDYING UNUSUAL ASPECTS OF THE REVS. HOW THEY THOUGHT. HOW THEY KEPT COMING BACK. WHAT THEY HATED. WHY THEY KILLED. I WAS HIRED TO WORK IN THE PSYCH DIVISION.
"IT WAS MY JOB TO DEVELOP A PSYCHOLOGICAL PROFILE... A WAY TO RECOGNIZE THE KIND OF PEOPLE WHO MIGHT BECOME ONE OF THEM. A REVENANT.
"YOUR MOTHER FIT THAT PROFILE: A LONER, AN INDIVIDUALIST, OBSESSIVE... PRONE TO FITS OF ANGER AND VIOLENCE."

"SHE WAS ALSO THE MOST INCREDIBLE WOMAN I'D EVER MET.
"SHE MADE ME SEE THAT EVERYTHING ABOUT THE PROJECT WAS WRONG, THAT WE SHOULD HAVE BEEN LOOKING FOR WAY TO CURE THE REVENANTS, NOT TO USE THEM.
"I DID EVERYTHING I COULD TO PERSUADE THEM TO STOP THE PROJECT. BUT THEY WANTED YOUR MOTHER. THEY WANTED TO TURN HER INTO A GUINEA PIG.
"SO WE LEFT.
"WE MOVED FAR AWAY FROM THE PROJECT, AWAY FROM OUR PASTS, ALL TO RAISE YOU.
"I HAD ENOUGH DIRT ON THE PROJECT THAT I COULD HOLD IT OVER THEIR HEADS, AND THREATEN THAT I'D GO THE PRESS IF THEY BOTHERED US. IT WAS ENOUGH.
"FOR A WHILE.
"WE STARTED TO GET VISITS. THE WANTED ME BACK ON THE PROJECT. AND IF I WOULDN'T TAKE THEIR OFFER, THEY WEREN'T ABOVE THREATS.
"I HAD TO KEEP THE TWO OF YOU SAFE. ONE OF THE OTHER DOCTORS, PHILLIPS. HE KNEW PEOPLE... HE WANTED TO HELP ME DISAPPEAR.
"SO, I SET UP A NEW NAME AND A NEW LIFE. I WALKED OUT OF THE DOOR ONE DAY.
"AND I NEVER CAME BACK."

SO... YOU KNOW... ABOUT MOM?
YES.
HEARD. IT BROKE MY HEART. KILLED ME. I WANTED TO COME BACK. I WANTED TO...
W-WHY DIDN'T YOU?
I'M NOT A GOOD MAN, HONEY. I'M... I'VE GOT PROBLEMS. GAMBLING AND MONEY... AND...
YOU WERE IN JAIL.
SO, NOW WHAT? WHY WERE THOSE THUGS AFTER YOU?
BEEP BEEP BEEP
IT'S... I HAD TO BORROW SOME MONEY... TO START SOME NEW WORK AND BUILD A LAB... AND...
OH GOD.
LISA!
BEEP BEEP BEEP

OH GOD... HERBERT!
WHAT ARE YOU DOING?!
BEEP BEEP
LOOK. I HAVE TO TAKE CARE OF SOMETHING RIGHT NOW. SOMETHING BIG.
NO... I JUST FOUND YOU...
I'M SORRY. PUT YOUR NUMBER IN MY PHONE. GO SOMEWHERE AWAY FROM THIS HOUSE. THOSE GOONS WILL BE BACK WITH FRIENDS. I WILL CALL YOU... AND... WE'LL START OVER OKAY?
YOU... UMM... BIG GUY... YOU LOOK AFTER HER FOR NOW, OKAY?
YES. HURRRM.
I'LL BE BACK. I'LL BE THE FATHER I ALWAYS SHOULD HAVE BEEN. I JUST HAVE TO FIX ONE LAST MISTAKE.

FUCK. *FUCK!*
ARE YOU... WOULD YOU LIKE TO... URR. TALK?
I CAN CALL **GEORGIA** FOR YOU IF YOU LIKE.
I... JUST... GIVE ME A MINUTE, OKAY? THEN... THEN WE CAN GET OUT OF HERE. I DON'T WANT TO DEAL WITH ANY MORE THUGS, Y'KNOW?
URR. YES.

I... URR... I WILL LISTEN TO OUR MESSAGE FROM LISA.

URRRM... YOU MIGHT WANT TO HEAR THIS.

HERBERT!
WHERE ARE YOU?!
JACK!
WHAT'S GOING ON? SCOTT AND RAMONA SAID THEY HEARD CRAZY NOISES FROM DOWN HERE!
NOW, JACK...
HEH EHE HHEEE...
DELILAH.
WHAT DID YOU DO?! I TOLD YOU TO WAIT!
I WAS AFRAID YOU'D LEAVE THE PROJECT JACK. THIS IS IMPORTANT WORK! I NEED YOU IN THE GAME!
GODDAMMIT!
SLAM!
WOOF!

HAHAHA HEHE.
DELILAH!
JACK!
NO
≠COFF≠
DON'T...

OH GOD, DEE... I'M SO GLAD YOU'RE ALIVE.
JACK... JACK... DON'T WORRY ABOUT THE STRAPS... JACK... JUST KISS ME.
OH, JACK.
STOP! JACK... SHE'S... BACK AWAY FROM HER!!
YOU DID IT... YOU BROUGHT HER BACK... SHE'S... BEAUTIFUL...
THE SENEX REV 5 WORKED, JACK. SHE FEELS. ≋COFF≋ SHE'S EXHIBITING EMOTIONS OTHER THAN RAGE...
SHE IS EXPERIENCING AN INTENSITY IN SENSATION. AN INTENSITY THAT I HAVE NEVER ENCOUNTERED BEFORE IN MY RESEARCH. THE VERY SAME INTENSITY WITH WHICH SHE ONCE EXPRESSED HATE AND THE RAGING DESIRE TO KILL.

NO, HERBERT. YOU'VE GIVEN ME ANOTHER CHANCE. I'M SO SORRY I DOUBTED YOU.
WE CAN START FRESH, DEE. IT'S **MEANT TO BE**. A SIGN.
YOU'RE BACK. OUR DAUGHTER FOUND ME TODAY. I HAVE HER NUMBER RIGHT HERE. I CAN CALL, AND WE'LL BE A FAMILY AGAIN. YOU, CASSIE AND ME.
CASSIE?
CASSIE?! WHERE'S MY GIRL? IS SHE **SAFE?!** ARE THOSE BOYS BOTHERING HER?!
HONEY... NO...
GHUH!
AHH!
I APOLOGIZE, MRS. HACK...YOU AREN'T READY YET!
FZAK!

GHUH... EMOTIONS...
HUHN... ALWAYS GETTING IN THE WAY...
YOU! YOU HURT MY HUSBAND!
DAMN YOU! FALL!
FZAK!
DID YOU TOUCH MY DAUGHTER, TOO? DID YOU TAUNT HER FOR BEING UGLY?
KRSSH!
FSSSH!

MY REAGENT!
WHUNH!
DID YOU HIT HER?!
KRAK!
YOU BASTARD. SHE'S A NICE GIRL. WHY ARE PEOPLE LIKE YOU ALWAYS TRYING TO RUIN HER INNOCENCE?!
HEY, CABRONA!
I DON'T KNOW WHAT THE HELL IS GOIN' ON DOWN HERE, BUT I CAN'T LET YOU HURT MR. LAZURUS.
YEAH, MAN.
HA. HAH HA HEE HEE!

WHUNNNNNHHH.
JUH... JACK?
THE ADDITIONAL REAGENT APPEARS TO HAVE WORKED WELL.
TOO WELL. DAMN.

HHHKKK!
GAH!

NEED SOME KIND OF HELP...

JACK'S DAUGHTER! PERHAPS... YES... SHE WILL HAVE TO DO...
CASSIE
(CALL)

MS. HACK? YES... I NEED YOUR HELP. IT... IT CONCERNS YOUR FATHER, JACK.
YES... I CAN'T EXPLAIN ALL THAT RIGHT NOW... IT'S A BIT OF A BAD SITUATION.

GHUUHHH...
URRR...
YES.

AHHHUHHH
YES, THE SOONER THE BETTER.

ROWF ROWF!
YURF YURF!
ROWF ROWF!
YURF!
WHUUUUHH.
DELILAH? WHAT'S... WHERE ARE WE GOING?
OH, JACK. SMELL THAT AIR. IT'S SO FRESH AND WARM. I'M SO GLAD WE'RE TOGETHER.
DO YOU KNOW HOW IT FEELS TO BE ALONE?
ALONE IN THE GROUND.
YOU WOULDN'T. YOU LEFT ME ALONE. ME AND CASSIE.
UHM... THAT'S NOT IMPORTANT NOW. DEE, TAKE US SOMEWHERE. SO WE CAN BE ALONE *TOGETHER*. I WANT TO MAKE YOU FEEL ALIVE. GOOD.
MOTEL
ADULT MOVIES
VACANCY
THE GOLDEN ANGEL CAFÉ
OH... OH YES. I KNOW *JUST* THE PLACE.
26

SQUAWW!
SPLOOK!
I GAVE YOU LIFE!
RUUUUGHHHRRRLL!
PSSSSS
INGRATE.
SPLLSH!
GLLLAGGH!

GHAH! DAMNED HOT GLASS!
GLAAAHG
HUK!

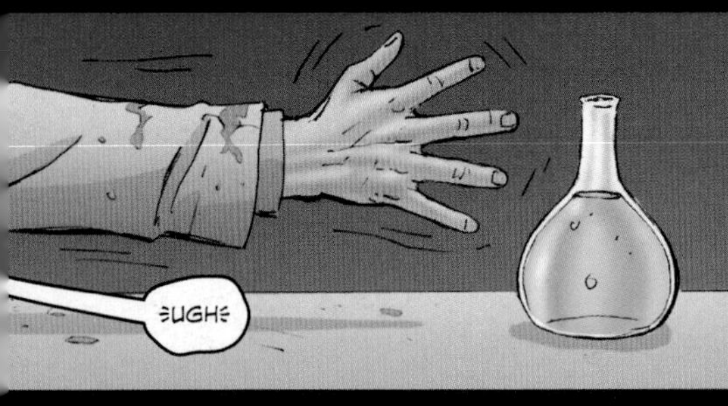
UGH

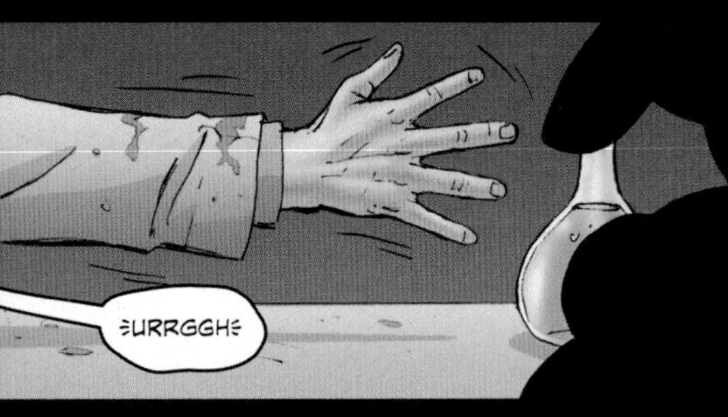
URRGGH

YEEEHEEIIIEH!**
POK!
GHAH!
**TRANSLATION: "REVENGE!"

DAMN!
GLLLURRRGLLL

GURK!

THANK YOU. YOU HAVE MY GRATITUDE...

YOU... AH, YOU MUST BE JACK'S DAUGHTER...

SAVE IT, GEEK.

WHERE THE FUCK ARE MY PARENTS?!
DO NOT MISS THE HORRIFIC CONCLUSION

SANTA FE, NEW MEXICO.
GOLDEN ANGEL
DINER
MOTEL
VACANCY
ADULT MOVIES
UNH
UNH
UNH
WUMP
WUMP
WUMP
OH GOD, YES!
YES!
WUMP
WUMP
WUMP
GOD DA-YUM...
SOUNDS BETTER THAN THE PAY-PER-VIEW SHIT ON THE TUBE...
OH GOD! FUCK YES!
WUMP
WUMP
WUMP
OH YEAH! YES! *FUCK!*
31
DO NOT DISTURB
WUMP
WUMP
WUMP
OH YES, JACK! *YES!*
WUMP
WUMP
WUMP

JACK! I MISSED YOU. OH, I MISSED YOU!
OH DEE... I LOVE YOU...
I THOUGHT YOU WERE GONE FOREVER... I THOUGHT I'D LOST YOU...
SPLUK!!!
SPLLUTCH!!
DEE?!
SPLLUTCH!!!
AHHHH!

NO! DON'T LOOK AT ME!
NO NO NO NO NO NO NO NO NO NO.
SO UGLY. SO UGLY... DON'T LOOK.
YOUR BODY IS JUST REACTING... IT'S... REVERTING. HERBERT REGENERATED YOU WITH HIS RE-AGENT. REPLACED DAMAGED TISSUE WITH BIOLOGICAL TISSUE.
YOU'LL JUST NEED MORE TREATMENTS OF HIS "STEW" TO MAKE IT PERMANENT.
DEE! IT'S OKAY SWEETHEART! IT'S... IT'S OKAY.
STEW? HA.
HA HA HA!
THE LUNCH LADY CAN MAKE A MEAN STEW.

INTERLUDE. NEF.
MOST IMPRESSIVE!
I/WE HAVE SELDOM WITNESSED SUCH SAVAGERY OUTSIDE THE REACH OF OUR OWN FEARSOME TENTACLES!
I/WE BELIEVE THAT THE WINNER IN THE BATTLE TO DECIDE WHO SHALL TRAVEL TO THE OTHERWORLD AND DESTROY THE MOST HATED CASSANDRA HACK, AND THE PATHETIC FAILURE LOW-BEAST HAS BEEN CLEARLY DECIDED!
KUMA. SPAWN OF NEF! PROUD SEED!
GO! AVENGE YOUR SPORE-PROGENITOR! AVENGE NEF!
HUCHRA FAGO DAH. AS YOU COMMAND.

SANTA FE, NEW MEXICO.
WELL, G'NIGHT CAMILLA.
BUENOS NOCHES, SENOR.
DELILAH! DON'T!
HUH?!
A NICE HEALTHY STEW.
DEE!
GHUH!
RUNNCH!
OH, DEE. GODDAMN IT...

NOW, JACK. REALLY. YOU KNOW YOU WANT ME THE WAY I'M SUPPOSED TO BE. YOU DON'T WANT THIS BODY. YOU WANT YOUR DEE.

WHEN YOU LOOK INTO MY EYES YOU WANT TO FEEL SOMETHING **GOOD**.

REMEMBER, JACK: IT'S JUST LIKE YOU ALWAYS SAID. IT DOESN'T MATTER TO ME WHAT ANYONE ELSE THINKS. IT ONLY MATTERS WHAT ***YOU*** THINK.
MOM
DIOS MIO.

IT HAS TO BE THE WAY IT ALWAYS WAS. WE'VE ALWAYS BEEN ALONE TOGETHER. US AGAINST THE REST OF THE WORLD. ME. YOU. AND OUR CASSIE. ALWAYS ON THE OUTSIDE. ALWAYS FREAKS.
THE ONLY DIFFERENCE NOW...

...IS THAT EVERYONE ***ELSE*** IS THE VICTIM.

INNER LIFE
HIT HIM AGAIN, VLAD.
FWAK!
GHUNH!
SO YOU'RE A DOCTOR, EH, WEST? I'LL TELL YA WHAT, I'M NOT.
BUT, I'VE SPENT SOME TIME DIGGING AROUND IN BODIES, JUST LIKE YOU HAVE.
IT'S PRETTY FAIR TO SAY I LACK THE SURGICAL FINESSE OF A DOCTOR LIKE YOUR-SELF.
NOW, IF YOU DON'T TELL ME WHERE MY PARENTS ARE, I'M GOING TO SHOW YOU MY VERSION OF A SEX REASSIGNMENT PROCEDURE.
THREATEN ALL YOU WANT. I DON'T KNOW WHERE SHE TOOK YOUR FATHER. SHE'S NOT SOME RE-ANIMATED CORPSE, SIMPLY GOING THROUGH THE BIOLOGICAL MOTIONS.

SHE FEELS. SHE THINKS. SHE MAKES COHESIVE DECISIONS. SHE IS COMPLETELY AND UTTERLY ALIVE!
THROUGH HER, I HAVE TRULY DEFEATED DEATH!
THAT'S WHAT THIS WAS TO YOU? A SUCCESSFUL EXPERIMENT?
YOU DON'T KNOW WHERE MY PARENTS ARE, YOU SMUG BASTARD.
THEN YOU'RE OF NO USE TO ME, SO I'M GOING TO KILL YOU.
JUST BECAUSE, FOR ONE SHORT SECOND, IT'LL FEEL GOOD.
BRRING
JUH- JACK'S... JACK'S PHONE!
BRRING
DAD.
CASSIE. I NEED YOU TO COME TO THE GOLDEN ANGEL DINER...
...AND I NEED YOU TO BRING HERBERT.

THE GOLDEN ANGEL DINER.
HGUK!

THAT'S MY JACK. NEVER A VERY STRONG STOMACH.
I'M SORRY, HONEY, I KNOW THIS ISN'T ONE OF MY BEST SMELLING RECIPES.

BUT ONCE DR. WEST GETS HERE WITH HIS CHEMICALS, WE CAN ADD THAT TO THE POT. I'LL BE GOOD AS NEW IN NO TIME.

AND HE'S BRINGING OUR BABY WITH HIM. OUR BABY CASSIE. ALL GROWN UP, AND SO BEAUTIFUL NOW.
AS BEAUTIFUL AS I ALWAYS KNEW SHE WAS, EVEN IF THOSE KIDS AT SCHOOL CALLED HER NAMES.

HM. DO YOU THINK WE HAVE ENOUGH? NO... I DON'T THINK WE DO. IT SEEMS LIKE DR. WEST HAD QUITE A BIT MORE.

FORTUNATELY WE HAVE MORE *INGREDIENTS*.

DEE. NO. IT'S... JUST LEAVE HER. I-I DON'T CARE WHAT YOU LOOK LIKE.

LET'S JUST GO BACK TO THE ROOM... WE DIDN'T FINISH... YOU KNOW...
AHEM
...MAKING LOVE.

YOU DON'T SOUND SO CONVINCED, JACK. DO YOU... DO YOU THINK SHE'S ***PRETTIER*** THAN ME? IS ***THAT*** IT?
I'VE BEEN GONE A LONG TIME. WHO HAVE YOU BEEN ***FUCKING***, JACK?
DEE. HONEY. YOUR FEELINGS ARE... YOU'RE AMPED UP... EVERYTHING IS STRONGER...

YOU LITTLE TRAMP! FUCKING MY HUSBAND!
NO! DEE! DON'T!
SHUK!
OH.
DEE...

HMM. PORNO AND A PLATTER. YOUR MOTHER CERTAINLY DOESN'T LACK IN REFINED TASTES, MS. HACK.
SHUT THE FUCK UP.
LOOK, MS. HACK. IF IT'S ANY CONSOLATION, I NEVER MEANT FOR YOUR FATHER TO GET HURT. I GENUINELY RESPECT HIM--
SHH!
--DESPITE HIS FAULTS AS A MAN OF SCIENCE. SO WHATEVER YOU MAY THINK OF ME, YOU SHOULD KNOW...
...JACK HACK IS A GOOD M--
FWUMP!
MUH...
DAD!
AH... CASS...
MENU

OH GOD, DADDY...
MOVE ASIDE, I'M A DOCTOR!
GHYUH!
WEST! I NEED YOU TO FIX ME!
ATTEND TO YOUR FATHER. I WILL GET WEST.
MY MOM.
NO. FIX MY DAD, VLAD.
KAFF
OPEN
I'LL DEAL WITH MY MOM.

MAKE IT, WEST! YOU'VE GOT ALL THE BLOOD AND SKIN YOU NEED. NOW FIX ME!
YOUR HUSBAND. HE'S... HE'S DYING OUT THERE RIGHT NOW. LET ME SAVE HIM!

NO... NO... I CAN'T LET YOU SAVE HIM. JACK HAS TO *DIE* NOW, WEST. AND THEN YOU'LL BRING HIM BACK. WE'LL BE THE *SAME* THEN. HE'LL UNDERSTAND.
MOM.

CASSIE! THIS IS SO PERFECT. WEST IS HERE, CASSIE!
HE CAN BRING US ALL BACK! ALL YOU HAVE TO DO IS LEAVE THIS MISERABLE OLD LIFE BEHIND. WE CAN MAKE UP FOR ALL THE TIME WE LOST! YOU, YOUR FATHER AND I.

IT'S... IT'S A REALLY NICE IDEA MOM. IT'S WHAT I ALWAYS WANTED... TO BE WITH THE PEOPLE WHO LOVED ME.

IT'S A REALLY NICE IDEA, MOM. THANK YOU...

...BUT I CAN'T.
KRAK!
GHNUH! CASSIE! HOW COULD YOU HIT YOUR MOTHER?!
LOOK WHAT YOU DID TO ME! WHY WOULD YOU WANT TO HURT YOUR MOMMY?!
HNF!
AHGK!

NUHHNNN...
HURRRR... I AM... SO SORRY.
I CANNOT SAVE YOU, JACK HACK.
IF THIS WERE ONE OF THE SHOWS CASSIE AND I WATCH IN THE HOTELS, I KNOW THAT BEFORE YOU DIED, YOU WOULD SAY WORDS...
WISE WORDS, YES? SMART, KIND, SAD WORDS, THAT WOULD MAKE PEOPLE CRY.
BUT THIS IS NOT ONE OF THOSE SHOWS. AND THE WORDS YOU WOULD SAY WILL NOT COME. SO, I WILL SAY THEM FOR YOU, JACK HACK.
I PROMISE TO LOOK AFTER YOUR GIRL, CASSIE. I WILL PROTECT HER. AS YOU WANTED TO.
WITH ALL MY LIFE.

=UNGH=
WHY, HONEY? *WHY?*

IF THERE'S ONE THING I PREFER ABOUT MY OTHER RE-ANIMATES...
...THEY DON'T ASK SO MANY QUESTIONS!
THUK!
UGH!

YOU HAVE TO RUN. GET THE FUCK OUT OF HERE! DON'T LOOK BACK, AND DON'T CALL THE POLICE.

AND FORGET YOU EVER SAW *ANY* OF THIS. COMPRENDE?

NO! GODDAMMIT! I *NEED* THAT GIRL! HOW DARE YOU DISOBEY YOUR MOTHER!
KRASSH!!!...

YOU DISOBEY ME, CASSIE. YOU DISOBEY AND YOU TALK BACK. I DON'T WANT TO DO THIS, BUT I HAVE TO PUNISH YOU.
THIS IS HOW I DID IT, HONEY. THIS IS HOW I PUNISHED MYSELF FOR ALL THE BAD THINGS I DID TO YOUR LITTLE FRIENDS. A DIP INTO THE POT... IT HURTS AT FIRST... YOUR SKIN BUBBLES, YOUR EYES MELT.
THEN IT STOPS HURTING. EVERYTHING STOPS HURT--
UK!
THIS ISN'T WHAT I HAD IN MIND FOR WHAT'S LEFT OF MY RE-AGENT, BUT YOU'VE FORCED MY HAND, MRS. HACK.
OVERDOSE!
A DOSAGE OF THAT AMOUNT WILL TRIGGER AN ENHANCED REACTION. DRAWING FROM YOUR REGENERATED CELLS, THE SENEX ENHANCED RE-AGENT WILL FLUSH YOUR MUCH MORE COMPLEX ORGANS, NOTABLY, THE BRAIN.
ESSENTIALLY, YOU'LL JUST SHRIVEL AND DECAY.

AS A SIDE EFFECT YOU'LL FEEL EUPHORIC. FOLLOWING THAT IS A SENSATION NOT UNLIKE THAT OF HAVING YOUR LIFE "FLASH BEFORE YOUR EYES".
THEN YOUR BODY IMMEDIATELY BEGINS, QUITE LITERALLY AND QUITE SPEEDILY, TO CONSUME IT-SELF. AN UNEXPECTED AND UNSIGHTLY RESULT OF TOO MUCH OF A GOOD THING, REALLY...
OH, CASSIE. YOU'RE SUCH A BEAUTIFUL BABY. I'M SO HAPPY...
IT'S SO HARD TO BE ALONE. I DON'T KNOW WHAT TO DO WITH MY LITTLE GIRL. NO ONE TOLD ME HOW TO BE A MOTHER.
I ONLY KNOW I WANT TO STOP ALL HER PAIN. MY LITTLE GIRL SHOULD NEVER HURT...
...THE WAY HER MOTHER...
...DOOOESSSSS...

JACK?
HE HAS... PASSED.

NOOOOOO. DADDY.

DAMN IT. ALL BROKEN.
NO... NO, THERE IS *ONE* LEFT.

HERE. THE BACK OF THE NECK AT THE BASE OF THE SKULL. YOU DO NOT HAVE TO BE WITHOUT HIM.

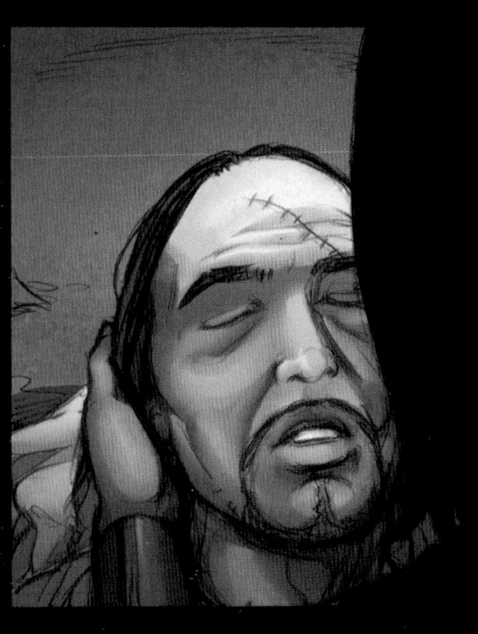

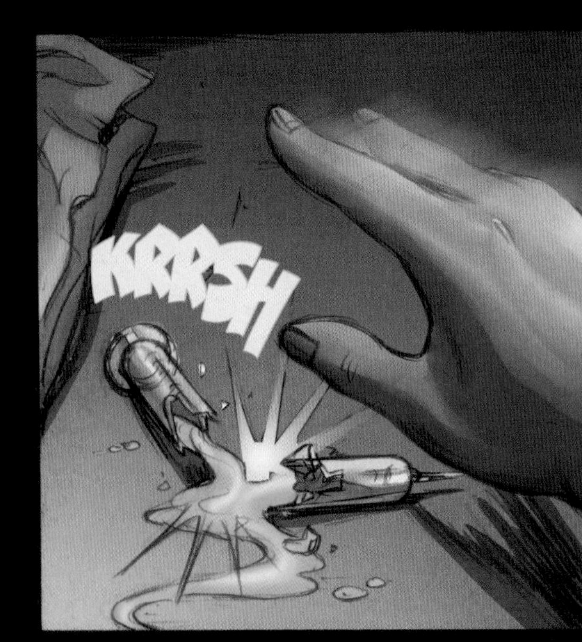
KRRSH

YEAH, GOLDEN ANGEL... NEAR THE HOTEL. BURNING! FUCKING HOT, TOO. MUST BE A KITCHEN FIRE.
WEST.
I WANT YOU TO KEEP WALKING. VLAD AND I ARE GONNA GO ONE WAY, YOU'LL GO ANOTHER.
BUT I WANT YOU TO KNOW SOMETHING. IF I EVER HEAR OF ANY OF YOUR EXPERIMENTS AGAIN...
WHEEEOOOOOOOOOOOO
WHEEEOOOOOOOOOOOO
...ANY EXPERIMENT, I'LL...
FUCK.

EMINENCE, INDIANA.
WE NEEDED THAT.
WE NEEDED ALL THREE HOURS OF IT.

YOU MAY BE A USELESS SLOB SOME-TIMES, BUT YOU MAKE A PRETTY GOOD BOYFRIEND, CHRIS.

I LOVE YOU, LISA. YOU KNOW THAT RIGHT?
I DO. AND I LOVE YOU, TOO. I GUESS I SHOULD QUIT QUESTIONING THE WHYS AND HOW...

"...AND JUST ACCEPT THAT SOME-TIMES THE EXPERIENCES THAT PEOPLE SHARE, DRIVE THEM TOGETHER.

"AND THE MORE ALIEN THE EXPERIENCE...

"...THE LESS PEOPLE HAVE TO HAVE IN COMMON TO FIND THEY NEED EACH OTHER."

MY WORK... ALL THAT PROGRESS AND DISCOVERY: **GONE**.
ONCE AGAIN, I MUST SLASH AND BURN TO COVER UP SOMEONE ELSE'S MESS, AND MOVE ON.
FIRST DAN... NOW JACK... BLINDED BY THAT ACCURSED HUM OF EMOTION THAT POISONS THEIR SENSES.
PERHAPS I AM ETERNALLY DESTINED TO BE ALONE IN MY WORK, UNABLE TO COLLABORATE OR SHARE DISCOVERIES WITH ANY OF THE WEAK-WILLED **INGRATES** AROUND ME.
YES.
ALONE.
DR. WEST.
I'M SORRY, YOU HAVE THE...
NO TIME FOR GAMES, WEST. YOUR **COUNTRY** NEEDS YOU.
THE PRESIDENT IS DEAD. WE'LL GIVE YOU WHATEVER YOU NEED...
SUPPLY ME WITH THE PROPER EQUIPMENT, MY FRIENDS, AND I CAN ASSURE YOU...
...**DEATH** IS JUST THE **BEGINNING**.
THE END?

COVER GALLERY

#1 Reprint cover A by **TIM SEELEY & EMILY STONE**

#1B by TIM SEELEY & WES DZIOBA

#2A by TIM SEELEY & WES DZIOBA

#2B by **MATT MERHOFF**

#3A by **TIM SEELEY & WES DZIOBA**

#3B by **BRYAN BAUGH**

#4B by **JEREMY HAUN**

#5B by **TIM SEELEY**

#6B by **ROSS CAMPBELL**

#7B by **SARA PICHELLI**

#8A by **TIM SEELEY & WES DZIOBA**

#8B by **MIKE BEAR & JEAN-FRANCOIS BEAULIEU**

#9A by **TIM SEELEY & WES DZIOBA**

#9B by **EMILY STONE**

#10B by **DAVID NAKAYAMA & EMILY WARREN**

#11B by JAMIE McKELVIE

ANNUAL B by **EMILY STONE & COURTNEY VIA**

ANNUAL C by **TIM SEELEY & JOSE AVILES**

ANNUAL D by TIM SEELEY, MS SHATIA HAMILTON & GINA FERENZI

ANNUAL E by **RION VERNON (modeled by ALICIA LI)**

#13B by **BRANDON GRAHAM**

#14B by JENNY FRISON

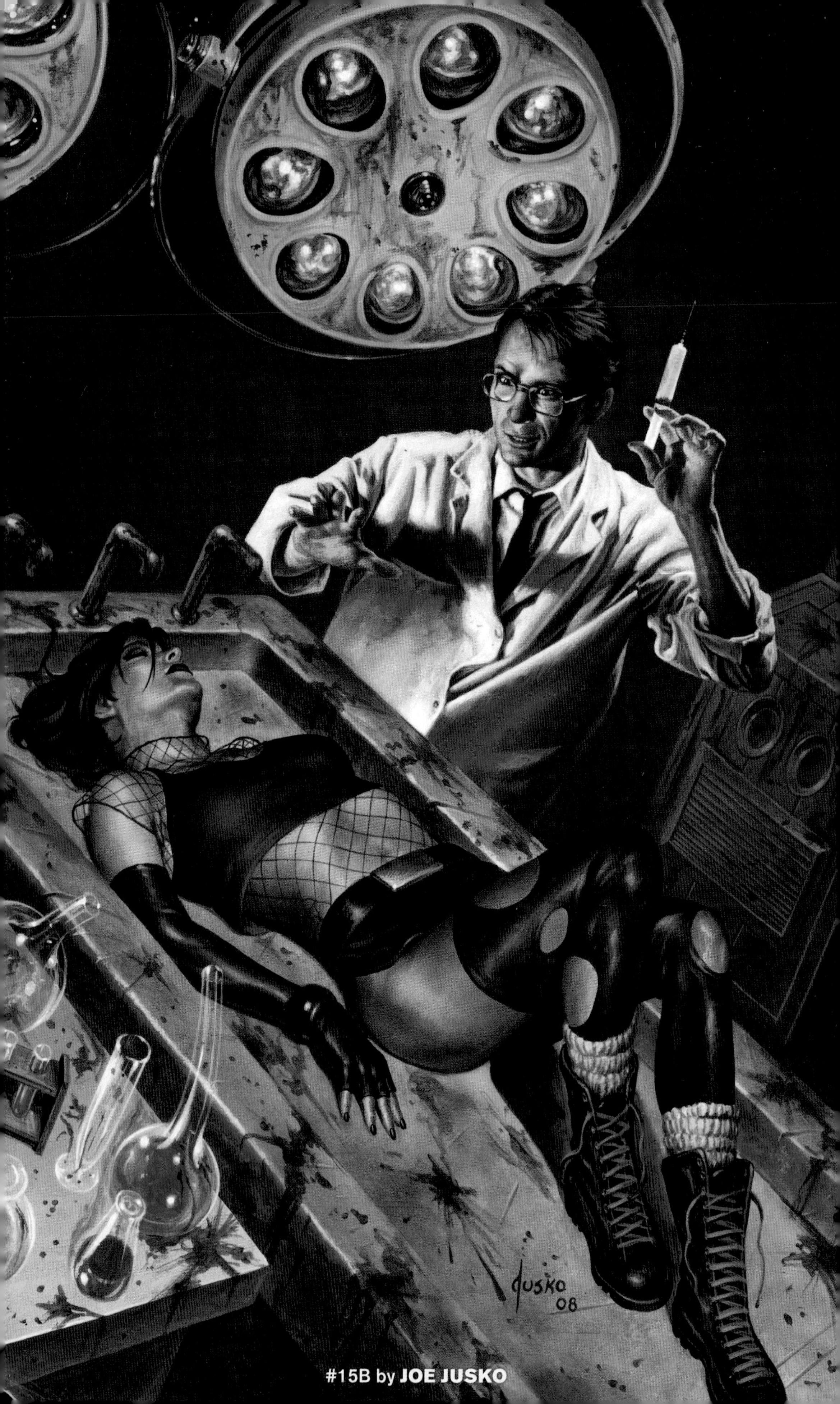

#15B by **JOE JUSKO**

#16A by **TIM SEELEY & JENNY FRISON**

#16B by **VINNIE TARTAMELLA**

#17A by TIM SEELEY & WES DZIOBA

#17B by **JEFF ZORNOW**

HACK/SLASH

PSYCHOFILES

PSYCHOFILES

THE LUNCH LADY

REAL NAME: DELILAH HACK

DEATH BY: HOT GRAVY

PRE-SLASHER OCCUPATION: SCHOOL CAFETERIA CHEF/SERVER

SLASHER TYPE: VENGEFUL GHOUL/PSYCHO MOMMY

SPECIAL ABILITIES: Resistance to pain and damage.

SLASHER WEAPON: KITCHEN KNIFE, VARIOUS POTS, PANS, BLENDERS AND OTHER IMPLEMENTS.

BODY COUNT: 11

THE STORY: Delilah Hack was always eccentric, but after the birth of her daughter, her bizarre behavior accelerated until her strange emotional fits drove her husband to leave them. Left to the task of raising Cassie alone, Delilah became very protective of the young girl. Observing her daughter's school hardships from her job as the school lunch lady, she eventually began to eliminate students she felt treated her daughter unfairly. After murdering them, she disposed of their bodies by introducing a new "mystery" meat to the school lunch menu. She was eventually discovered, but killed herself by stuffing her head into a pot of boiling gravy. But, Delilah eventually came back, choosing to continue her undying murder spree at Cassie's new all-girl's school. A scarred and terrifying monster, Mrs. Hack was eventually destroyed by her own daughter.

PSYCHOFILES

DR. GROSS

This asshole was one sick fuck and now I get to think of him anytime I try to wear sandals.

REAL NAME: DR. EDMUND GROSS

DEATH BY: N/A

PRE-SLASHER OCCUPATION: PSYCHOLOGIST, COLLEGE PROFESSOR

SLASHER TYPE: OBSESSIVE NUTJOB

SPECIAL ABILITIES: Dr. Gross possesses a resistance to pain and a keen intellect.

SLASHER WEAPON: SURGICAL TOOLS

BODY COUNT: 12

THE STORY: Dr. Gross was a professor at a prestigious Atlanta university, who regularly used hypnosis to sexually assault his students. When several students discovered photos of what he'd done to them, they decided to turn him in. Gross prevented this by killing each of them. Gross was arrested, placed on trial and sent to jail. While imprisoned he began a bizarre self-analyzation which ultimately led to him skinning himself in order to be closer to his "true self". Gross was removed from prison, and taken to a psychiatric hospital from which he escaped. He then set about murdering a number of his other students, occasionally convincing them to commit suicide or skin themselves.

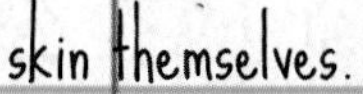

PSYCHOFILES

As bad as this guy sucked, I'd still rather hear Acid Washed than anything by Avril Lavigne...

SIX SIXX

REAL NAME: JEFFREY BREVARD

DEATH BY: N/A

PRE-SLASHER OCCUPATION: PART-TIME MUSICIAN, PART-TIME LAWN-CARE SPECIALIST.

SLASHER TYPE: FAUSTIAN

SPECIAL ABILITIES: Six is able to manipulate a variety of other-worldly magicks which appear to alter probabilities in his favor as well as granting him musical talent. The same magicks allow him to open interdimensional portals, and fire bolts of destructive energy.

SLASHER WEAPON: BLACK MAGICK GUITAR

BODY COUNT: 14

THE STORY: Jeffrey Brevard was a small town Floridian with big dreams of taking the musical world by storm. A terrible student who largely got by on his looks, Brevard formed Acid Washed, a retro hair metal band intended to evoke the halcyon days of rock 'n roll. The band, largely known for it's uninspired musicianship and terrible song lyrics booked only a few shows around Florida in three years until they met the mysterious benefactor who granted them power and success.

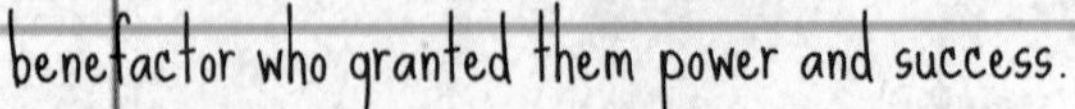

EMILY CRISTY

REAL NAME: EMILY CRISTY
ALIASES: THE OUROBOUROS
DEATH BY: STABBING
PRE-SLASHER OCCUPATION: HEAD RESEARCH ENGINEER, CEUTOTECH, INC.
FORMER MS. AMERICA,
FORMER NUDE MODEL.
SLASHER TYPE: VENGEFUL GHOUL.
SPECIAL ABILITIES: Superhuman strength, regeneration, resistance to damage, the ability to absorb the skins of others & use them as her own.
SLASHER WEAPON: NONE **BODY COUNT:** 12
THE STORY: While studying biology at Franco-Belle University, she took various small jobs to pay for school, at one point modeling nude. Eventually her good looks and personality got her as far as the Ms. America pageant, which she won. Shortly thereafter, the nude photos resurfaced and were published by GIRLIE magazine. This, of course, caused a large controversy, and Cristy was eventually forced to give up her crown. Determined to help women and utilize her intelligence, she eventually took a job at Ceutotech, Inc, a cosmetics firm she had once been a spokesmodel for. Cristy headed the Regenerative Research Division, tasked with studying the regenerative qualities of slashers and the potential youth-restoring effects that could be derived from them.

During a breakout, The slasher known as Acid Angel stabbed Emily, a wound which eventually caused her to bleed to death, but not before she injected herself with the concentrated slasher-derived chemical called "Hate Juice".

When Emily later returned to life, she discovered she could steal the skin of others. She escaped from a government lab and returned to her alma mater to kill again.

FATHER WRATH II

REAL NAME: SAMUEL LAWRENCE

DEATH BY: N/A

PRE-SLASHER OCCUPATION: PREACHER'S ASSISTANT

SLASHER TYPE: OBSESSIVE NUTJOB

SPECIAL ABILITIES: None

SLASHER WEAPON: CROSS

BODY COUNT: 3

THE STORY: Samuel Lawrence was the nephew

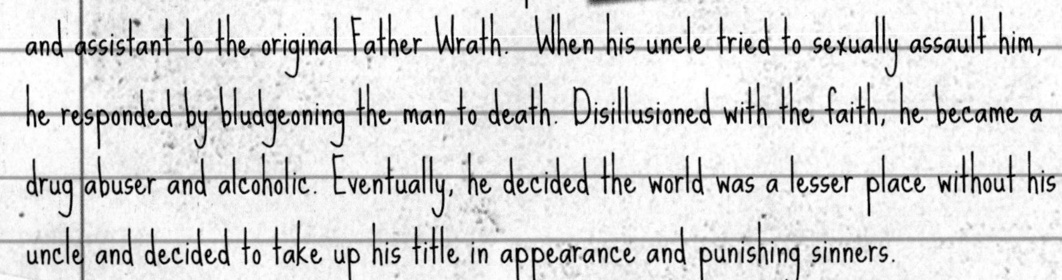

and assistant to the original Father Wrath. When his uncle tried to sexually assault him, he responded by bludgeoning the man to death. Disillusioned with the faith, he became a drug abuser and alcoholic. Eventually, he decided the world was a lesser place without his uncle and decided to take up his title in appearance and punishing sinners.

THE CHILDREN

REAL NAME: UNKNOWN. DR. PHILLIPS CALLED THEM ROMULUS, REMUS, PHOEBE, LUPA, ARTEMIS AND SONIA

DEATH BY: N/A

PRE-SLASHER OCCUPATION: N/A

SLASHER TYPE: BACKWOODS PSYCHOS

SPECIAL ABILITIES: NONE

SLASHER WEAPON: NONE

BODY COUNT: UNDETERMINED. AT LEAST 2

THE STORY: The children were an assortment of feral kids, collected from various places around the world. Dr. Howard Phillips' attempt to cure them with slasher derived cells only further devolved them, creating fierce, cannibalistic creatures who lived in a wolf pack-like organization.

PSYCHOFILES

TIN WOODSMAN

REAL NAME: KENT WOOD

DEATH BY: SUICIDE

PRE-SLASHER OCCUPATION: ACTOR

SLASHER TYPE: VENGEFUL GHOUL.

SPECIAL ABILITIES: Superhuman strength regeneration, resistance to damage. Wears protective tin armor

SLASHER WEAPON: AXE

BODY COUNT: 2

THE STORY: Kent Wood was a little person actor who made a living appearing as an extra, or in various character roles in Hollywood productions. A volatile, intense individual, Wood eventually took a job as a Munchkin in a "Wonderful Wizard of Oz" remake filmed in Texas. There he met and fell deeply in love with Sarah Blake, another Munchkin cast member. Blake cheated on Wood with lead actor, Rick Ross. This caused Wood to become deeply depressed, and in an attempt to punish Blake, he hung himself on set. Wood eventually returned as a vengeful killer, appropriating the Tin Woodsman costume to commit heinous murders.

PSYCHOFILES

DIABOLIQ

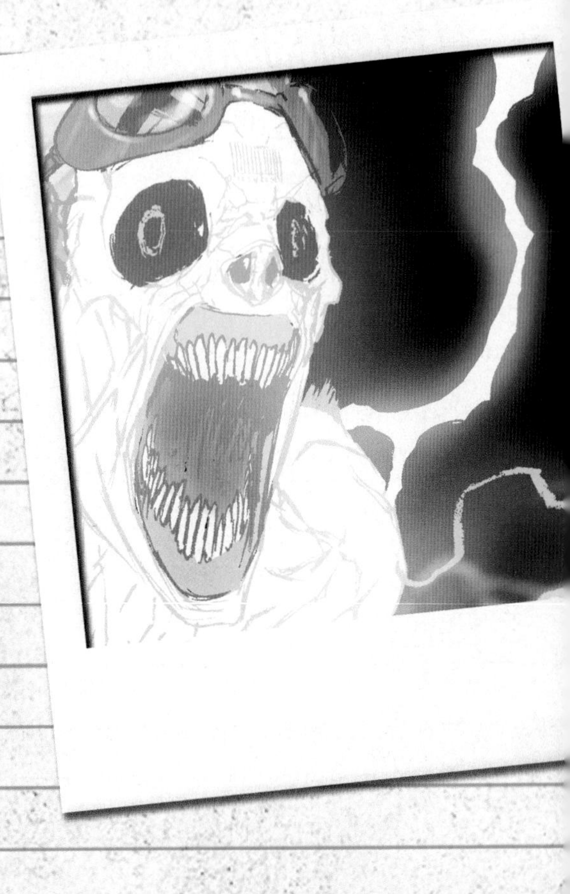

REAL NAME: IAN MATHESON
DEATH BY: ELECTROCUTION
PRE-SLASHER OCCUPATION: BLOGGER. PART-TIME I.T. STAFF.
SLASHER TYPE: VENGEFUL GHOUL.
SPECIAL ABILITIES: DIABOLIQ is able to reside within electronic equipment as well as power lines and wi-fi signals. He is also temporarily able to possess a human being and control their body by manipulating electrical signals in the brain.
SLASHER WEAPON: NA
BODY COUNT: 7

THE STORY: Ian Matheson spent much of his youth as a sequestered computer geek who got along better with machines than humans. The arrival of the internet opened a new world to him, and he became a well known blogger by the age of 15. After 7 years, he'd developed a large following, mostly among the cybergoth subculture. Matheson's sociopathic rants against humanity often also included observations on the future of humanity and the internet.

Eventually, Matheson decided that all prior rules and morality should be cast aside for a new age, and thus he murdered an innocent homeless man and blogged about it. This lead to a confrontation with police, and Matheson's death. But, Matheson's "essence" was somehow transferred via a bloody USB drive into the internet, where he stalked the Suicide Girls he held responsible for his demise.

PSYCHOFILES

DR. HERBERT WEST

REAL NAME: HERBERT WEST

DEATH BY: N/A

PRE-SLASHER OCCUPATION: MEDICAL RESEARCHER.

SLASHER TYPE: N/A.

BODY COUNT: Herbert has never directly killed, but a number have been killed by his experiments.

THE STORY: Herbert West is the inventor of a special solution that when injected into a main artery of a recently deceased person causes the body's mechanical, living functions to return. However, most subjects that have undergone the "re-animation" process have turned violent and often must be destroyed.

After being expelled from the Zurich University Institute of Medicine in Switzerland, Dr. Herbert West arrived at Miskatonic University in New England in order to further his studies. He rented a room from fellow medical student Dan Cain, and converted the building's basement into his own personal laboratory. West's attempts lead to the accidental death of a rival researcher, whom West then reanimated, but was forced to decapitate with a shovel. The head, now undead, attempted revenge on West, which led to the death of Cain's girlfriend, Megan Halsey.

West and Cain eventually attempted to reanimate Halsey, but needed a new body for the dead woman, succeeding in creating a creature from various parts. Halsey's heart rejected the body and she committed suicide, leading to the end of West's partnership with Cain.

West continued his experiments, but when one of his creatures committed murder, West was sentenced to prison, from which he eventually escaped. While in prison, West had encountered a psychologist named Dr. Jack Hack.

Seeking to continue his work, West sought out Hack and the two began new experiments in reanimation.

SKETCHBOOK

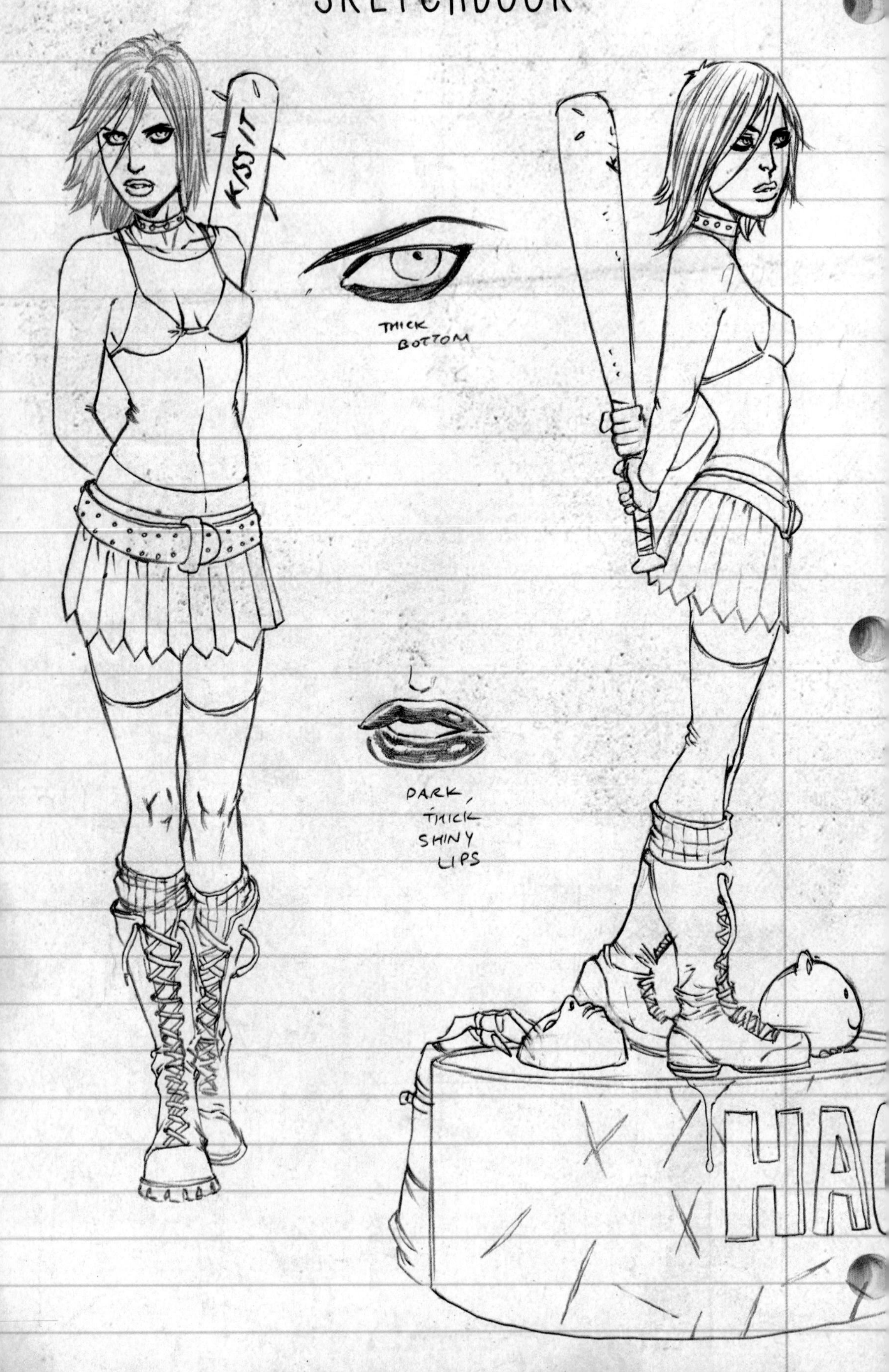

SKETCHBOOK
"FREDDY"-ESQUE
CLAW
HACK/SLASH

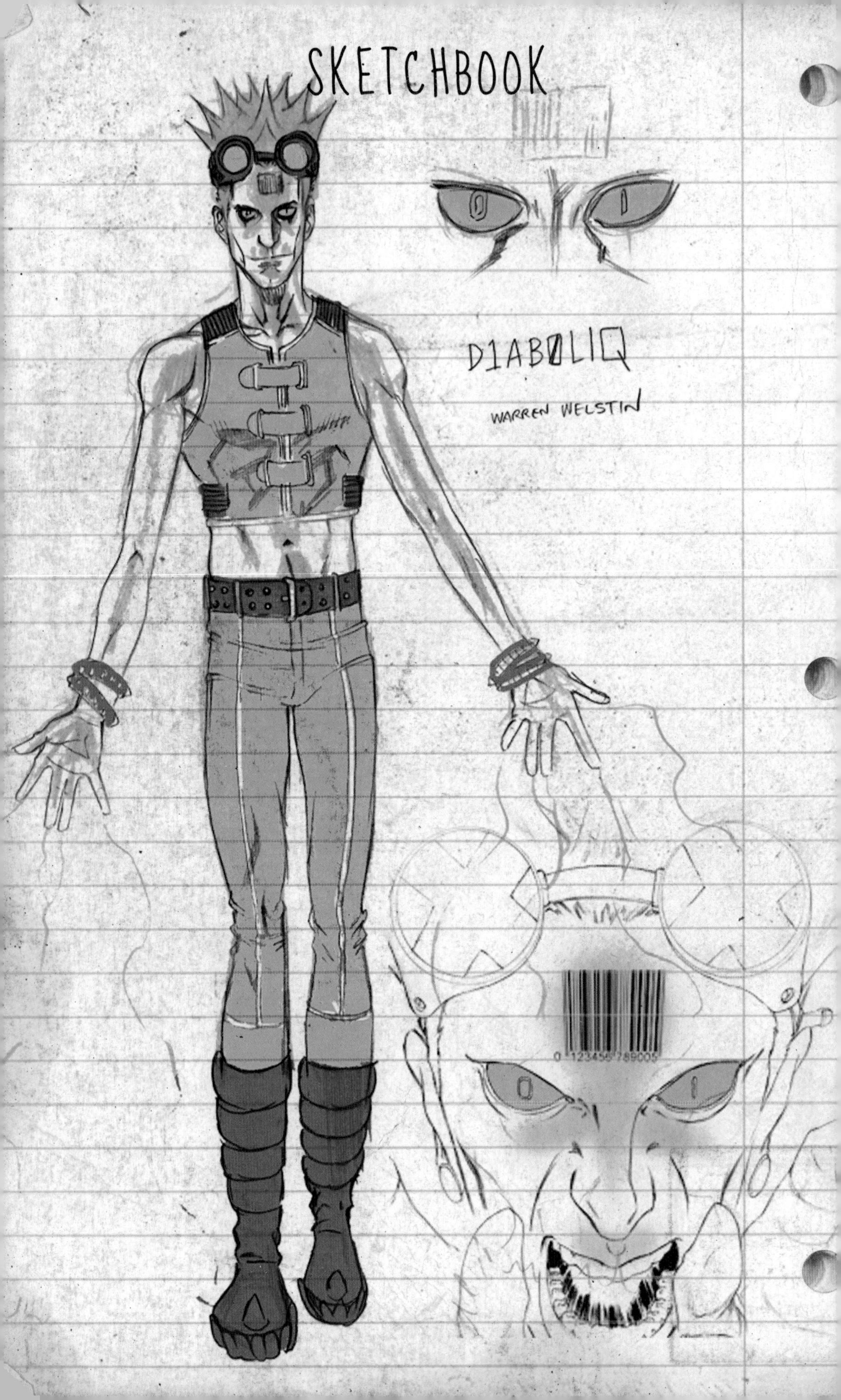
SKETCHBOOK
D1ABØLIQ
WARREN WELSTIN
0 123456 789005